BELOIT FICTION JOURNAL

Volume 28
2015

Cover art courtesy of artist Adrià Fruitós.

All stories are works of the imagination. *Beloit Fiction Journal* is printed by Badger Press, Inc., Fort Atkinson, Wisconsin.

ISSN 0883-9131

Beloit Fiction Journal publishes one issue each year. Subscriptions are available for $10. Manuscripts are read from August 1st to December 1st. Submissions must be accompanied by an SASE. Simultaneous submissions are accepted with notification. Address all correspondence to:

Beloit Fiction Journal
Box 11 Beloit College
700 College Street
Beloit WI 53511

General Inquiries: bfj@beloit.edu
or
(608) 363-2681

www.beloitfictionjournal.org

Beloit Fiction Journal
Volume 28 Spring 2015

Contents

Announcing the winner for the inaugural Hamlin Garland Award for the Short Story

"Waiting for Jubilee" by Laura Steadham Smith

The richness of its descriptive language and depth of characterization seemed noteworthy. The story finds a way to not only take a longer view of a human circumstance, but to make that longer view into a living action. "Waiting for Jubilee" involves a number of tensions that yearn for resolution: generational conflict, environmental degradation, economic hardship, ethnic differences and competing ambitions between a husband and wife. The notion of miracle is introduced early, serving to accentuate the pressing need for remedy. The final beach scene brings the main characters to a transformative place, and they momentarily rise above and see beyond the tensions that have defined them; it also directly involves them in an action that seems miraculous because of the simple fact that they are doing it. I think most everyone has had the experience of participating for a short while in something extraordinary—an action with a higher purpose—and have felt rejuvenated by the effort, stronger in facing personal problems. It was a pleasure to be reminded of that.

– David Rhodes,
author of *Driftless*

Laura Steadham Smith

Waiting for Jubilee

I have never seen a miracle. I have seen fish and eels jump onto the shore by the hundreds, summer nights in Mobile Bay. When the wind blows east, when the silt drains from the rivers and fills the bay, brackish and thick. What fishermen call a jubilee. I have seen revival meetings in church gyms, seen tire salesmen call themselves prophets. I saw a Buddhist monk in west Mobile, standing barefoot in a Walgreens parking lot. The one who later killed a man over food, killed him with a wooden spoon. I have never seen my father pray, not even in the Melkite church where we visit my uncle in Cleveland, where they place the host on our tongue, the one where they speak Aramaic. Not even when he got word that his father was sick, back home in Lebanon. Not even when he checks the books, sees that we are in the red again this month. Asks me to drive to Bayou la Batre, to see about a new supplier. So I am not hopeful.

But Monday morning I drive to Bayou la Batre anyway, maybe because I am a good son, or maybe because my wife is pregnant, or maybe because I own a seafood market and I don't know what else to do. I wake early, leave Molly bunched under the covers, her knees pulled up as close as her belly will allow. She is six months along, her stomach firm and large. I kiss her cheek, and she stirs but doesn't wake. Her blonde hair lies in ropes across the pillow. She has left tiny lists all over her bedside table. Post-it notes about job applications, grocery lists, cleaning chores. I grab a handful, think about throwing them away, but then I place them back on the table, by an old cup rimmed from red tea. It's how she relaxes, by getting clutter outside her head. I go to my truck, parked behind our rental house, and I cross the bay. The water is calm and glassy. The sun is yellow and hot in my rearview mirror, close above the dark trees shrinking on the eastern shore. Ahead, Mobile's office buildings stand tall and clean.

I drive through the city and south, all the way down to the coast. Since the oil spill, fewer customers have come in for local seafood, and we've found fewer fish and shrimp to be caught. My father and I prefer to work with small fishermen, ones who take their own boats in the bay or along the lip of the Gulf, only one or two crewmen to help. The bigger rigs put out longer, spend whole months in the Gulf. They come back with flash-frozen seafood, good quality but not as fresh. But since the big hurricanes—Ivan in 2004, Katrina in 2005—and now the spill, the smaller fishermen are harder to find. Our main supplier sold his boat, and we can't keep the store stocked.

I meet the Vietnamese shrimper at a boat launch in Bayou la Batre. The sun sears the harbor water, stains the surface yellow. I park by a withered oak tree in the middle of the sandy parking area. I have never done business with a Vietnamese man before, but my father worked with them in Bayou la Batre for years, before the hurricanes lifted their boats and dropped them in the pinewoods. We've all seen the pictures of trawlers that wait along the coast, their nets caught in saw palmetto and scrub pine. My father has warned me to be polite, that Vietnamese shrimpers want to talk.

The man's name is Thiêu. He is waiting on the tailgate of his truck, big igloo coolers full of the night's catch behind him. Across the parking lot, several small trawlers are docked in shallow water, swaying. I nod, approach Thiêu, and we shake hands. I say hello, try to pronounce his name.

"Call me Joe," he says.

Probably one third of the shrimpers in Bayou la Batre are Vietnamese. There are more Buddhist temples than Baptist churches in the south part of Mobile County. They immigrated in waves after the war. My father imagines that the swampy edge of Mobile Bay, blistering in summer and balmy in winter, is the closest American shore to Vietnam. He thinks they keep themselves too isolated. "Like incest," I've heard him say. I am surprised that Joe doesn't have an accent.

"Sam's Seafood?" Joe asks. "In Boatyard?"

"That's us," I say. My father owns the business, started it in the '80's when he came over from Lebanon.

Joe and I make small talk. He is trying to make a connection, I imagine, in the hope that we will work together for a long time. I cannot tell him that Molly keeps reminding me that her brother is hiring, the one who owns a truck contracting company in Birmingham. He has done well for himself, may be able to set something up for us, if we want. I cannot tell Joe that Molly has family in Birmingham, some cousins, her younger sister. That she wants us to have security, options, when the baby comes. That I see her point.

"Got probably a hundred pounds," Joe says. "If you want to look through."

He steps aside and lets me open the coolers. The shrimp inside are on ice, their bodies limp and gray, almost translucent. A few of them still twitch. I put my hand in the mass of bodies, slimy and cold. I sift through. Since the spill, deformities are common.

I know what I am looking for: white or pink clumps, tumors that bulge from beneath the carapace. Blank heads, empty of eyes or sockets. Black goo in the abdominal plates, thick like tar. I pull out a few shrimp with tumors on their heads. But I see the black shrimp, and I stop.

A tiger prawn. The black shrimp is half the length of my forearm. A giant. Looks more like a lobster than a shrimp. Yellow bands ripple across its tail. It is an invasive species, one that could push the native brown and white shrimp out. I lift the limp giant from the ice.

"You see a lot of these?" I ask.

"Too many," Joe says.

"Tough business," I say. "The storms. The oil." I slip the tiger shrimp back into the cooler. "Now these."

"We are unlucky," Joe says.

I remember a news story I heard. A Vietnamese woman from Bayou la Batre drove her four children to the Dauphin Island Bridge. Parked in the middle, and threw them over into the Mississippi Sound, one by one.

"Maybe our luck will turn," I say.

Joe shrugs. "When theirs does," he says and points to the coolers.

My father's name is Samer. Samer Hammoud. Few people know his name. He goes by Sam in America. Sam Hammoud, with his khakis and his Chevy pickup, is American. I, Todd Hammoud, am American. The Samer Hammoud who was a young man in Lebanon is a mystery. The young man who hid his brother from Muslims that wanted to kill him in a bunker in Beirut, the city that always smells like diesel fuel. The man who took the money his family raised to send him, the only child they could afford, to a latter-day promised land. Who is agnostic, now. Who refused to teach me Arabic.

"You live in America," he told me. "You don't need Arabic."

Who consults the almanac religiously. To learn the tides, seasonal storm patterns, when the fish will bite. Who governs his store according to the waning of the moon. And who tries to predict the impossible: when a jubilee will come, when the bay will mysteriously fill with carbon dioxide, whether from rotting detritus or an influx of fresh water no one knows, and the water will strangle the fish. When they will swarm the shallows, and we can gather them in buckets, free and plentiful. Who scoffs at his religious brother, holding onto the old ways in a new country. My father is agnostic and practical, but neither of us can depend on the sea and become atheists. He must be both businessman and mystic.

Sam Hammoud still works at the seafood market. He will die before he retires. He built the business from the ground up. When Alabamians make a comment about where my father comes from, it is usually in reference to the store. "How wonderful," customers say. "That you built your own business. That you came here with nothing, and you made a life."

I take the full coolers of shrimp back to the store. My father meets me out back, and we load the coolers onto dollies to roll inside. He is not a tall man, but he seems large anyway. Stout and strong, like a live oak.

"Not much to show, for all that," he says, looking at the coolers. They seem small, in the back room of the shop. They are not enough. Even if we sell them all, they alone will not bring a profit this week.

Then, "Molly called. Said you wouldn't answer your cell phone." He rubs his chin. "Sick again." Some women have morning sickness again in the third trimester, we've been told. Nothing to worry about.

I nod. "I'll call her in a minute." My wife is pragmatic, but she is sensitive.

My father is stern and precise. He looks through the shrimp again, to see if there are any I missed. Hidden tumors, another shrimp without eyes. He moves quickly, efficiently. His wedding band glistens through the gray bodies. The big shrimpers sell the deformed ones, too. Peel them and freeze them, so customers never know the difference. But we sell them fresh, never frozen, so customers can see the heads for themselves. We cannot hide.

It is true that the shrimp are tested extensively. That the diseased shrimp often pass, don't contain any oil or chemical dispersants. But their parents did, or maybe their grandparents, and the oil has entered the genome. No one knows what this will mean for the next generation.

That night, my father drinks. We stay late in the store. My mother stays with us. She runs the café half of the business. Fried crab claws and shrimp, oysters on po-boys. Recently, more and more farmed catfish, red beans and rice. My mother was a cheerleader at the University of Alabama. Blonde, tiny. She married my father as an act of rebellion.

My father pulls a bottle of whiskey from somewhere, refills his glass. I can count the number of times I've seen him drink on one hand, though it is always hard liquor. He refrained during the spill, during the recovery, when we lost suppliers, but tonight he gives in, quietly. He sips slowly, pulls the glass away and swirls the liquid. When he raises it to his mouth again, his hand shakes.

"You ought to be home with Molly," my mother says and looks at me.

I know Molly has called her. Has complained that I'm never home, that when I am I don't pay attention to her. I am not an idiot.

"He doesn't have to hurry," my father says. He wraps his hand around his glass. If he could, he would pull all the oil from the Gulf with that hand. If such a thing were possible. I know he racks his brain, planning. If a man could heal fish, my father would be a savior.

My mother pulls a pair of booties from her purse. They are pink and tiny. She crocheted them herself.

"I thought I'd do a few more like these," she says. She already has a pile of soft blankets she's crocheted, that she's been waiting to give a grandchild since I was born. I haven't told her that I look at Molly and feel sick. That I see her belly and am terrified. That my heart pounds like it will jump from my chest, that it rattles my seat belt when I drive. My father knows. He suggested that I join a church. See a pastor. "Free counseling," he shrugged.

I haven't told them that I have been meeting with a Presbyterian preacher. The man believes in predestination, so he doesn't evangelize. He tells me to let go and trust. Have faith that things will work out, whether in Boatyard or Birmingham. But here the counseling breaks down, because he believes that Someone holds the Gulf in His hands, and I know better. I know that when jubilees happen, the fish are killing themselves, but not for our sake.

My father is unhappy with Joe's catch, so he asks me to try another shrimper. Down in Weeks Bay, a small offshoot of Mobile Bay. Weeks Bay is on the eastern shore, maybe more sheltered from the Gulf. We've heard fewer stories of tar balls in crab traps in the bay estuaries. There is no beach in Weeks Bay, only brown grasses and bogs red with pitcher plants, dusted with goldenrod. So on Wednesday, I drive down. Watch herons wade through the marsh. I pull my truck off the county highway by the Fish River bridge, and I pull under to the boat launch. I am tired. Molly isn't sleeping well, and the hunt for new suppliers is exhausting. We have to keep the store stocked, and this is easier when the fishermen deliver their catch themselves. But we have to inspect the quality firsthand, before we let these men come to us. Before I leave these men to come to my father. My father and I, we run a quality business. We take care of our own.

I am looking for a good old boy from Summerdale, a man named Donny Campbell. I park and get out of my truck. Donny said he'd be wearing a blue T-shirt. Only one other man sits by the launch, a sunburned man with a wad in his cheek. His shirt was once white. Now it is yellow, stained with sweat and time. The man leans against a rusted out Ford. The water is calm in the smaller bay. A brown pelican drifts by, then dives and surfaces with a fish. I pull out my cell phone to call Donny, see where he is.

The sunburned man leans against his truck, an open can of Coors beside him. He stares at me, but I look away. Any night fishermen ought to be in by now. The bay is narrow here, where it tapers into the river. Across the water, the other shore is a faint line, where Weeks spills into Bon Secour and Mobile Bay. This is the farthest south that jubilees are possible.

Donny doesn't answer. I close my phone. It is the cheapest kind Verizon sells, not one of the smart phones. I have no choice but to wait.

The sunburned man leans, spits. Crosses his arms. Out of the corner of my eye, I see him study me. I turn and look at him. He needs to shave. His eyes are narrowed, staring.

"You one of them Arabs?" the man asks. He pronounces the first *A* wide, lingers a little too long.

I bite my lip, judge his stance. He is leaned toward me, his head up. Not aggressive, just waiting. He sucks at his lip, and a muscle tenses in his cheek. I think, I could kill him. If I tried. If I needed to. The water ripples against the shore, the docked boats. A small breeze brings salt, the faint smell of fish. The pelican wheels overhead, an endangered species like the rest of us.

"Yes," I say.

The man nods, laughs to himself. Leans and spits a second time. When he speaks again, it is clear he is Cajun. "Them Arabs got all da money, man," he says. "All da money."

I look at my work boots, cracked across the toes, and I wonder how closely the man is looking.

"All da oil," he says.

"Except what's in there," I say, and point towards the bay.

The man stops, jaw sagged loose and open. Then he throws his head back and laughs, long and loud. He stomps, laughs some more.

"Oh man," he says. "That's good, you know?"

I look at him, and I have no anger in me. I feel sorry for him, a disgusting kind of pity. For his dirty clothes, his drunkenness, the dirt and grime lodged in the cracks of his skin. I check my phone. Nothing. I would have heard something come through, anyway.

"I was a fisherman," the man says. "Caught it all, you know. But those booms didn't do nothing."

I agree. I've seen the helicopter photos, orange booms placed around Weeks Bay to stop the oil. The sheen of an underwater plume thick and glossy, surging through. Swirls of color in the water. Like an angry, demon god, undeterred by human sin offerings.

"Put you out?" I ask.

The man nods, picks up his beer. "My crabs don't have claws," he says. "Ain't nobody want to eat mutant crabs."

"Probably not," I say. I know.

He tells me about his daughter, about to graduate high school. She wants to go to technical college. He sways a little, and I know this is not his first beer. He tells me about his boat, how he sold it and mortgaged his house. Told his daughter to take out loans.

"And you know what's next," he says. "The bees. All them honeybees, getting sick. Gone be the next big food collapse." He raises his finger, shakes it at me. "You just wait and see."

I am relieved when the boat approaches. The man in a blue shirt onboard must be Donny. I am relieved when the sunburned man stumbles away, gets in the passenger seat of his Ford like he's going to sleep it off. But something throbs behind my eyes, a white, sharp pain, for myself and my father, when I run my hands through Donny's diseased catch and I see that it is no better and no worse than Joe's, when I see that it is the same.

That night, Molly wants to go out to eat. I am hesitant, concerned about the expense, but I give in and we drive to a Mexican restaurant in a grocery store parking lot. Molly eats the free chips and salsa, and I sip my water.

"I've been thinking," she says.

She tells me that she wants to put in her two weeks' notice at the Panini place where she waits tables. Tips are good for a pregnant woman, but she may be able to get a teaching job outside Birmingham. Her brother knows a principal in Shelby County.

"May get us somewhere," she says.

This Mexican restaurant is tacky. Too many bright colors, murals of mariachi players with sombreros. I fold my napkin, wipe my mouth. I know that the Gulf is sick. But I think of my father's hands sifting through the shrimp. He has already lost his country, I think.

I say, "I can't go to Birmingham."

Molly's green eyes turn glassy. I can tell that her heart is racing, that she is feeling panicked, but she doesn't let herself cry. She picks up a chip and stirs the salsa instead.

"Don't say that," she says.

I have never seen a miracle, but I am not ready to give up.

"I know that family is important to you," Molly says.

This is the one thing my father carried with him from Lebanon. That family is most important. This is why he visits his brother in Cleveland every chance he gets, why he has spent his life building the store for mine. Why he has no savings now. Why he helped his brother get settled in Cleveland, his cousin in New Orleans.

I offer to order her queso, and she drops the subject. She is tired, too.

That night, she curls against me to fall asleep. She smells like lotion, shampoo. Fresh and clean. My heart hammers, but I hold her close and warm until her breathing slows. Then I pull away, though I do not sleep. The night is long.

On Sunday, we rest. My mother takes my father to a park and they feed ducks in a manmade pond. Molly asks me to walk with her, and we circle our rental neighborhood until her feet ache and she asks to go home again.

I spend the afternoon reading about rental properties in Birmingham. Molly shows me ones she has bookmarked on a realtor site. We don't talk about *when*, only *if*. She knows not to ask. She drags me into the kitchen, and we spend hours chopping vegetables and stirring spaghetti sauce. Her grandmother's recipe. I stand behind her when she washes her hands, put my arms around her. I put my hand against her belly, palm flat, and it pushes back, firm and solid. We feel the baby kick. The motion is beautiful and terrifying, like God choking inside Molly, and I close my eyes and hide my face in Molly's hair. My heart pounds, and I know I should be happy, but I think I may be sick. But then I open my eyes, and it is just Molly, just my wife, whose smile is a little uneven, who loves pugs and Alabama football and laughs a little too loud, and for a moment I know where I am.

At 11, my father calls. "Todd," he says. "May be a jubilee tonight."

He has made this call plenty of times before. The almanac predicts them, but it's a fool's game. The bay is 70 miles from north to south, and a jubilee can happen anywhere along the northeast shore. The best way to learn about a jubilee is to have friends who live on the water, in just the right spot, who can call you when they see it start. I hear the hope in his voice, so I tell him to get some sleep, and I go to do the same. I am tired, and I fall asleep quickly. I dream of Molly before she was pregnant, when we were college students at South. When we felt unattached, thought we might travel to Oregon or Maine. A shore other than our own. In my dream, Molly smiles, but I am nervous.

The phone wakes me at 2:30. Our bedroom is dark. I fumble for the receiver, pull it to my ear. Molly stirs, puts her hand on my arm.

"Steadman's Landing," my father says.

I tell Molly, and we pull on our clothes in the dark. The night is warm, air thick with sweat, crickets deafening in the trees. We drive back roads to the boardwalk at Steadman's Landing. 100 years ago, a dock stood here. Now, old pilings corrode in the seawater, a barnacled perch for pelicans and seagulls.

I have buckets in the back of my truck. The moon bleeds cool light over the parking area by the landing. Where the pines thin and sand begins, it throws a silver veil across the churning water. From here, the water looks alive, like it is writhing from beneath. Mobile rises over the shore on the other side, 10 miles away, the horizon blushed from city lights. To the north, the interstate bridge forms a chain of pearls hovering just above the water.

Others are already here, filling ice chests all along the sand. Someone has clipped a spotlight to a piling, and it brightens a single swath of water. Bugs swarm in the light, and the water is brown and murky. A few kids run around with butterfly nets. Men in cutoff T-shirts wade into the water and haul buckets in and out.

My father is already on the beach. I walk to him. He wears a baseball cap, even though it is night. He looks younger than he should, wide awake and energetic. He holds two buckets, and he hands one to me.

"Todd," he says. "Look."

I look at the water, swirling with creatures. Crabs, eels, flounder. Clambering over each other into shallow water, to breathe. Their scales glisten green and yellow, the colors of bay mud at night. They writhe until the water turns to foam, until the water churns and gulps.

"Not as many diseased ones," my father says.

He is right. Here, farther north in the bay, rivers empty into the delta. The current probably keeps more Gulf water out, more oil away, though the freshwater provides challenges of its own.

"Come on," he says. "Help me."

Molly paces behind us on the beach, and we straddle the border where water meets sand and fish bubble over. My father's hands are steady, his arms stout and strong. He leans and fills his bucket, and I follow his lead. He bends with the waves, catching the wealth of the sea and tossing it back. I understand now what he is doing. I fill my bucket, toss the animals back into the bay. Foam and fish swirl around my ankles.

"That's great," he says. "Keep moving."

I wipe saltwater from my eyes without dropping my bucket. We scoop them up and throw them back. Flounder with eyes bunched together, long eels like water snakes, snapping blue crab. Saltwater catfish with fins like knives. We find a rhythm, scooping and tossing, scooping and tossing. The clamor around us quiets. Others see what we are doing, and they back away onto the beach. Only the bay murmurs, a deep cadence beneath the fish, in and out, across and back, a constant heartbeat of salt and water and life below the surface. I have never seen a miracle, but in this moment, I see my father and myself, standing inside that heartbeat, beneath the wide sky, throwing fish against a mysterious wind. I see crabs scuttle against the tide, from side to side, evading their suicide dance. We catch them, and we throw them back, to protect the next generation.

My father smiles. Water soaks his shirt, his arms, splashes onto the brim of his hat. In the spotlight's glare, he is blinding, his shadow stark against the water behind him. Salt fills my eyes, my nose, briny and sharp. I look at Molly, and she has a hand to her face, and I know she is letting herself cry, but she smiles. The fish churn and leap, rough like sandpaper against our legs. And we work, we catch the fish and we throw them back, and I don't know about the next day or the next or the ones after that, but in this moment, the rhythm of the bay and my hands is enough.

John McNally

The Creeping End
(a triptych)

1

The dead man was discovered in a parking garage stairwell, the same garage where Detective Jankowicz had found a lost pug 13 years earlier during an ice storm. The dog had been shivering when the detective found it, its crooked teeth clacking, so he lifted the black pug off the concrete and zipped her up inside his jacket. Before he brought her home to show his wife, Sharon, he whispered to the dog, "You better be good, okay? If you're not good, she'll murder us both. I'm not shitting you, little dog."

The dead man in the parking garage was wearing a leather bomber jacket and Ray-Ban aviator sunglasses, but there was no wallet on his person. He had been shot once through the heart–that much was clear.

From the dead man's hand, Detective Jankowicz retrieved a cell phone to search for clues–it was the same model as his own cell phone–but the call history already had been erased, as had all of the text messages. The detective swiped the screens back and forth, but there were no Google or Facebook apps on any of the screens. There was an address book full of hundreds of names and phone numbers, most of them accompanied by an avatar too small to see. Most significant were the photographs. There were thousands of them, and all of them were of a penis. From the angle that the photos had been taken, the penis presumably belonged to the owner of the cell phone. It was quite possibly, although not conclusively, the dead man's penis.

The detective scrolled and scrolled. Though the subject was the same, the photographer had made use of the camera phone's various features. The penis had a vintage look about it in some photos while in others it was sepia or solarized. A few of the photos had been shot in negative, making the penis look otherworldly, like a photo Neil Armstrong might have taken of his own penis while sitting in a Moon Buggy. A few were wildly distorted, as though reflected in a funhouse mirror–bulbous at the top, pencil-thin at the base. There was an aqua penis, a cinnamon penis, a bleak penis. Most disturbing was the photo in which the man's penis was surrounded by an antique frame. It looked like a daguerreotype taken by a perverted prospector during the Gold Rush. An old-timey penis, Detective Jankowicz thought.

In more photos than not, the penis was erect and firmly gripped in the man's hand, much as one would patriotically hold a flag while marching in a Fourth of July parade. It was, the detective had to admit, a large penis–or, at least, larger than his own–and he could almost understand why the man had taken so many. Each photo was like a hip business card that offered little more than an image that told you, in some oblique but evocative way, what the company had to offer, and if you wanted to know more, why, you simply asked the person who gave you the card.

The coroner said, "Well? Should we call it a day?" He was an old man with hands so gnarled and veiny, they looked like skin-covered tree bark. He and the detective were both atheists. The topic of God had come up one night in a bar after a few too many shots, but it wasn't something they would ever mention in the light of day–not here in Winston-Salem, at least.

The detective pulled out his own cell phone and took several photos of the dead man. When he was done, he clapped the coroner on the back and said, "It's a day all right."

The detective, afraid that he would be blocked in by all the other emergency vehicles, had parked down a side-street. It was bitterly cold out with a blank, grey-white sky overhead–much colder than one would think it could get in North Carolina. The sky was churning. Jankowicz thought, *It's going to snow*, and that's when he saw across the street a woman standing by herself.

The woman was in her 30s, thin, and with long, black, curly hair. She looked South American. Possibly from Brazil. He'd had a Brazilian girlfriend in college. Sofia. The woman across the street wasn't wearing a coat, so her arms were crossed, and she bounced lightly from foot to foot. She might have been waiting for someone, but it was difficult to determine intent. When she saw the detective looking at her, she cocked her head and then turned around, facing an abandoned storefront. The detective hesitated a moment before walking on.

Inside his unmarked squad car, he examined the phone again. There were over 7,000 photos of the man's penis. 7,142, to be precise. The detective had taken an art class from a hippie in college who saw penises in every painting he showed them. "Look," he would say. "The phallus! Do you see it? The phallus is everywhere in this painting. Just look! It's here. And here. And here. And here. And here. And here. And over here." And for a while, the detective began to see penises everywhere he looked–the bottle he drank out of was a glass phallus, his own penis was an ironic phallus, the shoes he wore were two giant phalluses. *I'm wearing a couple of size 12 dicks*, he thought ruefully one morning as he tied their laces. He had begun pointing out penises to his girlfriend, Sofia. "Look at the ice cream cone that little boy is holding," he said one night after they had left the movie theater. "It's a giant penis, and it's dripping!" He shivered. "Disgusting," he said, turning Sofia away from the sight. Before spring break, Sofia broke up with him. He could see it in her eyes when she started to speak. He knew it was coming. After she delivered the news, she reached over and pulled a thread off his shirt, as though cleaning him up before sending him out into the world alone.

The detective eventually quit attending the hippie's class, unable to see the value in recognizing phalluses everywhere he turned, and yet here he was now, almost 30 years later, a cell phone in his hand, and it was, as the professor had promised, a world full of phalluses. The hippie was onto something, after all.

2

During the last six months that he and his wife lived together, before the separation, Detective Jankowicz developed a sensation inside his head that he could only describe as his brain shivering. His brain shivered, or so it seemed, inside its skull. What followed the shivering was a sensation of chemicals filling up his head, resulting in simultaneous feelings of euphoria and pending death. And then he'd wake up, trying to catch his breath.

The detective visited a neurologist, who thought he was having simple partial seizures and prescribed anti-seizure medicine, but the medicine didn't stop the brain shivers from coming. They stopped only after he and his wife of 20 years separated. He wasn't even aware at first that they had stopped. He had been too preoccupied by the financial logistics of his divorce. He hadn't had a brain shiver, or whatever they had been, for a month by the time of his sleep study–a study he had scheduled for himself out of desperation–but he decided to keep his appointment anyway in case the shivers returned.

On the day that he was supposed to go–the evening of the day that he had worked the case of the dead man with the cell phone–the sleep study clinic shut down because of a freak snow storm. In fact, the entire city of Winston-Salem had shut down, as though in the grips of a historical blizzard, though little more than an inch of snow had accumulated.

"We can reschedule you for next week," the receptionist told him over the phone, "or, if you like, you can come in Saturday night. It'll be a reduced staff, though. And you may be the only patient here. But that's an option, honey."

Saturday night, Detective Jankowicz parked behind the clinic and, clutching his pillow, walked to the back door, which was lit by a single bulb. He was wearing his sleeping clothes–sweatpants and a T-shirt–under his heavy coat. As soon as he rang the buzzer, the door opened. Had the man who opened the door been peering through the peephole the whole time, waiting for him to arrive?

"Hello, Detective. Let's get you in out of the cold." The man wore hospital scrubs and a stethoscope but was not a doctor. He reminded the detective of backwoods preachers he'd had dealings with: short and mustached with a high-pitched voice and a fierce light burning in his eyes. "I'll be taking care of you. Name's Thomas."

Thomas led the detective to a room that looked like a motel bedroom and motioned for him to sit in the room's sole chair. He explained that he would be hook-ing him up to all kinds of electrodes and wires, and that he should relax. "Pretend you're getting a haircut," he added. He slipped over the detective's head a machine connected to a chain. The machine covered most of the detective's torso. Jankowicz felt ridiculous, as though he were a Halloween robot or an old school hip-hop artist wearing the most preposterously large medallion imaginable. How could he possibly sleep wearing a machine of this size?

"You're a homicide detective?" Thomas asked, and the detective nodded. "Well, now, that's something," Thomas said, plugging wires into the machine and then attaching the wires' electrodes to the detective's head. "And you've been involved in some big cases, too, now isn't that right?" he asked, rhetorically. "The Baldino murder in 2004? Now, that's a story, isn't it? Killed by a power drill? Oh, man." Thomas smiled and shook his head. "Or the case of Elaine Riggs. She smothered her twin boys in their sleep, right? How on earth does a mother do that to her own two children?" He sighed. "You're not from North Carolina originally, are you? From Chicago, right?"

Detective Jankowicz nodded. The only way that Thomas could have known any of this information, Jankowicz realized, was if he had Googled the detective ahead of time. The detective was about to ask Thomas why he had Googled him, if that was standard procedure before a visit to the sleep clinic, which the detective was pretty sure wasn't, when Thomas said, "Twice now, I've died and come back to life."

"I beg your pardon?"

"I saw you looking at the scars on my arms. You probably saw the scars on my head, too."

The detective had not noticed any scars at all until Thomas pointed them out, but now that they had been pointed out, it was impossible not to stare at them. The scars were thick, like putty attached to flesh.

"First time," Thomas said, "I fell off the roof of a house and was pronounced dead." He used to work as a handyman, he explained, and he used to drink on the job. His fatal descent began when he lost his footing on a steeply pitched roof. Thomas said, "I grabbed onto the lip of the gutter on my way off. Might as well've grabbed onto a razorblade." He held up his right hand. The tips of three fingers were missing. Why hadn't the detective noticed this before? Thomas leaned in close, his breath smelling of coffee and Certs. "Hit my head on the concrete and cracked open my skull. They pronounced me dead at the hospital. For three solid minutes, I was officially dead." He leaned back, put a hand on the detective's shoulder, and said, "Now, how many people can say that?" He averted his eyes, possibly out of embarrassment, and said, "Second time, I drank myself to death."

Jankowicz, who did not believe in an afterlife, was haunted by the nothingness that lay beyond him. Two years after his college girlfriend, Sophia, had broken up with him, she died in a car accident, a head-on collision, with a drunk driver. Even now, he suspected her death had affected him more than he could ever admit, which was why he tried not to think about it.

"What was it like?" the detective asked. "Being dead?"

Thomas remained silent while he attached the final electrodes, and then he said, "Does Detective Jankowicz need to pee before he goes beddy-bye?"

The detective nodded, and Thomas helped him off the chair and led him down a corridor to a restroom. Inside, Jankowicz caught sight of himself in the mirror. He looked like something from a science fiction movie–part man, part machine, his innards a tangle of wires, his chest a circuit board. How the hell was he supposed to piss, he wondered as he fumbled with the sweatpant's elastic band, unable to see beyond the wires. He finally gave up and shuffled back to the fake bedroom.

"Okay, now," Thomas said, helping the detective to the bed. "If you want to stay up for a while, you can do that. Here's the light switch. Make yourself comfortable. I'll be in another room monitoring you. There's a P.A., so if I need something, I'll speak to you through the P.A. If you need something, just ask me. I'll be here all night. In point of fact, we're the only two living souls here."

Jankowicz tried to get comfortable on the bed but couldn't with all the rigging around his head. He noticed a video camera mounted to a wall and wondered if Thomas would be staring at him for six straight hours, occasionally jotting down notes.

On his way out, Thomas paused for a long, almost loving look toward the detective. "It's how I'd always imagined it," he finally said. "Only better."

"What?" the detective asked.

"Death," Thomas said. He said, "I can hardly wait for the third time." He peered up at the room's ceiling vent, as though tucked away inside the vent's darkness were the secrets of the universe, and said, "Praise Jesus."

Unable to move comfortably and certain he would not sleep for even a minute, Jankowicz said, "Amen."

3

Among the over 7,000 photos on the dead man's phone was one that was not of the man's penis. It was of a woman sitting on a park bench and smiling at the photographer. She looked foreign, possibly Brazilian, and she was wearing sunglasses on top of her head. He had seen her before, this woman. She had been standing across the street from the parking garage. Why hadn't the detective gone over to speak to her when he'd the chance? Was the divorce making him unable to read people the way he had once been able to? In the photo, the woman's eyes betrayed the smile, and Detective Jankowicz loaded the photo onto his computer at work so that he could enlarge the image.

The woman sat on the bench with her knees almost touching but not quite, her hands clasped in her lap. It wasn't fear in her eyes, but it wasn't happiness, either. They were eyes the detective had seen before, back in college, when his girlfriend Sofia told him it wasn't going to work out between them. Her eyes, he remembered, told the whole story, expressing genuine sadness but also relief. It's over, the eyes said. It's finally over.

The detective's screen saver had come on and he was rubbing the bridge of his nose when the phone on his desk rang. It was his wife–his soon to be ex-wife–Sharon.

"Yeah?" he said, trying to make his voice as emotionless as possible. This was new to him, talking to her as though she were just anyone at all.

"It's Alice," Sharon said. "She's not doing well."

Alice was their stocky black pug that had been riddled with health problems for years–mast cell tumors, arrhythmia, two back legs that no longer worked. Her latest health issue involved her jaw. The bones in a pug's jaw were frail to begin with, but after years of grinding down food with crooked teeth in a too-small mouth, the jaw bones had become as thin as floss. Their vet, Dr. Lannigan, had repaired the first fracture months ago, but he had warned them that it might not hold.

"I'll be right over," Jankowicz said.

When Sharon opened the front door of the small house she had rented after the separation, she was holding a pillow with the old dog resting upon it, the way a child princess would be carried around the royal court. For the first time ever, the dog did not acknowledge Jankowicz's presence. Her eyes, unfocused but moving quickly, laid bare the pain.

Jankowicz reached out to scratch the old dog's head, careful not to bump the dog's lower jaw. The jaw hung all the way open while the dog's tongue, a slab of dry flesh, futilely attempted to aid the throat in swallowing. Sharon wasn't crying, but the skin under her eyes was puffy and wrinkled, and her nose was chapped from having repeatedly wiped it.

"I think it's time," Jankowicz said, and Sharon nodded. "Why don't you bring her to the house in a few hours. I'll call the vet's office, make sure they can get her in right away."

What Jankowicz didn't say, but what they both knew, was that he needed to go home first to dig a hole. He was always stunned how difficult it was to dig deeper than a few shovelfuls of dirt. He'd have to dig deep enough so that the body wouldn't be excavated by whatever wild animal scurried near the grave, catching a whiff of death. He had buried four dogs in his lifetime. Alice would be the fifth. Fortunately, the temperature had risen considerably the last few days, and the melted snow softened the ground.

Detective Jankowicz was standing in the driveway when Sharon arrived.

"Want me to drive?" he asked, and she nodded.

They took his unmarked patrol car to the vet's office. Alice lay on a towel on his wife's lap. The detective drove without speaking, but every now and again he would reach over and scratch the top of the pug's head. Whatever had gone wrong in his marriage had gone wrong years ago, so there was no point in analyzing or discussing it. They'd both agreed that relationships had an expiration point, and they'd lived long enough to reach theirs: 20 years.

It took 10 minutes to reach the vet's office. The harder Jankowicz tried concentrating on what was going to happen to Alice, the more vividly he saw the Brazilian woman on the bench instead. He thought of her eyes, sad and relieved. He wondered who she was or if he could ever find her. He wondered if she would know who killed the man who had taken her photo. He wondered, not unreasonably, if she had killed him.

The detective helped Sharon out of the car by lifting from her lap the towel with Alice wrapped inside, but Sharon wanted to continue holding the dog so he handed the bundle back to her and opened the door for the lobby. The one thing Jankowicz never got used to in his job was the smell of death, and the dog's putrid breath hinted at the creeping end.

The receptionists already knew Alice's fate when they walked in, and the three of them, wearing stiff blouses with cartoon dogs and cats on them, stood together behind the counter to greet Alice.

"Such a good girl," they said to her, reaching over to touch her one last time.

"We're so sorry," one of them said to the detective and his wife. "How old is Miss Alice?"

"Fourteen, fifteen years," the detective said. "We're not really sure."

"He found her in a parking garage," his wife added, motioning toward her husband. "He saved her life."

The door to the hallway that led to the exam rooms opened, and a young vet tech asked for them to follow her. The detective was aware of the dog's time ticking down, that this would be the last time she would travel this hallway, the last time she would enter this exam room and lie upon this steel table, the last time she would be with the people she considered, in whatever mysterious way she considered things, to be hers.

Normally they would have had to wait, but Dr. Lannigan stepped inside right away. He was a bald, tan man in his late 50s, and he stopped as soon as he saw the dog that he had brought back from the precipice so many times, this dog he called his miracle pug. Today, however, he said very gently, "You've had enough of this world, haven't you?" He walked over to Alice and put his bald head against her graying head and whispered, "It's okay. You've been a good girl." The detective looked up at Sharon, whose eyes were wet now. She pulled a Kleenex from her purse and blew her nose. The detective was holding it together, not giving in to what he felt, but then Dr. Lannigan wiped his eyes, and the detective thought, *oh, shit,* but still he managed not to cave. All three of them put their hands on the animal as though it were a sacred thing in possession of restorative powers. Then the vet pulled from his pocket two syringes–one to make the dog slip into sleep, the other to make the dog slip into death.

While Dr. Lannigan tried to find a vein in the dog's bony arm, the detective held the dog around its torso, his thumb pressing in the exact spot of the dog's heart. The heart was thumping harder than usual. When a door slammed in another part of the building, the pug jerked up to see what was happening. *She's aware,* the detective thought. *She knows what we're doing to her.* He tightened his grip on her and said, "Shhh, it's okay, sweetie, it's okay."

The side of his hand touched the side of his wife's hand, the first time their skin had touched in months. The dog's heart sped up as the doctor punctured her skin and injected the first liquid.

"She's going to go to sleep now," he said, and he ran his hand across her head, as a magician might, as the dog lost consciousness.

The doctor said, "Okay," and he inserted the second syringe into her leg. He barely pushed the plunger with his thumb, filling her vein, when the old dog's heart stopped beating. The detective waited for another beat, but it never came. "It's done now," the doctor said. "She's gone."

Sharon wrapped the towel around the dead dog and then the detective lifted the swathed pug and carried it out to the lobby while his wife stayed behind to take care of the bill. This was, Jankowicz understood, the last thing he and Sharon would ever do together as husband and wife. His hands, he saw now as he reached to pull open the door, were caked with dirt and clay from the enormous hole he had dug. He had dug deep and wide enough to bury not just the dog but to bury all three of them. He had dug in proportion to his grief.

He popped the trunk and gently set the dog inside atop paperwork for murders he was still working, mysteries that no one had yet solved. Cold cases. After he shut the trunk and leaned against the car to wait for his wife, he answered the buzzing phone in his pocket.

"Hello?" he said.

"*Alô*," a woman said, and Jankowicz felt dizzy.

Although he had not seen her in almost 30 years, he knew the sound of her voice as well as he knew his own. It was his college girlfriend, Sofia. But how was that possible? She had died when she was 24. The detective had gone to the funeral in Murphysboro. He had helped carry the coffin to the hearse, and he had watched as it was lowered into the ground.

"Don't you still love me?" Sofia asked. "Why haven't you called me? I've been worried about you."

"Yes," he said, his eyes blurring at last. "Of course I still love you. Where are you?" He swallowed. Was this really happening? Shyly, he asked, "Can I see you again?"

There was silence. Then the line went dead. When he looked down at the phone's screen, the detective saw that he was holding the dead man's phone and not, as he had thought, his own, and when he pulled up the information about who had called, he saw the photo of the Brazilian woman sitting on the park bench, her eyes staring back at him. He had made so many mistakes lately. What he had mistaken for sadness and relief in her eyes were only reflections of the day's clouds.

The detective, wiping clean his face, composed himself. He hadn't eaten much today or had any water to drink. He would call this woman back later tonight and break the news. He would ask her to meet him for coffee so that he might ask her some questions. He would take his own photo of her with his phone, but he wouldn't be sure of his motives for doing so. One day, perhaps not as far in the future as Jankowicz would wish, a stranger would find, among the many photos of dead people still populating the detective's phone, a single image of this Brazilian woman. Who is she, the stranger might wonder. Who is she, and what could this beautiful woman possibly have meant to a sad and rumpled man whose final breath had already dispersed in the air around them?

Alain Douglas Park

Dig Deep Magnolia

Kathryn knew it was dangerous. He was married now. She hadn't seen him in years.

And yet here she was in her car, on a Saturday mid-morning in March, among the empty and stacked coffee cups, the wadded napkins, the heaps of clothes she kept meaning to donate, digging around for her phone in her huge bag, the one she loved but in which she could never find anything when needed. Had way too much shit in it. Over the years with all the moving, she'd gotten used to keeping everything close to her and now it was habit. Inside there were crumpled receipts for things long gone, old makeup, torn notebooks, dried pens, tampons, floss, cigarettes, power bars, loose money.

She found it finally and dialed his number and looked out the car window towards his house until he answered, a little out of breath.

She told him, sitting there with the engine off, that she was still about a half-hour away, if that's still okay. Traffic's terrible. He said, sure. *We*'ll be here. *We*'re not going anywhere. *We*'ll keep an eye out for you.

She switched the phone to the other ear.

"Alrighty then. See you when I see you."

Then she hung up and put the phone back in her bag and took the floppy thing onto her lap. Before, *they* had been *we*.

Outside the car it was a nice day—sunny, a little cloud cover. Pleasant. A spring day, completely enjoyable to be in. According to most, Austin had more nice ones than bad ones. And people didn't complain about the weather here, although they didn't particularly praise it either when it was good, and Kathryn could tell by this—by the way they ignored their surroundings—that Austin was going to be a nice place to live.

She had parked several houses away—down the block and across the street, under the Texas Ash and out of sight—so she could look at his place for a while, ingest it all before she went to meet him. His house was grey, the only one on the block. Not a drab grey, but a warm grey, with black trim, the front door a bright cheerful yellow. It all worked well. It was very deliberate.

As was his lawn, which was freshly mowed. She knew this because he had been outside before cutting it and watering the flower beds. She had watched him and waited to phone him until the mower was off, until she was sure he might hear the ringing inside. Which he had. Which she had to admit made her happy, since he reacted so quickly, rushed off inside, taking the front steps in two bounds to reach it in time.

He came back out now and resumed the yard work. He was more or less how she remembered, even from a distance. Tall, but not muscular. Still intense, still focused on whatever he was doing at the moment. Still quick with his motions. A decade didn't really age some people. For others it did.

Kathryn looked in the rearview at her face. She had done her eyes, heavy and dark, but nothing else. Never needed much else. Her mouth always carried its own color.

What did he used to say? About her lips? *Ripe.* He used to say they were *ripe* and ready to be eaten.

Then he would eat them.

When Kathryn was young, her mother used to tell her you're only as good as your worst day. It was a line Kathryn heard a lot, because her mother had wanted Kathryn to believe it. That it's a hard life, hard for a reason. Get used to it. You're bound to stumble.

And after Kathryn left her mother's house—because in the end it was her mother's house—when she was just 17, this was what she came to know herself.

Yes, I am only as good as my worst day.

Over the years she'd found her own lines, things she would tell her boyfriends and the different men she would date and live with to prepare them as well—*It's a bottom-up life, so don't expect much,* or, *It's all a test, sweetie, but no grades, only pass/fail,* which only begged her favorite, *And just so you know, I'm a lover of failure.*

She always knew she was performing a little with these lines, creating moments, but there was, she felt, at least some kernel of honesty in her methods.

Like Jeff on his knees now, pulling weeds from the beds in his baggy shorts and old concert T-shirt. He was definitely less pasty compared to their Chicago days but the color looked good on him. It all seemed so healthy: him, the yard, the house.

Her mother's house had been grey too, although that wasn't in any way deliberate. Just was. Had actually been white at one time. But why don't you try keeping house for a teenage girl as a single mom—the inside was hard enough, forget the outside. Things get dirty.

She lit a cigarette and watched as Jeff finished, raking the clumps of mowed grass together and sweeping the sidewalk of any remaining clippings. He was whirlwinds of action. Then there was nothing.

When she got out and started walking, the little yards she passed were all nicely kept, just like his. Everything she'd seen in Austin so far was nice. People had yard sales. Antique shops put their stuff out on the sidewalks. She'd bought a desk recently, an old quarter sawn oak desk, beautiful and huge and heavy with a tooled leather top, completely too expensive and impractical, but it was just too good to pass up. She'd wanted it, had always wanted one she told herself, so she spent more than she should have and got it. She blamed it on the nice day. Everything seemed that way here. Blame it on the day. Jeff seemed like a nice man now. She guessed he always was. He'd always been nice to her.

Looking back, it felt like such luxury, how they lived in Chicago, so young and careless, though, really, it was probably just the opposite. The dumpy apartments. Sleeping all day. Taking any job she could get.

She'd been having the same dream lately. Waiting tables again, a busy restaurant on a busy shift and there she was, showing up without something she needed to work. Sometimes it was her apron, others her pen or order pad. When she arrived she'd have to scramble to get this thing, whatever it was, so she could work. She'd have to borrow and plead and beg and ask her co-workers to help who were so sick of helping her because she was always forgetting something. She was *that* coworker. So she was always starting her shift to eyes rolling, 10 minutes behind and flustered.

She was a nurse now, and, in truth, it was the same kind of work. Feast or famine. Slammed or dead. She was good at it. Nothing really bothered her, not blood or gore or anything else that oozed. Their pain didn't bother her either. She was good at acknowledging it but it never stayed her hand. She never froze. She had empathy but little sympathy, a perfect balance actually. She could drive a needle in and think about lunch. She didn't take it home with her. (Which was good since her place was miniscule and even an unwanted thought could overwhelm the space, her cramped attic apartment up that narrow staircase with the impossible turn in the middle. Her desk had been hell for the delivery guys, but at least they did it; her queen-sized bed was wedged for three days until she finally relented and swapped it out for a single, resisting to the last because it felt so much like going backwards.)

Here it was only sprinklers that hissed at you. Snapping flags on porches. Two kids on bikes rode by her from behind, moving around her like she was a rock in a river. An ice cream truck appeared, its chime all digital and tin metal.

And just like that she was directly across the street from his house. She finished her cigarette and dropped the useless butt of it on the concrete and crushed it with the toe of her shoe. A kid walked past her holding up a dripping cone, limping on a viciously skinned knee. He must have been crying before, because his cheeks were large clean rivers where the tears had washed his dirty boy face. Someone was going to have a hell of a time cleaning that thing. Not her, though.

And she couldn't remember how long she'd been standing there either, so she got going again and started across the street, squeezing herself between the parked cars, sidestepping and looking at her shoes, trying not to touch her bare legs to the metal, and as she stepped out from between the bumpers and put a foot in the road there was a flash of brown and a roaring engine and a wall of wind smacked her face. She was hit by something not unlike hot air, a suction pressure down the full-length of her body, pulling her violently into the road. She had the vague notion of seeing a UPS truck taking the corner at high speed. Her face and body felt wet. Everything was flushed and compacted, only inches from her skin. *Holy shit that was close. Fucker almost hit me.* The moment stayed with her, filled her up, just how close it really was, holy fuck, locked in her joints, but somehow she still made it across the street, up the steps, and through the open yellow door. He asked if she was all right—he'd seen it through the window—and it was only then that Kathryn's head came back to her to some degree and she saw his face, up close and in front of her again after 10 years. It was only then that Kathryn was able to use her mouth and utter the most useless of hellos.

And then she was sitting, not quite knowing how, on a couch in a living room with a glass of water in her hand. She put it down on a coffee table and looked around the place. All normal things. Jeff's things, she thought. Although there was a pink bouncy seat across from her and a playmat beside it. And next to the TV there was a large round basket filled with a mountain of baby toys which Kathryn stared at as if they were clues.

Right, Jeff had a baby. She knew this, but the toys still only seemed like pieces of things and all Kathryn really knew was that they were colorful and shiny and rounded and that these things had their own basket in Jeff's living room.

He came in as she was studying the heap of toys.

"She's sleeping," he said. "In case you're wondering why it's so quiet."

"I wasn't," she said. "But that makes sense. Thanks."

He sat down in a chair across from her, and leaned forward with his elbows on his knees and put his hands together. He had on a red polo shirt, buttons open at the neck. The concert shirt was gone. He had a weird look on his face, smiling but funny.

This confused her. "Are you okay?"

"Of course," he said. "It's you I'm worried about. You should drink a little. Take a breath."

Kathryn sat in her seat. "Is the baby with her mom?"

He laughed a little. "Baby's sleeping. Sara is running today, a half-marathon. Then she goes out with friends."

"You married a runner?"

"Well, I guess. But it was after the fact. She started running a couple years ago."

Kathryn nodded. Her neck was stiff.

He took a drink of his own water and said, "I take it you don't run."

"No, I don't." She looked at him. "You still smoke?"

He shook his head. "You?"

"Sometimes," she said. There was still a flushing pulse in her ears and her hands felt prickly with pins. "But you don't run, right?"

"No," he said. "I don't."

She touched her forehead. "I'm sweating."

Then she was alone again and she noticed some art on the walls, large oversized photographs, what looked like blurry landscapes, odd focus depth, maybe the prairie or desert or tundra. One of her previous boyfriends was an artist and she remembered one of his shows about the Iraq war when that was still fresh and horrifying, a video projection on the gallery wall of civilian war dead, what had been a staple of nightly news everywhere else in the world but not over here. It'd been a quick, rolling feed, but one of the images was of three boys lying down like they were sleeping, arms folded and spooning each other, almost a sweet image until she noticed the head of one, the top crown missing. When she'd stood there, waiting for the picture to loop again, she thought it hadn't looked right. The wound looked too clean, almost like it had been erased, but she knew too that her boyfriend didn't retouch anything. At least that was what he'd said.

She needed a bathroom, had no idea what she looked like. Down the hall she could see a bedroom, the master probably, a corner of bed visible, a glass of something on the nightstand, big headboard. She walked towards the room, wanting a better view, but the bathroom came up quickly so she went inside. She turned on the light and a loud suction exhaust filled her ears.

She found the sink but it was full of small rubber ducks, about a dozen of them, piled up on each other. She turned the water on anyway, stopped the drain, and slid her hands underneath the stream, the coolness washing over her palms and fingers. It felt great, rolling over her knuckles. Some of the ducks started bobbing at her as the basin filled with water, nodding their heads to what she was doing as they spread out on the rising surface. There were a lot more than she thought. She immersed her hands all the way in the water, through the ducks, and it felt like some party game. What she wanted was her face in the water but the ducks were taking over. They closed in around her wrists, swam in her way, and she started to pull them out, one at a time, lining them up along the sink, but their numbers didn't seem to shrink at all. There were a lot of ducks.

Her last job had squadrons of squeaky toys to distract the kids. A private practice pediatrician with a two-year waiting list for his work on head trauma—which was funny since right now her own head felt like it was going to split and it would be great to have his hands on her temples. Although, to be honest, he didn't even need hands to do what he was known for, didn't even need to see the kid's face, just lab work and a couple brain scans and he could say exactly when the trauma had happened, how long it had been going on, the meat of all that litigation work they got, proving one way or the other if abuse had happened, if shaking had occurred, and really, he was so good at it. Kathryn picked up a duck and squeezed it. No squeak but there was a hole underneath and water inside the little body.

She had helped him sometimes late into the night, compiling the data, and refining the algorithms that he'd publish which would help others diagnose the same things. At one point, as part of some project, she had read a list of perpetrator statements taken from the police or social workers, descriptions from the parents themselves of what they had done to their own kids. She had to do this to match the statements—the kinds of self-reporting, the language the parents used—to the known scans of the victims, so that they could know, and then everyone could know, how, say, the damage of this given brain aligned with the statement from the parent who caused it. And they did learn things because of her work. Like how saying *held*, *jostled*, and *shook* usually meant the same thing. How it was a good idea to double the time any parent said it was happening. Two months meant four. Five times meant 10. It was important work. There were pages of statements she had to read and use, as part of her job. She still could remember large portions of the list.

The water hit the spill line and started flowing down the back drain. She shut off the tap and the remaining ducks rode on the waves. Phrases popped up here and there, *I had to hold him under the arms since he was so heavy, I held him tight and I didn't support his head.* She thought of them. *I was exhausted, and, I was feeling terrible, and, I was crying just like he was.*

She pushed the ducks aside and cupped her hands around some water and raised it to her face, but then she stopped, remembering her mascara, her thick eyelashes which she had fussed over so much and gotten just right. She had sat for a long time at that new desk of hers, her free hand stroking the tooled leather edge, the mirror propped against the wall, as she applied it, getting it right, just like she used to.

She looked in the mirror. Her face was red, and tired, her hair messed, fly-aways galore, all of it like she had just woken up, but her eyes: her eyes at least looked good. She dropped the water and stood there quietly in the tiny room until she heard knocking at the door.

My movements were rough. I wasn't being careful. I picked him up and held him close because I was exhausted, like him, and I was crying, just like he was, and *I was worked up* and *I held him.*

Jeff had her glass of water with him, said she looked kind of hot. Maybe they should get some air?

Then before Kathryn had a chance to take in more of the place—because she wanted to—they were through the house and into the backyard and she was sitting again by herself, this time in a wicker chair under a magnolia tree. The tree was huge and gave wonderful shade, flowering above her with enormous purple-pink blossoms on the branches, the whole tree thick with color, the air spicy from the blooms. She sat back in her chair and breathed finally and took a sip of the water in her hand. It was lemonade.

She was starting to feel a little better. She could sense that her heart was in her chest again, that the beats were slowing and no longer pushing out through her temples. The slats of the wicker chair were cool lines on her back and the bowl of the seat cradled her body as it gave slightly when she shifted weight, wicker-tender and pliable. It felt like she was floating in a net, the gentle give, the pavers beneath her feet stained with crushed magnolia petals, like a bleeding watercolor, and the sunlight, filtered and patchy, swayed gently in front of her. There was running water, a fountain somewhere, and chimes, wooden or bamboo, and the green backyard seemed to grow into the distance.

A screen door swung behind her and Jeff came out and sat down next to her, placing a baby monitor on the little matching wicker table between them. All the garden furniture was painted white, rough and honest, peeling a little in the shade.

Closer now, his face really was the same. Just only a little older than she knew, the creases a little crisper. But it was the same boy. The same flecked green eyes.

"God, Kate. It's really good to see you. I mean it, just really good." He handed her a napkin. "Really good. Even dazed and confused."

"I'm sorry," she said, wiping her forehead. "Guess I'm a little shaken."

"Understandable. That was really close. Those UPS guys drive way too fast."

"I'm feeling better now."

He scratched his cheek and sat back. "You're looking better."

She took another sip. The lemonade was sweet and sharp and Kathryn felt the summer coolness of it wash down her throat. He had a cup of coffee for himself and he blew across the surface and tasted it. They did this for a while, alternate sips, as the wind swept the grass and touched the chimes overhead.

This wasn't how she wanted to start, off-edge and recovering. She had wanted to be the one in charge, to come in with the power. But she had no energy.

He seemed to sense her mood and launched into a ten-minute monologue about his life since her. His moving back home. His job building houses with his brother, which still left him time for music, although not as much as he'd like. He'd pick it up later, he was sure. And he liked Texas now, even with all the Republicans. They're not so bad and people tend to leave each other alone here. And Austin was different than the rest of Texas anyway. The heat was the hardest part to get used to after living in Chicago, but he didn't even notice it anymore.

He started asking her questions, the small talk she apparently had glossed over in their emails. How long had she been in town again? (Three months.) And where before? (Seattle.) And before that? (Portland.) Anywhere else? (Let's stop there.) So, what's here? (A job, I'm a nurse now.) No more restaurants? (Not if I can help it.)

"A nurse? That's great. I can see you doing that actually," he said. "What kind?"

"Kids," she said. "Babies. Neonatal."

He raised his chin. "Oh, sure," he said.

"You know, preemies. Intensive care," she said.

He said it sounded intense but she told him it wasn't really. It might still be new for her, the NICU, "but it's harder when they're older, because older kids can tell you all about what's happening to them. They can tell you exactly how it hurts. The babies can't talk. Which actually lets you do more." Like a case they just had, a Down syndrome baby whose lymphs were leaking and they couldn't find it so they gave him methylene blue to track the fluid. Funny thing though, she told him laughing, was that the whole baby turned that bluish methylene green, like a dull turquoise, as the compound permeated his skin and tissue. He looked like a little alien, all puffed up and dyed, though the baby didn't care, didn't hurt him at all, but can you imagine a 10-year-old turning blue?

He was nodding, leaning forward again. She had forgotten about his eyes, the intensity in them. How when he looked, he really looked *at* her. Into her. She told him how the really tiny ones, the severely premature, couldn't even cry, their bodies too underdeveloped for it. She had an image of the two of them younger, his eyes up close to hers, an inch or two away on the pillow, like pools of bright organic space, she used to think, like some perfect planetary nebulae, perfectly round and glowy green, gaseous and cloudy and wet. Looking at him, she still thought it.

She kept talking about her work, the previous job, the one with the private practice pediatrician, how tough it had been—especially when she started screwing around with him—which didn't help—how quickly that got messy.

Jeff was listening to her with his beautiful eyes and smiling at her, taking small sips of his coffee, which, she was sure, must have been cold by then. And she must have been nervous, because she had been talking for a long time, just rambling on about feeding tubes and core temperatures and catheters and fluid delivery, all so much easier when the patient can't talk.

She stopped and raised her lemonade to drink again. She took long sips, thirsty sips, tipping her head back for the last of it as the cold ice slipped down to rest against her lips. Drinking, she thought how her lips must look to Jeff. She felt his eyes and then mouthed a cube, almost kissed it instinctively. She was immediately embarrassed. She let out a breath into the glass which came back to her face foggy and cold. She looked away to the yard. A breeze coursed through the blossoms above her and she kept her eyes straight and fixed on the grass, that large expanse of growing green in front of her.

Her mom had been a gardener, vegetables and things. Their whole backyard was covered in beds, her mom always out there, wrist deep in the dirt, and Kathryn watching from the back window. She remembered tomatoes and sunflowers and corn, so much back there but Kathryn had never wanted to help, never responded to the coaxing, her mom's invitation to just stop standing there and come out and join her for once. Kathryn even had her own gardening gloves, a few different sizes over the years, which her mom kept buying in the hopes that Kathryn might change her mind. They hung clean and dirt-free next to her mom's well used pair.

Jeff leaned back in his chair. He breathed deep and looked at her.

"So how are you doing, Kate?"

Kathryn continued to sit in the garden and smiled and shook her head ever so slightly back and forth.

That was supposed to be her question to him. How was he doing? That question—when posed right, when asked at just the right moment—which can trigger so much: a chain of events. How is he doing? What are his hopes? What does he want out of life that isn't there? What are his regrets? What would he do differently? What does he want? And, more specifically, what does he want now? What does he want to do about it now?

Those were her questions. What she wanted to know.

And, also, what, if I may ask, was so wrong with us then anyway? Why did it end? What was so wrong with me? And, if I could press just a little more, what's so wrong with me now? Why don't we now? Couldn't it still, somehow, even after all this time and with all this complication, still somehow work?

His red shirt was bringing out the color in his skin. The tattoo of the phoenix bird on his arm, the one she used to trace with her fingers, her tongue, was peeking out from his shirt sleeve. He looked so healthy and fit. She remembered his body, his long, lean body. She thought sitting there that she'd very much like to hold him again and feel the spasms and coursing flow when she did.

Then there was a piercing birdlike noise. A shriek, otherworldly, electric, vaguely intelligent, coming from the monitor between them. After a second, Kathryn realized that she was hearing a baby crying. Of course that's what it was, on the other end of the monitor, a baby crying through a garbled speaker. She heard it then, the same sound from the window of the house, the noise echoed in stereo.

He apologized and got up and went inside. A few seconds later she heard in the monitor a door open and quiet shushes as the crying trailed off, rustling and muffled talking, Jeff stringing words together, soft questions said to the baby that didn't need answers.

He was changing the baby, engaging the baby, talking to her tenderly as he worked. Kathryn listened to his fatherly movements. She reached out and touched the monitor. She was keenly aware of the plastic feel on the tips of her extended fingers. Like those parents who kissed the incubators. She heard his voice and felt the pressure contact. The plastic was warm.

This, she thought: This is Jeff.

She'd been so precise before with her emails after they'd reconnected, taking time between responses to really gauge what their effect would be. She'd mentioned needs, dropped the word innocently like a pebble in water to see where it went. *I need to buy some groceries*, then later. *I need some air. I need to get out more.* Needed to get to a computer to check her mail, see if he wrote. Until finally, *I need to see you.* She had asked, half-joking after some quick back and forth about the internet and living remotely, *is phone sex cheating, ha ha.* He didn't answer. She could almost hear the screen thinking.

The sounds in the monitor were gentle.

This, she stroked, this is Jeff.

And he had written to her, he had, asking why it was that he kept thinking of streetlamps in winter, of snow falling in a circle of light, which she knew, *knew*, was the view from her Chicago window, the one next to her bed where on certain nights you could lie on your back and watch the huge clumpy flakes fall slowly through the dark.

She felt him.

"This," she said. This is—

More sounds in the monitor, footsteps, more rustling, louder and less connected. Someone else was the room. Another voice was in the monitor, the words still muffled but Kathryn could tell it was a woman. She straightened herself and withdrew her hand and looked around the yard again. They were going back and forth, the voices, talking low. Kathryn couldn't make out most of what they were saying but there were words she caught—*finished early* and *who?*—and she did hear the whole question clearly, no mistake—*She's out back?*—followed by silence. Now whispers.

She uncrossed her legs. She swallowed and touched her hair, her pulse in her throat again.

Then the screen door cracked against the jam and Kathryn turned her head and saw a tall, thin woman in running shorts and a tight half-top walking towards her. The woman wasn't really smiling. She was a tower of swift movement and before Kathryn even had a chance to stand she was shaking this woman's hand still sitting in her seat. The woman's cheeks were reddened and her hair was dark and shiny, pulled back in a tight ponytail. Kathryn felt the heat coming from her body.

"Sit, sit. Don't get up. You must be Kathryn. I'm Sara," she said, continuing to shake Kathryn's hand. "I'd hug you, but I'm still all sweaty." The woman said this like they were old friends but only the corners of her mouth curved up. "I haven't met many of Jeff's old friends so, really, this is great." She took a seat on the bench across from her.

Kathryn nodded. "Thanks for having me over. I hope it's not too much trouble."

Sara shrugged. "Well, not for me," she said. "I didn't know you were coming." She scanned Kathryn's face for a second and then laughed and flipped her bangs. "If I knew, I wouldn't look like this," she said, leaning back and waving a hand down her front.

Kathryn followed the motion and looked at Sara. Her tight, defined abs. Her skin glisteny and tanned. Kathryn didn't know what to say.

Sara stared back. And then she smiled, a smile wide with teeth, bright and straight. "You'll have to forgive me. I'm usually much more talkative." She held up a finger and raised the glass of water she'd brought with her and downed the entire thing, gulp after gulp disappearing. When she was done she let out a huge sigh and said, "I can usually hold up whole ends of conversations."

Kathryn made a motion like it was nothing to worry about.

Sara leaned forward, the same way Jeff had done earlier, elbows on her knees, hands together, her head thrust into the space between them. "So," she said, her eyes fixed on Kathryn's, "How are you liking Austin?"

Kathryn shifted her weight in the wicker seat. "It's nice, but I haven't seen all that much. The job's so new and busy."

Sara was nodding as she started untying her shoelaces.

Kathryn looked up to the branches above her. "I like your tree."

"Thanks," Sara said, gazing up with her. "Me too. It's great when it blooms like this. But they'll all start dropping pretty soon. Then it'll be a mess. Have you been to the wildflower center yet, at UT?"

Kathryn shook her head.

"Oh, you should. It's beautiful. Especially now." Sara got her shoe off and gestured with it at Kathryn. "You'd like it."

"Okay."

"We'll go sometime," Sara said. "All of us." She smiled again and it seemed like even more of her mouth was in it this time.

Kathryn mumbled something by way of response and tried to drink her lemonade but only got a thimble's worth of melted ice instead.

Sara set her shoe down and started rubbing her foot. "You know, I have to admit," she said, kneading the heel and grimacing, "I've heard a lot about you. Didn't really know what to expect." Her face looked pained, but her mouth was still smiling. It hadn't stopped smiling this whole time. "The *Great Kate*," she said. She paused and straightened. "Oh, I'm sorry. I shouldn't assume, should I? Can I call you Kate?"

Kathryn was about to respond but she heard the screen door again as Jeff made his way outside to join them with the baby. He sat down in his seat again, straight backed and calm, his face more animated than before, smiling more, as he bounced the little girl softly on his knee. He looked back and forth between his wife and Kathryn, not saying anything. Finally he turned all the way to Kathryn.

"This is Brit," he said. "Say hello, Brit." He waved a little hand at Kathryn.

Brit was six months old, sitting up very well on her own, with bright, big eyes and only the tiniest bit of hair. She looked at Kathryn blankly, all over her face, studying her intently. Brit looked exactly like Jeff. Kathryn smiled and glanced at Sara and saw that Brit looked exactly like Sara as well.

"Want to hold her?" Jeff asked. "She'll come to you. She's good with strangers."

Kathryn said yes and accepted the baby and then the little thing was in her lap. The baby had no expression at all, just staring at Kathryn, pulled back a little, with her wet eyes and open mouth. On her lap now, Kathryn could hear Brit's shallow baby breath, air going in and out, passing thinly over her lips.

Kathryn held this baby—like the hundreds of others she'd held in her job—and she knew this baby. She knew everything there was to know about a human at this point in their life. She looked at the tiny, big eyes looking back at her and felt the weighty heft of her on her lap and she knew her.

A tingle moved up Kathryn's cheeks and she felt her face go prickly with heat. The magnolia branches swayed above her and she started to well up. She tried not to, but she started to cry sitting under the tree, just a little at first, trying to smile between bursts, trying not to jostle Brit too much, but soon it was more. Soon she was crying hard. She looked at the tiny face, the face that now showed signs of consideration, a pout responding which then turned to tears of its own—sympathy crying, they called it—and Kathryn couldn't stop.

Sara and Jeff seemed at a loss at first but they quickly moved in. Sara drew herself close, right next to Kathryn, their knees touching as her hand came over to caress Brit, stroking her daughter's face softly and shushing the baby on Kathryn's lap. And Jeff came over too, as if to hug Kathryn; he embraced her and put his arm around her—to comfort her, to rub her back gently, to hold her—although, really, he only did these things so he could take the baby away from her.

Steven Kurutz

Party George

Though he was no charmer in bars, or in nightclubs, restaurants, stores, offices or public spaces, George Castle believed he thrived in the depressurized atmosphere of a party, where girls were friendly, receptive to chance, and where with the assistance of an open bar he transformed into *Party George.* It was as this looser, more self-assured character that he first met Emily.

The men's style magazine that employed him was celebrating its first-annual "Real Men" issue. Cooked up by the new editor-in-chief, the theme seemed to cast doubt on what typical months featured. Regardless, it meant a party at a fashionable downtown hotel, and there he spotted her standing under a Warhol. She had on an elegant blue blazer over a crisp white shirt, her long dark hair cinched like an equestrienne's. That she was his physical opposite, with the tiny waist of a child, a smallness enhanced by his looming bulk, didn't discourage him.

Some men were made lustful by arresting curves, a walk. George Castle, 24, newish to the city, a low-born striver, was stirred by superior tailoring.

He floated his standard Party George opener: "So, what brought you to the party?"

Miraculously, she responded. Her boss at an interiors firm had designed the hotel's lobby, she said, and in a voice friendly and searching she asked, "What's your reason?"

Normally, his face would have gone numb. And later Castle would discover the problem with meeting someone as an imagined version of your best self. But now he was Party George.

He did a funny bit on the celebrity DJ and the absurdity of the profession. He spoke with winning self-deprecation of his junior editorial duties and plans to march up the masthead. He listened with interest yet remained protectively detached. It was, he thought later, alone on the subway, a commanding performance. If he was aiming for commanding he should have stopped then.

Her West Village studio from the moment he heard of it loomed in his imanation. Like the rest of the huddled yearning masses, Castle suffered the tyranny of a roommate. One night, after a month of feverish wooing and selling of himself—a bankrupting trial of drinks, dinners, a play, even a symposium at the 92Y on the films of Orson Welles hosted by Peter Bogdanovich, one Icarus saluting another—Emily invited him up.

The little apartment inside a townhouse was beautifully furnished like he'd imagined, with brass-leg tables, a French writing desk and a proper couch instead of a flimsy, post-college futon. Castle washed up in the bathroom, and when he pressed a towel to his face, it felt like drying with a summer cloud.

Emily moved about nervously, tidying up and apologizing for an imaginary mess. She seemed, for all of her allure to Castle, inexpert at hosting men, but he was too distracted to notice. He was studying a framed photo, hung prominently on the center wall, of her family—a large, smiling, tight-knit clan posed on a deep front lawn—and picturing himself squeezed in among them. He next scanned her oversized art books and her CDs, a mix of 90s Britpop and Gershwin.

When he held up a small box covered in worn brown leather, Emily exclaimed, "Isn't that *great*? I got it in Spain," and spoke nostalgically of a post-college summer studying Gaudí in Barcelona. Castle had spent a post-college summer working at an adult diaper factory back in central Pennsylvania. His grip on the box tightened.

In Lumber City, the rugged little town from which he'd escaped, the girls had a hard, fleeting beauty. By 15, most were screwing older guys who cruised town in mud-caked pickups and dipped Skoal wintergreen. Castle loved these girls' unapologetic sluttiness, their fuck-it attitude towards school and their own reputations. But he had neither a truck nor an interest in getting lip cancer, and instead dated a quiet girl who was considered weird because she openly read books.

At the state university he attended, his longing shifted to the well-groomed sorority girls from the Philadelphia suburbs, whose meals he served while working in the dining hall.

In New York, he'd so far been out with a sassy, quick-talking music publicist, who in one marathon date recounted her entire life story then vanished from his life, and an aspiring poet, a friend of a co-worker, whose fierce creative independence was undercut when during their date she called her mother three times. Then came Emily. She was the type of smart, stylish, well-traveled girl Castle had become aware of since moving to the city the year before and saw himself attracting much later, after he'd scratched his way to success and owned a German luxury car and a Hamptons beach house. Only he was years ahead of schedule. He could hardly contain himself.

Sometimes he wondered why Emily was single. Why wasn't she in one of those hermetically-sealed relationships where you curse the dude who got there first?

Now that he'd been allowed into her sanctuary, Emily revealed an ex-boyfriend. He was the son of a close business associate of her father. She'd loved this boy from childhood, she confessed, and had waited, virginal, for him to notice her. They finally got together during college. Then, senior year, she made a surprise visit to his Cornell fraternity house and found him under a tangle of bed sheets with a tarty British girl.

"He's such a *shit*," Emily said with fresh bitterness, and Castle, who knew no Britons, dimly saw in himself a safe harbor. Whatever keeps me snug in this apartment, he thought.

There'd been no one serious since, and now, on the cusp of 25, Emily had a busy, sexless routine: she socialized during the week and spent Saturdays at home, clipping pages from foreign editions of *Vogue* and watching old movies on TCM, a pleasure Castle shared. "I need the weekends to recover from my job, anyway," Emily said, sounding weary and without direction. After NYU, she'd wanted to become a dress designer but couldn't face artistic rejection. She'd tried fashion journalism but hated the freelance hustle. She discovered she was too dreamy for corporate retail, not frumpy enough for the nonprofit world. Interior design was her latest stab at a career and her good taste and easy sociability suggested a fit. But she worked for a high-strung woman who reacted to delayed furniture shipments with the drama of a hostage crisis. Lately, she'd been mulling grad school for psychology.

"I need to figure out my life," Emily sighed, burrowing under a Hudson's Bay blanket. On the little TV next to the bed Robert Osborne was introducing *Double Indemnity*.

Soon they were fucking. Or Emily was, gripping his big shoulders and smiling as if she were thrilled by their weight. Castle was *making love*: to the Warhol, to the crisp white shirt, to the little townhouse apartment, to the leather box from Spain, to the thrilling sensation he had penetrated the upper crust. He made love to everything but the actual, real person spread before him. Afterwards, with rising warmth in her voice, Emily told him that he reminded her of her beloved grandfather. An impoverished Polish immigrant, the grandfather had pedaled scrap metal in the streets of Newark and, in the post-war boom, built a flourishing business supplying high-grade steel to the builders of Manhattan skyscrapers. This same grandfather had married early and for life, put Emily's father and his siblings and their children through college and singlehandedly changed his family's course.

Castle had made a mockery of high school shop class, and lacked the native blue-collar facility for handcrafts and machinery. His own surname seemed too sturdy for him, somehow. He was puzzled by her comparison.

Emily propped up on one elbow, turned to him and said, "You have the same drive and purpose."

It pleased Castle to hear he projected an up-from-nothing ambition that harkened back to a teeming-immigrant America. Since his mind was so often filled with wealth fantasies and career schemes, he felt it presaged his own fortune. He'd yet to discover that a job in publishing won't get you a beach house in Montauk—or even Manasquan.

If Emily had stumbled a bit in love and work, she regained her footing around Castle. While scrambling eggs in a T-shirt the next morning, she pulled up her hair to reveal her pale, tender neck. She looked directly at him. She said, "You like it when I wear it this way, don't you?" Castle stood stunned. Not just because she articulated this secret turn-on, but because he was totally ignorant of her desires. Emily was a mirror that reflected back his aspirations; his only insight was that he was hopelessly drawn to her.

"Yes," he said. "Yes I do."

Soon they were out together several nights a week. Bleeding money and uneasy around new people, in particular anyone who might outshine him, Castle lobbied to stay in. But Emily spent her workdays trapped in the land of hysterics. "Enough TV," she'd say. "We can't meet anyone in this apartment."

"Haven't we already met someone?"

"You know what I mean. Let's go *out*."

Out they went. To gallery openings. To book parties. To events manufactured by PR people. Several of Emily's friends also worked in fashion, so they usually ended up at one or another bar/restaurant popular with the fashion crowd. Castle had stumbled into this world. Only a year before he'd been a schoolteacher, a position that in a poor, rural community carried high purpose and even esteem. But he was troubled by the thought that he'd arrived at his destination too early, that he'd be living the same day in an endless loop. He sent off a flurry of letters to jobs posted online and one found its way to the legendary editor of a style magazine. The editor was from a Pennsylvania coal town and partial to applicants like Castle. A twist of fate, a new life. So he was half-astonished to be frequenting tiny, subterranean bars in downtown Manhattan packed with stylists and photographers who were just back from a six-day swimwear shoot in the Rio slums.

One night, he and Emily doubled with her publicist friend, who was sleeping with a member of the Strokes. Admittedly, he was a minor Stroke. But there was George Castle, knocking back 7 and 7s in an East Village bar with a rock star. Past midnight, he and the Stroke got into a drunken musical debate, with Castle making the case that Paul, not John, had had the greater solo career. "Motherfucker, take another listen to 'Jet,'" Castle slurred, thumping his meaty fist down on the table to roaring laughter from the girls.

Party George was back!

Somebody snap his picture!

But then the Stroke said coolly, "So we're playing Tokyo next week," and he and Emily and her friend, who'd all been there, traded little observational bits about the city. Roppongi was nonstop, they all agreed. As Emily raved about the "mind-blowing" sushi at a fish market whose name Castle couldn't pronounce, he listened silently for what felt like weeks, a frozen smile on his face.

Whenever he got distressed over their differences in background and worldly experiences, he liked to think of Emily's grandfather. It reassured him to know that Emily, too, came from poor immigrant stock. Never mind that she was two generations removed from a pushcart, while his relatives had never stopped scuffling.

He thought of the grandfather as they walked from the bar back to her apartment. Crossing Astor Place, empty at that late hour, Emily said, "You got really quiet tonight around my friends."

Castle heard in her tone a critique. In a move that ran counter to his usual approach, he was honest.

"I didn't have much to say. I've never been anywhere."

"I like it better," Emily said, "when you're funny and outgoing."

They continued in silence. Soon they passed the bright-lit outer lobby of one of the many banks that were colonizing the city, and Emily's gauzy yellow top was made briefly, beautifully translucent under her unbelted trenchcoat, which fit her perfectly. Whatever feelings of despair and even anger towards her he'd had one minute earlier suddenly turned to desire.

The following Friday they were at Emily's apartment after work. Castle was still stricken from reading his latest credit card statement and announced he was going on "lockdown." No dinners out. No anything. Toward restaurant checks and rent payments Emily displayed a casual ease that suggested parental support. Yet she also used coupons at Duane Reade. She was no snob, either. Visiting Castle's dingy Brooklyn walk-up the first time, she didn't blink an eye (though she didn't rush back). He expected her to respond, in poorhouse solidarity, "We'll stay in, eat ramen." Instead, Emily's mouth tightened and she fixed him with a stern, almost enraged look. The look said coupon clipping was a choice—it wasn't going to be a lifetime sentence. A certain standard had been passed down, and would be maintained, with or without him.

Afraid of displeasing her, Castle said he would go out, but no cabs, and when later they came home, in a cab, he vowed never to talk about money.

In fact, he upped his spending.

For Emily's birthday, he took her to a temple of French cooking said to be the priciest restaurant in the city. Second priciest wouldn't do. So starchy was their waiter, so haute was the cuisine, even Emily appeared uneasy, reading the menu and saying, "Are you *sure*?" But his mouth curled into a reckless smile and he told her to order anything, *everything.*

Which fork first? What the hell was cucumber foam? Castle was adrift in uncharted waters, so nervous about making gaffes he was nauseous. As he handed over his credit card to pay the $800 bill, he thought of his mother and father back in Pennsylvania, freezing, with their thermostat turned down in winter to keep the bills affordable. He was a character out of Grimm, chasing a dazzling light, growing more lost with each step.

One night around this time Castle heard from a hometown acquaintance named O'Brien. They'd moved in the same small town teenage orbit, going to DJ dances in the Catholic Church basement, hanging on the corners, driving into the surrounding woods to smoke dirt weed. But it all felt to Castle like a lifetime ago, and his focus these days was on shedding that rural life. After O'Brien's call, he recovered a hazy memory of an all-night keg party in the woods; of being shaky on his feet; and of O'Brien, who virtually lived behind the wheel of an 80s Mustang painted sunrise orange, driving him home the next morning.

O'Brien said he was a roving union welder now. He was working on a big job out near Kennedy. During the week he and four other guys shared a single motel room in Bay Ridge to cut costs; on Fridays after work, he raced home on I-80. Commuting 270 miles and three states so he could make good money without leaving their dying hometown.

O'Brien suggested they meet up, and named a bar near the mouth of the Verrazano Bridge. When Castle arrived the next night, he found working men on worn vinyl stools and a white-haired woman behind the bar. Waiting for O'Brien, he watched a scrawny guy who looked exactly like Dickey Betts walk across the worn linoleum floor to the jukebox and select "Ramblin' Man," without irony. O'Brien, two weeks in the city, had found shitkicker turf amid all that concrete.

Castle had a busy work life, and a handful of friends he'd made through the magazine. But he thought of them as distinctly New York friends. He found himself surprisingly happy to see a familiar face. Tall and solidly built, with longish hair and a chestnut beard, O'Brien carried his size more confidently than Castle. He didn't walk so much as saunter through the door in the style of an oil roughneck. "I heard you were up here, man," he said, extending a steady hand. "Got your number from your brother."

O'Brien sauntered off to the bar and returned with the first round. After a brief, reacquainting silence Castle motioned outside. He could never get over the immense scale of New York compared to their town. "You could fit every person in Lumber City into a couple of these high-rises," he said.

"Yeah," said O'Brien. "With room leftover for the ones in jail."

On the way there, Castle had rehearsed a speech for the newbie packed with tips for adjusting to city life, hard-earned nuggets of urban wisdom. He remembered his own early days in New York as a heady mixture of excitement, bewilderment and sheer terror. He once took the wrong subway line at 2 a.m., and almost pissed himself out of fear, actually felt a few dribbles. If only someone had given *him* a little speech.

But before he could relay his strategy for handling disturbed subway bums, O'Brien launched into a story of seeing a Spanish man in the Times Square station dancing the tango with a sexy puppet, and another tale of going out for "a sixer and cigs" and wandering lost for an hour. O'Brien's tone was one of amusement; the city was a daily adventure. Where was the fear? The feelings of alienation that Castle battled? He tabled his speech.

Instead, they drank and talked about Lumber City and the characters that gave the place its scrappy charm. Like the old man who drove an antique tractor everywhere, even though he wasn't a farmer. He just liked to tractor around at a snail's pace. Remembering a kid they knew who had three different teenage girls pregnant at once, O'Brien declared, "It's a goddamn white trash record!"

"Speaking of characters," he added, "I saw your uncle last weekend."

"Rick or Curt?" asked Castle, referring to his father's brothers, one a hard-partying fuck-up, the other a drifter head case. When telling New York friends about his family he edited out the uncles.

"Curt," said O'Brien. "Guess he got booted from wherever he was living. Been sleeping on people's porches. Man, he looked it."

"I hope it's not hereditary," Castle said, only half-joking. He downed another beer, but instead of feeling drunk, around O'Brien he felt sturdy and centered.

O'Brien himself drank enough to tranquilize a jungle beast, displaying lower primate brain function only as they stood to go. Eyes glassy, he suggested they sneak into a park one night and throw a keg party.

"A kegger?" Castle said. "What should we do afterward? Race four-wheelers up and down Park Avenue?"

Earlier in the evening, O'Brien had called out Castle on his slick new appearance, pointing to his shoes—a pair of Italian loafers, the same ones the magazine had featured in a spring fashion spread—and saying, "What happened to the boots and grungy flannels? You went Hollywood."

Castle had reminded him they were in Bay Ridge.

"Hollywood is a state of mind, and those shoes"–O'Brien turned up his nose as if they were faerie booties–"are some Clooney shit."

O'Brien's remark stung. For all his upward striving, Castle believed he still held firm to his roots, even if he didn't openly show it. But keg parties were clearly one of the local folkways he'd left behind, along with fire hall weddings, canning gardens, God. No matter how much he missed these and other things—and sometimes he missed them like a severed limb—he didn't see where they fit with his present life and ambitions.

"You're wasted," Castle said now.

"So?" O'Brien said. "What difference does that make?"

Days later, Castle found himself calling O'Brien to meet a second time at the bar. And a third and fourth time in the weeks that followed.

As a reward for her servitude, Emily's boss flew her to Tuscany, to help furnish a hedge fund manager's villa. She returned home amorous. In bed, after, she said, "My whole family will be at my uncle's house next month. He's turning fifty and wants to distract himself with a big party. You'll come and meet everyone."

Castle didn't fully register her invitation. He was lying on his back, naked, and stewing over the way Emily liked to role-play in bed, inventing parts for him that bore no resemblance to his actual self. Previously he'd been Kip and Jean-Luc. Tonight, she'd cast him as Aldo, the suave heir to an Italian sports car dynasty, while she played herself as Aldo's wife. He hated this sexual playacting, once blurting mid-stroke, "*I just want to be George Castle.*" But did he? He worked at becoming a savvy New Yorker like a job and kept details about his hometown vague, relying on Emily's disdain for her suburban Jersey upbringing and tendency to romanticize. Emily knew only that he was from the vast middle of Pennsylvania that was neither Philly nor Pittsburgh. Into this outpost of Appalachia she'd invented a small town out of a Frank Capra movie, designing it the way she designed rooms. "I bet there's a soda fountain!" she squealed. It sounded better to Castle than empty stores, caved-in row houses, a prescription pill problem. A rust-belt city in miniature. If he was role-playing out of bed, what expectation could he have of being treated as himself in bed?

"This is your father's brother?" he asked her. "So your father will be there?"

In his prior relationships Castle had specialized in girls from busted-up families. In these fatherless households he needed only to show up and not be a raging asshole to be held as a shining example of manhood. From what he knew of Emily's father—corporate lawyer, backyard griller, organizer of family trips—he seemed very much involved.

In bed, Emily gave him gentle prepping. "Just ask my father his opinion about the war in Iraq or, I don't know, Bush's immigration policy. He's a political junkie." Castle made a mental note to watch *The McLaughlin Group*.

"My grandfather will be there, too," Emily said, referring to the man whose lifeblood was somehow present in Castle. "I told him about you."

She stretched a toned leg out and up as if doing horizontal plies, a post-sex habit that drove him wild, and asked, "Do you have a summer suit?" The question implied a closetful of suits, for every season and occasion. In one swoop, Castle thought miserably, he'd gone from needing one suit to needing ten.

He admitted he didn't, and Emily became excited about dressing him, tossing out looks rapid-fire: "How about gray linen?" "Do you think seersucker is too bold?" "Actually, wouldn't a khaki suit look very Robert Redford in *The Great Gatsby?"*

Castle pictured himself dressed, in the end, as the fictional Italian playboy Aldo. No, he'd buy the suit himself, he told her. But he said this too harshly and watched her leg fold up and slip back under the covers.

At work, he consulted the magazine's dapper, silver-haired fashion director, who sent him to a British menswear shop off Park. Accustomed to the fluorescent clamor of big-box stores, Castle stepped inside the pin-drop quiet boutique and felt every muscle tense, as if he were a thief breaching an unlocked townhouse.

A thick-necked salesman in a blue chalk-striped suit approached, his eyes falling to footwear.

Castle admired the way rappers and billionaire tech moguls wore sneakers to even formal events. But in copying the style, he now realized, the essential ingredients of success and money were missing and he just looked like a guy in a pair of scuffed-up Adidas.

"I'm here to buy a suit," he said, adopting a businesslike tone.

"Follow me," the salesman said, gruffly but not unkindly, and ascended a carpeted staircase lined with photos of famous clients: Winston Churchill, Prince Philip, James Bond. Now George Castle! They stopped at a rack of pants and jackets in luxurious fabrics. Beside it stood a tri-panel mirror and a wooden stool, upon which Castle stepped. The salesman measured Castle's big body, inherited from a line of Eastern European laborers, and said, "Let's see if we can work a miracle."

In guiding the fitting process, the salesman's style was reminiscent of a sports coach. "Now you'll want to go with a soft shoulder," he said, circling Castle, dispensing tips in his ear. "Watch your sleeve length. 'Attaboy." After Castle's measurements were recorded in a bound ledger and a suit selected—a navy two-button—the salesman grabbed two dress shirts, one white, one salmon. Leaning in close, as if revealing an important secret, the salesman whispered, *"Sea Island cotton."*

Castle had resolved not to ask the cost, since any budget above zero was theoretical. He was going to have the fine things he wanted whether or not he could afford them—it was his right as an American!

But he felt a powerful need to do something first. Slipping into the dressing room, he called Emily, who was in a nearby department store. When she swept in like Jackie Kennedy in dark sunglasses carrying shopping bags, the salesman instantly read the situation and shot Castle a look of disappointment, as if he'd wasted his coaching on the wrong guy.

"Wow!" Emily said. "Look who cleans up well."

Castle beamed. Like it was a compliment.

One evening, Castle rode the J train deep into Queens and walked along a noisy boulevard of gas stations and tire shops. Following the directions he'd been given, he turned up a hill into a thickly-forested city park. The sun was a red fireball floating on the horizon. The warm evening air contained the live-wire energy of late spring.

Where the dense path opened Castle saw a parking lot, empty but for O'Brien's truck, and O'Brien and another guy lifting a square red beer cooler from the bed. More guys in dirty jeans and work boots stood around with beers, talking and laughing.

When O'Brien had called Castle earlier that week, he'd just gotten out of a three-hour editorial meeting. The whole staff was still recovering from the loss, six months earlier, of the legendary editor, who'd dropped dead of a heart attack while power lunching on prime rib at the Four Seasons. His replacement, a baby-faced guy with a spiky haircut, was clearly out of his depth. He responded by coming up with 500 ideas a day, most of them contradicting his ideas from the day before. The baby-faced editor liked to sit the staff around a large conference table and ask everyone for insights into "our guy." Fearing for his job now that his patron saint was gone, Castle studied the habits of the metrosexual like an anthropologist. When it was his turn, Castle announced that "our guy" was increasingly using facial creams and suggested a trend story. The baby-faced editor loved the idea.

Now Castle and the others tramped with the cooler into the greening spring woods and down a ravine, until they reached level ground and a set of old LIRR tracks no longer in use.

Bottles littered the scrub grass beside the rail bed. A rocky cliff had been transformed into a hieroglyphic wall of graffiti:

FUCK SKOOL.

MANNY IS 4 REAL.

Castle looked around and realized the city, unbelievably, had vanished behind them.

"One of the guys I work with," O'Brien said, pointing, "partied here in high school."

"No keg?" Castle said. "I feel cheated."

"Can't have everything."

O'Brien fished into the cooler and came up with a Yuengling bottle. His face radiated contentment.

O'Brien introduced his work buddies to Castle. Muscled guys with chests like engine blocks. Castle was certain none of them used face creams.

"Where's your girl?" asked O'Brien. "I said on the phone bring her along." He held up his beer to the surrounding woods. "This is the Lumber City experience right here."

Keeping Emily from the Lumber City experience was a daily mission for Castle. He'd invented excuses each time she'd asked to meet his "Dear Friend from Pennsylvania," as she called O'Brien, or he'd asked to meet her.

"She had a work thing tonight," Castle lied.

Someone had brought along a boom box. Out blared the demented opening wail of "Crazy Train."

A guy with a bald head set off by an unruly goatee made a loud whoop. "If I couldn't hear 'Crazy Train' ever again I'd shoot myself," he said. "Just pull the fuckin' trigger. I won't live in a world where I can't listen to 'Crazy Train' while enjoying an adult beverage."

Castle chuckled. "That's no life at all. I feel sorry for the Pilgrims."

"Me, too," the guy said solemnly.

Two pipefitters from Bensonhurst were trading piss-test stories nearby, recalling tense waits for NIDA-5 results. They sounded like chemists detailing the process to flush coke from the bloodstream. Castle listened to them talk, enjoying himself royally. Away from the Manhattan bubble he felt relaxed and self-assured. No pressure to appear cultured. No fear of someone waving around an Ivy League degree like a loaded gun. (It was a moral failing that *he* liked to be the credentialed member of any group.) Standing beside O'Brien at a beer party in the woods, he felt reconnected to some trashy, rustic past.

In moving to New York, it dawned on him, large parts of himself had been covered over and forgotten, the way a modest house is bulldozed in an upscaling neighborhood. Not that long ago, Castle would have been happy just to live in a town with a McDonald's and a movie theater. Why was he now spending four grand he didn't have to dress like James Bond? Somehow, New York had awakened in him a monster of greed and ambition. He couldn't blame the city. People moved here all the time and weren't disfigured by it.

O'Brien scratched his boot across the gravel, bringing Castle back. "Well, this is it. After next week I'm gone."

"Why? Are you taking time off?"

"No, man. Job's done. Just some polish work left." O'Brien polished off his beer in exclamation. "I'm headed down around Lancaster to work on a Walmart Supercenter. Construction's booming."

Castle became very aware of his face; it felt heavy, formless, sagging. Like he'd been punched. He knew O'Brien's comforting presence in the city was fleeting, yet, insanely, forgot. Trying to work his features back into a dignified position, he said, "Can't you get another job here? Can't you get hired to rebuild the World Trade Center or something?"

"Nah. I'm ready to go back. I saved enough for a down payment on a house. I'm getting married in the fall." O'Brien laughed wistfully, as if the experience had already passed into memory. "It was fun, but this place isn't my speed. I got to hand it to you, I don't know how you keep up."

Is that what I'm doing, keeping up? Castle thought. He wanted, at that moment, to renounce New York, to drive back with O'Brien and teach history to eighth-graders, but knew the minute he did he'd be restless for something bigger. This was his impossible contradiction. As Castle worried over it once more, the opening piano notes of "Against the Wind" echoed from the boom box. The music made him picture horses running free on a beach, like every Bob Seger song.

"I might be able to get to the bar one more time," O'Brien said. "I'll let you know." Then he slipped into the leafy darkness to get another beer.

When finally the day of Emily's uncle's party came, they drove to Jersey under one of those cloudless skies that offer no cover. The uncle lived in Bergen County, in a neighborhood that approximated forested isolation yet was two minutes to a Starbucks.

"Here it is!" Emily said, pointing out a large stone house newly-built, its driveway packed with nice cars.

Castle forced his old Accord onto the driveway's edge. He killed the engine and watched, amazed, as Emily stepped from the passed-down heap as regally as if by chariot, whereas he slinked away catlike, as if he'd just shit on her uncle's lawn.

As they approached the house, Emily said, "Just be yourself," though what help to him was that?

Inside, she rushed ahead. Castle trailed her in his new suit across vast rooms and out French doors to a deep backyard, where his legs buckled at the sight of her family and a crowd of friends, drinking on the patio, gossiping at tables, splashing in the pool. The mythic leisure class—at leisure.

A Hispanic caterer walked past, balancing a tray of hors d'oeuvres, and Castle felt the sudden need to grab a tray and join him as a server.

Emily waved him over. He waited a moment, so as not to seem totally lap doggish. Then he went to her anyway.

"Mom, Dad, this is George." Emily's mother had let her hair grow long and gray in a bohemian way, while her father, unlike the square-jawed provider he'd imagined, had birdlike features and the lean muscled arms of a swimmer. Castle braced himself, expecting, as a prospective son-in-law, to be made to pass through some gauntlet. But her father just said "Glad you could make it" before he and his wife excused themselves to greet an arriving couple, leaving Castle with a stillborn sensation and an unused anecdote about the Oslo Accords.

Castle beelined for the open bar and gulped two Jamesons to calm his nerves. When he returned, Emily was talking to the most elegant older woman he'd ever seen. Outfitted in tan slacks and a buttery-brown leather coat, with matching leather boots and a jaunty brimmed hat, she looked dressed for a chauffeured safari. Something about the diamond compactness of her body reminded him of Emily.

He felt a strange sexual attraction to the old woman, whom Emily introduced as her grandmother. As at the magazine party where he and Emily had met, the alcohol now emboldened him, turned him into the more confident *Party George.*

"You look incredible!" he flirted.

"Well, I should," the grandmother said, touching his arm. "My husband paid a fortune for these clothes."

"Grandma!" said Emily.

"What? I'm having fun talking to your charming friend."

At the mention of Emily's grandfather, Castle grew curious to meet the man to whom he'd been compared. But Emily frowned and said, "Grandpa isn't feeling well. He's inside, lying down." Castle waited a minute and then excused himself, saying he had to use the bathroom.

Inside the empty house cooled air pumped wastefully. Moving through the kitchen, Castle overcame the intruder's fear of being found out. He went room to room, and at the end of a dim hallway, he found Emily's grandfather in the den. Faced with the home's shiny grandeur, the old man had retreated, purposely it appeared, to a room whose musty scent and cozy dimensions were tenement-like. Back in Lumber City, Castle knew plenty of people worn down by a lifetime of work, his own relatives included. But Emily's grandfather looked as if his very *essence* had been ground to nothing. He sat sleeping on a recliner, covered with a fraying green blanket, his face shriveled like a piece of fruit sucked of its juice.

For a long time Castle stood in the doorway, watching the grandfather slurp little gulps of oxygen at sporadic intervals. He saw no resemblance between himself and this worn-out old man who sat alone while the people he had sweated for and carried on his back drank and laughed in the sun. None whatsoever! But when the grandfather gave a stir, Castle turned, and as fast as he could, ran back to the party.

Eliana Ramage

Elder Watching

The last time we were all together was the first time I saw Kituwah. Kituwah is the place we came from, the place where water spider carried over the first fire in a basket she wove on her back, and the place where God gave us the laws about how to be the people. When we spread out into towns across the mountains of the Southeast, embers from that first fire were carried by messengers to all the different towns during the Green Corn Festival. They'd light a communal village fire, and everybody stoked their home fires with that village fire the whole year through. So we would always be connected, so we'd always have Kituwah pulling us back home. When they tore us from the mountains, we hauled the embers clear across to Oklahoma in battered tin buckets and yes, 4,000 of us died and yes, we kept those embers lit.

But to white people that place was called Ferguson's Field. To them, it was a mound that took thousands of years to build and a couple seasons to plow down because the Fergusons were farmers and farmers like flat.

It took 13 hours to get to North Carolina for Tri-Council. 13 hours of plastic-wrapped sandwiches, Ruth's head leaning back down on my shoulder faster than I could slap her away, the same Country Top-40 coming in on every station, fading into static, coming back again from the Ozarks to Appalachia. 13 hours just to get Daddy to his tribal council meeting, and the moment we got there he just ran off to see his council friends.

Mama whisked us into the hotel for check-in and a costume change. First, there was the matter of Ruth's tear dress—the screaming and the searching of the room and the calling down to the front desk for an iron.

Mama fussed. Here, let me take a wet wipe to the beading on those moccasins. It's filthy. Haley Beth Duncan, I don't know why it was too much to ask for you to polish your crown before we left. Are you girls trying to punish me?

She used to put us in Tiny Tots dance competitions at powwows, which was pretty normal for an Indian mom to do, but then it got out of hand. Pretty soon she was driving us to pageants for Little Cherokee Ambassadors, then Junior Miss, then Miss. I spent every summer spread out on the roof of our apartment building, working on my tan so I'd be ready to beat the next full-blood girl come into town with a hunted deer slung over her buckskin-clad shoulder. She never showed up, but blood still haunted me.

Mama had always been there to sew our tear dresses, bead our moccasins, do our hair, and quiz us on Cherokee language and history before the competitions. The walls in our apartment were thin, and I fell asleep to the clack of Mama at the sewing machine. She stayed up real late into the night, machine fixed to the applique setting as she sewed geometric designs on our cuffs and hems. She woke up early the next day and drove us to school in her bathrobe, and the whole ride there she made us answer practice interview questions: "What in your opinion is the greatest strength of the Cherokee Nation?" (Answers: *Our language, our culture, our traditions, our elders; and our children–who are the future.*)

But our Tiny Tots days were long over and we had moved on to being the public face of tribal womanhood.

Mama took a step back and stared at us in the mirror. Tear dresses had never been flattering on me. The older I got, the worse I looked in them. I was wearing the dress I had worn on my float in the Cherokee National Holiday parade: purple florals with a plain band of decoration where the fabric ballooned at my arms and waist.

There are two stories about tear dresses. Some people say that we started wearing them after the Trail of Tears, when we didn't have any scissors and the bulky pattern was torn straight from bolts of fabric. And then there's the story about Miss Indian World, some Cherokee girl in the seventies who shamed the entire Nation by having to wear a Choctaw outfit at her crowning. They say that a group of Cherokee aunties got together and invented the tear dress, so Cherokee women would have something to call traditional.

If that were the case, I wished they'd designed it a little more forgiving. I had, as Miss Beth said, "filled out"—a statement I appreciated even less than my dress's drop waist.

Mama did my makeup, which I could've done myself. Someone in the next room had the news on high volume.

"Can we go yet?" I asked.

Mama licked her thumb and rubbed an invisible spot on my crown.

"Mama?" Ruth crossed her arms and sighed. She looked stupid, posed like a surly teen in what was basically a floor-length calico pioneer dress.

"Fine," Mama said. "Let's get on."

The councils took roll like a steep drive through the Ozarks: slow, and pressing tight to the side you know. It was the first year we'd ever had a Tri-Council meeting, the first time the Nation had been united since the Trail of Tears, and we were careful not to mingle too much. Each of the three bands sat together. Each council looked like old friends at a favorite booth in a bar, and that's exactly where they'd head after the meeting. Least, that's where Daddy always went with his council friends.

Eastern Band wore ribbon shirts and bolo ties and tear dresses, and I guess they said whatever the Eastern dialect is for "present"—I didn't catch it. UKB wore more or less the same, and they said "ahani" or "v'v." As for Cherokee Nation, we're known for our stubbornness almost as much as our low blood quantums: our guys wore suits, and when you called their names they said "here."

The announcer spoke like she was wading through creek words, tossing out extra syllables to the vowels she liked best. She had to be Eastern Band.

"Before we begin with the resolutions," she said, "We've got a couple performances. First, we'll have Miss Martin's first grade class from the Cherokee Nation, and then we'll have Miss Eagle's kindergarteners from the Eastern Band."

A group of five kids came shuffling onto the stage. The girls pulled at their tiny tear dresses, and the only boy fiddled with a black and red finger-woven sash. The sash was all he had, Cherokee-wise, and he wore it tied around what had to be a slightly older brother's basketball shorts and wifebeater. He tugged the ends around his neck and looked like he was fixing to strangle himself. A young-looking teacher yanked it from his grip and ran back off stage, and then the children sang a short song I almost understood: *usdi yona, usdi yona, osda tlegi, osda tlegi.* Little bear, little bear, good something, good something. Again and again.

I bet non-Indians would think it's cute. Maybe beautiful. If this were in the newspaper I know there would be words like "reclaiming," "survival," "strength," and "the next generation." They'd probably put in a short paragraph about the horrors of the Trail of Tears, just enough to feel bad but not bad enough to do anything about it. Like when Mama said, "if there's anything I can do" at Auntie Beth's mother's funeral when there wasn't anything Auntie Beth would ever ask for or that Mama would ever do for her. I watched the kids onstage tug at the outfits their mothers sewed and I felt tired knowing what would come next.

After the Cherokee Nation kids ran back to their seats, on came 20 little Eastern Band kids. Their girls were in tear dresses, too, but it was their boys who went all out. Those little boys outdid us, right down to the white trade shirts and buckskin leggings.

They sang *Amazing Grace*, the song Mama couldn't get Ruth to learn during the drive from Oklahoma. They sang the whole song, even the last four verses that everybody skips because, honestly, by the end of the second verse, we get it—you're great.

I heard Miss Eileen and Miss Sandra whispering to each other in the seats in front of us. They did that at home, too.

"It's what I'm always saying," Miss Eileen said. "These Eastern folks always gotta show off to us. Why can't they have some sense?"

"Eastern people, I swear, they think they're so special."

I tried to catch Ruth's eye, but she was texting behind a propped-up notebook. Elder-watching had always been our favorite sport. We thought there should have been a show: *Indian Elders say the Darnedest Things,* or maybe, *Indians Behaving Badly.*

The announcer said: "We will now move to our first item on the agenda. Are the council members prepared to vote on Resolution 101-A?"

The morning passed slowly, and I was grateful for Mama's reminder that I pack some beading. Ruth was still in her needlework rebellion phase ("Give her time," Mama said), so I was helping Mama get Ruth's new moccs beaded before the end of her term as Junior Miss.

Mama and I had decided on an Eastern Woodlands pattern, with octagonal buds you'd find on Cherokee beading going back maybe a century but never in nature.

When I was little, and everybody was going on about our land and how we lost it, I wasn't so interested in the traditional stories and the history that tied us to these mountains. I thought our land was magic because of the beading patterns, and how the flowers and leaves back East were the kind that couldn't exist anywhere else. I guess I half-expected them to be made of Czech size 11/0 opaque beads.

A few hours in, the UKB tribal council tried to put Resolution 7 on the table: *Resolution to condemn the closing of the casino of the United Kituwah Band.*

I looked up. Mama sighed.

The announcer hesitated. "I'm sorry, I'm afraid that resolution is not on the pre-approved agenda."

The UKB councilman said the issue needed to be addressed.

Miss Beth laughed. She reached across Daddy for the nearest microphone and flipped a long strand of shiny black hair over her shoulder.

"Jim," she said, "Y'all haven't got any tribal land in federal trust. You can't operate a casino as the UKB if you've plopped it down on Cherokee Nation land. Now, we're not the ones saying it's illegal, the U.S. government is."

She smiled then, and looked out at the audience. "But, you know, now isn't the time or place to get into that."

The UKB man, Jim, sat down, but not before announcing to the whole Tri-Council that the UKB would be suing the Cherokee Nation right away when we got back to Oklahoma.

Miss Beth muttered something nasty about Eastern Band and how rich they are now with the new Harrah's, though Lord knows how that was related. Daddy grabbed her elbow and pulled her back down.

After that no one seemed to remember what was related, or that we as a nation ever were. The three chiefs banged on their plastic folding table and said that we were all family—and Jim said sure, but some of us are more related than others.

Miss Beth stood again and walked right up to him. Daddy didn't follow her, but he still held his arm up, hand still shaped to her elbow. Miss Beth asked Jim if he had a problem with intermarriage.

He said, "Your white tribe wants to call me out for racism?"

Chief Kingston yanked the mic from the announcer's hand. "Lunch break," he said. "Everybody out."

I told Mama that Beth was losing it.

She shook her head and gathered up her beading. "Don't talk like that about an old friend," she said.

She signaled for Daddy, but he was already near the exit with Beth.

"She sure is memorable," said Mama. She threw her beading in the bottom of the bag and I knew we'd have to untangle the hanks on the drive home.

It was the quietest hog fry I ever attended. There was supposed to be a smell, grease in the air like you could feel it, fresh-cut grass, kids running wild and too many shades of laughter. But they'd made the food beforehand, and it sat in the cafeteria cold in aluminum pans. Talking was all whispers within bands. Nobody wanted to gossip with the wrong person.

We prayed a long prayer and lined up in the order of people raised right: elders, almost-elders, grown-ups, and kids. That's pretty much pan-Indian, and Mama had a story about the time she went to Gathering of Nations Powwow in New Mexico and some teenager cut my wheelchair-bound grandma in the frybread line. Kid nearly got skinned alive, she said, by which she meant the elders chewed him out and questioned his lineage for rude tribal ancestry.

But after the morning's drama we were all on our best behavior, even taking second helpings of traditional bean bread when nobody likes it. We spoke softly, and reigned in the children when they stuffed kanuchi up their noses.

Mama sat on Daddy's right, and Beth on his left. Mama held his hand, but mostly kept quiet and ate. Daddy and Beth talked politics, going way back to how UKB abandoned the homelands in the early 1800s when those who would become the Cherokee Nation held tight till the bayonets came out.

Daddy and Beth went way back themselves, and sometimes those two reminded me of Grandma and Grandpa. They leaned in close, laughed, went off on the Eastern Band and how they hid in the mountains instead of coming with us on the Trail. "Cherokee people can't do that," Grandpa used to say, "You go where the people go, even when it kills you."

I always wondered: are we pissed at UKB because they left our land, or are we pissed at Eastern Band because they chose it? I never really learned how those two grudges made sense together, but it was coming on 175 years since then, so I knew we were good at being pissed.

Mama took Daddy and Auntie Beth's empty plates and piled them over her own. She dropped Daddy's hand and stood there for a minute, three plates, three forks, three knives, three cups in her arms. Daddy said something to Auntie Beth and she laughed.

I dragged Ruth to the auditorium and made her eat with me. I told her if she didn't, I'd tell Mama about her white boyfriend Jesse. We ate our pork and dumplings in silence and threw out the bean bread. I didn't want her to see what I saw.

Mama and Daddy had met working for the Nation. Mama still had the same job she'd had back in high school, working behind the check-out counter of the museum gift shop. Her blonde hair made her more approachable, and even when it greyed you could still tell she was low blood quantum. Tourists asked her questions at the counter about the Indians, questions they were embarrassed to ask the brown people who worked at the Ancient Village: *Where are the teepee exhibits? Where can I find out more information about my Indian great-great-grandmother? How many Indians are alive these days?*

Daddy had spent his entire adult life in tribal politics, but when he met Mama, he was a Cherokee re-enactor in the Ancient Village. He could do great things with a blowgun, but he never learned to do his own hair. It was long and black, and Mama showed up early every morning to braid it. Your daddy was a piece of work, she said. Always talking, looking around, jerking that half-finished braid right out of my hand with his laugh.

Daddy used to joke about that job, about how when he and Mama were dating, he'd spend his lunch hours with her because of the gift shop A/C. Mama sometimes joked about the way he'd flirt with the girls from the stickball exhibit, how tacky they were in their buckskin tops and sports bras. But the delivery always fell short; Mama wasn't a funny woman.

I was in a bathroom stall. I sat still with my head in my hands, breathing. I did that at home sometimes, too, when the apartment felt too small. I sat there and breathed in the smell of antibacterial soap. Hand-dryers hummed; a quarter clinked down the tampon dispenser.

I sat in that stall, trying to wrangle four yards of heavy calico and hold it high, away from the seat, while Miss Eileen stood at the mirror and talked about my father and "that girl on council."

I imagined Sandra shaking her head. "That's nothing," she said. "I saw him coming out of her room at the Holiday Inn this morning."

"They must be morning people," Eileen said.

I flushed and left the stall. I scrubbed my hands harder than I ever had. I stared straight ahead.

I saw Eileen look at Sandra through the mirror. They switched from English and huddled close like mean high school girls. They spoke quiet, muffled Cherokee; short sentences that meant so much.

I turned and looked straight at them.

"'Siyo," I said.

They stared at me.

"Tohiju? Ayv tohiqu ale alihelisdi ahani. Nasginasque edodi."

I ran out of the bathroom, surprised at myself. If I'd said it right, they'd know I understood them. They'd know how rotten they were, no question.

If not, they'd know I was just one more mixed kid with an English-Cherokee dictionary.

During the first afternoon recess, I went looking for him. The individual councils were spread out around the school, so I started with the higher grades. The sixth grade had Cherokee language diagrams of photosynthesis on its classroom door, and the fifth had hand-drawn family trees. The school's third graders had a small exhibit of traditional pottery lined up on a plastic folding table outside their door. They had a long way to go towards shaping anything round.

I saw them then, through the window of the door of Miss Eagle's kindergarten classroom. They sat side by side on the teacher's wooden desk, calves dangling. They read from Daddy's council notes. Dad pressed his palm to her thigh.

I touched the door handle. It was cold in my hand. His fingers slid higher, and closer to the pick-stitch hem, and I turned away, and I let go.

You can't trust a word Miss Eileen says. Miss Sandra, either. That's what my father told me when he left us.

He still wanted to be chief someday, so he had to be subtle. I guess Mama let him because she was tired. She never said a word about it. After he left the house was quiet, except at night when Ruth and I were in bed and the door was closed and the machine was on and she sobbed through the whir of the needle.

She sewed us each new jingle dresses. We hadn't danced jingle at powwow in years, but we knew better so we ignored the crooked ribbon applique and uneven hems and we said thank you, ma'am. We said, how did you know?

I walked straight to the hotel in the rain, and I didn't take off my moccasins even when I felt the tear of asphalt ripping underfoot. Heavy, wet, muddy black, they had just a few sparks of beading visible.

I fell asleep. Beth's room was down the hall. I missed my only responsibility, which was letting them take my picture with the other princesses, and I missed dinner, and I probably missed a couple more council fights. But I woke up for Kituwah.

They called us up to the mound. It used to be huge, though I've forgotten how huge. The Kituwah I know is the Kituwah that was sold and plowed after Removal, a mound maybe five or six feet high. It's wide around, though, and it took a while for us to quietly find our places.

They came. Grandmothers rolled in wheelchairs with toddlers on their laps, grandfathers on canes and walkers with grandsons in their grip. Children and grandchildren walked slowly, taking tiny steps and carrying their elders in such a way that they would not realize their weight was not their own. Arms wrapped under shoulders, around waists. Hands held hands and fingers and wheelchair grips. They walked together across the grass, all our parents' parents.

It was 50 feet from the road to the mound—a long way for a frail person. We stood, quiet. We waited.

Mama had made us bring dirt from home. She'd gone out in the backyard in

Oklahoma and filled four bags. A Ziploc of damp soil from the garden, a Kroger bag of sand from the sandbox, a paper bag of red clay from under the porch, and a second Ziploc of black earth she had to dig deep to get to. She'd labeled each of these with our names and set them out on our suitcases the night before we left.

We stood at Kituwah, Mama, Dad, Ruth, and me, with bags of dirt at our feet. From across the circle I saw Beth. She wore a sleek fitted pantsuit, the kind that made my mother look short. She rested a hand on the back of her mother's wheelchair and smiled at my father. I grabbed Ruth's hand. She rolled her eyes at me, but didn't pull away.

After the blessings and speeches, after the sun had gone down below the green mountains that held us from every direction, we came forward. We poured the dirt from our homes into a turtle shell, and we turned that over onto the center of the mound. In this way Kituwah was supposed to grow tall again, but it would take time.

When we had finished, all of us–the people who couldn't stand on their own and the people who held up their people and the kids silent with the whispered threats of spankings–the three chiefs said what a blessing it was to be together again. How we were torn apart when they stole our land, and how we were never meant to be broken like this. How we were one nation, and we'd always be one nation. Then an old man came out into the center of the mound. He carried a walking stick and it poked holes in the ground when he leaned on it too hard. He spoke in Cherokee.

I like to think he talked about home. About family and forgiveness, about the Nation as a family and family as the people who will stand by you. The people who will protect you and be good to you, who will hold up your world from the sky vault *Galunlati* like the four birds who hold the ropes in each direction. Like the water beetle who swam to the bottom of the ocean again and again, coming up each time with the grains of mud that would form our land. Like the buzzard, who flapped his wings across the new and muddy earth to dry it, who flew too low in our homelands and created our mountains and valleys with the trail of tired wings.

But his Cherokee came from another world, one I couldn't put together with my piles of do-it-yourself phrasebooks. I couldn't tell when those deep, cracked syllables broke off to separate words, I couldn't tell when they held strong. I only remember one word he said that day, or that I'd like to think he said: *O we nv sv.*

Home.

Elliot Sanders

Pleasure Seekers

When Don and Beth maxed out the Visa, they decided to sublet the basement. Not that they were entirely keen on having a stranger living with them, but the basement was like a mini apartment. It cried rental—at least this is what their real estate agent had told them 11 years ago. But back then, they had two small children and used the basement as a playroom. When the kids got noisy, Beth and Don would retreat upstairs. Two floors up, they could barely hear Silas and Izzy; just some soft knocking against the sheetrock, the occasional vibration when Silas (seven) got into the dumbbells. "Sounds like mice in the walls," Don told Beth at the time. "Or cats," Beth added.

The kids were grown now, away at college in California. 3,000 miles, was it? Silas was at San Diego State, and Izzy up north a ways, at Stanford. It had been a shock, their children moving so far for college. But when Izzy had been accepted to Stanford, how could they argue with that? Of course, they'd asked Silas to stay local for college, but he'd given them a month-long guilt trip about the essential unfairness of Izzy being in bright, shiny California, and him stuck in Western Mass, with its long, moody winters and muggy, mosquito-flecked summers. *Okay, okay,* they both agreed, finally. Now the kids had been gone nearly two semesters and the house was oh so quiet. They both felt a bit cheated by unexpected loneliness.

Beth had spent the past few months repainting the basement and arranging furniture. It was, after all, such a nice house: an airy four bedroom with a loft and palace windows. There were two flagstone patios, one out back and another attached to the basement, surrounded with azaleas and leafy hostas and bushy rhododendron that Beth tended spring and summer.

But college tuition was expensive and they needed the money. "It'll be like having a new neighbor," Don said. "Only closer." The space was probably best suited for a college student, but U-Mass Amherst was a half hour drive, and many students, like Silas and Izzy, were without cars. Plus, college kids came with noise, parties, empty beer cans. That was the last thing they wanted, their house turning into a frat dive. They'd advertised in the paper, but no calls had come in. It seemed like a good deal: cheap rent, fully furnished, and everything carpeted except for a storage room containing the furnace.

"We could try Craigslist," Don said over breakfast one morning.

"God no," Beth said.

"What's wrong with Craigslist?" He reminded her that they'd practically furnished their whole dining room on Craigslist.

Beth admitted that, yes, they had. But that was years ago. Back then they were poorer and more naïve. And Beth had always sent Don in with the money while she waited in the car. It made her uncomfortable anyway, she said, Don walking into a stranger's house with a wad of cash in his pocket.

"We're going to get a smoker," Beth said. "I can just feel it."

"You used to smoke."

"I hope we get a girl," Beth said. "Or a mom with a kid. That could work."

"A single mom?"

"No, that's sad. I take that back."

Don stood up, scratching at the nest of wires and adhesive tabs under his sweater. The heart monitor was a recent development. Almost every night now, he woke to a red-lined, stuttering heart. The blood was squibbing and squirting in all the wrong directions. That's what it felt like, anyway. Three in the morning, he'd get out of bed and grope blindly to the bathroom mirror, where in the glow of the nightlight he studied his pale, haunted face. Each time he was absolutely sure this was the moment: he was going to drop dead right here on the tile. The only consolation was that his kids wouldn't be the ones to find him.

He panicked again on the exam table at the cardiologist's office, hooked up to the EKG. Words drifted through the air:

V-fib…

tacky-caaaardia

atrial valve…

Catheter ablation

Catheter what? Don had said. And if that didn't work, then what? What was the worst case scenario? He hated the hospital. He'd been admitted for something unrelated a few years back, and remembered it for the beeping, sleepless nightmare that it was.

Eventually, Don and Beth did use Craigslist, mostly at Don's urging. A week later, a young woman named Julie phoned and said she'd take it right away. Beth wondered if they should conduct some kind of interview, but Don said that would just freak her out—she sounded so nice on the phone.

The day of Julie's arrival, Don and Beth watched at the front window. Here came Stan Roderick with his giant mastiff. Every day, Stan and his dog walked down the street, stopping at the corner of Don and Beth's lawn. Then Stan reached into a pocket and put on a ball cap, at which point the dog squatted in their lawn and did his business. Stan never picked it up. It was infuriating, senseless. What bothered Don worst was the donning of the ball cap. He was certain it was some cue. Stan had *trained* the dog to shit in their lawn. But why? They'd never done anything to the Rodericks. They were as invisible to each other as all the other neighbors.

When Julie's Nissan Sentra pulled up, Don and Beth put on their coats and shuffled down the driveway. "She's pretty," Beth hissed in Don's ear. And she was—spongy brown curls and a soft, earnest face with blue eyes. She wore a kicky little wool blazer and a tight turtleneck that showed off her chest. Julie saw Don and Beth and stepped into the yard to greet them, but when she put her foot in the grass, she immediately lifted it up to inspect her boot.

"Oh, shucks," Beth said.

Julie wiped her boot clean on a chunk of snow. Beth apologized.

"No biggie," Julie said. "I grew up with three Great Danes. Our yard was a practically a sewage plant." She stuck her finger in her mouth in a mock gag.

Don helped Julie carry boxes from her trunk to the basement, making a path through the slush. Beth followed them back and forth with a barrage of questions. Was Julie in school? Did she work? Did she have family nearby? Would she be having much company? Was there a boyfriend?

They stood by the glass slider. "Well," Beth said. "If you need anything, you know where to find us." She pointed her index finger straight up.

"Wow, three stories," Julie said. "If these were medieval times, you guys would be nobles. And I'd be like, a serf or something, tucked away in the cellar." She laughed. "Oh, in the future, just call me Jules. It's sort of my go-by. Toodles."

Don thought Beth looked like she had wanted to give Julie a hug, but was holding herself back, sticking to lesser-lessee protocol. In the absence of their own children, Beth seemed ready to glom onto anyone under 30. But this *wasn't* Izzy. This girl was 22, and totally different from Izzy, and disturbingly attractive—so attractive that Don felt anxious each time they made eye contact. It frustrated him, his inability to squelch desire at this age (52 next year!). With the heart monitor poking at his chest, he was a goddamn walking medical experiment.

Turned out, Jules wasn't hard to live with. They saw little of her. Which was surprising, considering that she didn't seem to work. She was practically interred down there in the basement, and Beth wondered what she was up to.

"Maybe she's one of those trust fund puppies," Beth said. "She'll be set until thirty. Then she'll be lost."

"Or homeless," Don said. But Jules paid her rent. She had given them three months up front. The only thing that did bother them—and it was a little thing, really—was that certain items seemed to be disappearing from the fridge. A bottle of ketchup. A jar of pickles. Sometimes the gallon of milk looked a bit lower in the morning.

"You know what bothers me about this," Beth said. "Why doesn't she just *ask*. If the girl wants a pickle, ask for a pickle."

Neither of them was even sure when Jules was in the kitchen. It was disconcerting, imagining her sneaking upstairs after they went to bed, if that's what was going on. Don was home all day (he worked from home), and he rarely saw her. One morning they woke up and, strangely, their bedroom door was wide open. Beth swore she'd closed it, but of course they couldn't be sure.

A week later, perhaps to ease their misgivings, they invited Jules up to the kitchen for dinner. "She must get lonely down there," Beth said. She sent Don down the stairs to knock on the bedroom door. There was no answer. He knocked again. The door was unlocked and he pushed it open. Jules lay in bed with an oxygen tube up her nose. Her eyes were closed. Don startled. Oh shit, he thought.

Jules opened her eyes, then giggled when she saw Don's face. "Didn't mean to scare you," she said. "Just catching my Os."

"Os?"

"You know, oxygen? Sometimes I use it when I get tired. It's supposed to wake you up. But the funny thing is, it usually ends up putting me to sleep."

Over dinner Jules explained that she was a hospice nursing assistant, but in between jobs right now because her recent patient, a 90-year-old named Jeb, had just died.

"Oh my," Beth said.

Jules said, "Jeb fought at Omaha Beach and then spent the next forty years working in a box factory."

"Isn't that something," Beth said.

"If you ask me, it's terrifically shitty," Jules said.

Beth picked up her napkin, refolded it, set it back down. Don had the sudden urge to smack her. "So," she said. "What's a hospice assistant do?"

"Well," Jules said. "I deal with octo's mostly."

"Octo's?"

"Elder care. Eighty and up." Then Jules explained the medical hierarchy, and the fact that a lot of nurses don't like to get their hands dirty with the really nasty stuff, like changing bed pans and giving sponge baths and cleaning up fluid leaks.

"Fluid leaks?" Don said. He had just served himself another helping of casserole and put his fork down.

"Yeah," Jules said. "All kinds of things leak at that age. Most people couldn't even imagine."

But Don could. Though he was trying hard *not* to. He concentrated on Jules' eyes, and on all the features of her face that were so intricate and so perfect. Then he thought of that morning at the gym. He'd been swimming. Four days a week he swam. Aside from showers, it was the only time he was allowed to remove the heart monitor, which he wrapped in a T-shirt and stuffed in a gym locker, deeply embarrassed of it. He often changed facing a corner so nobody could see him peeling off the sticky tabs, which had left a hairless triangle around his heart.

Twice a week, the pool held a water aerobics class, where there was a poolside boom box and an instructor performing yoga-like maneuvers. Octogenarians bobbed in the pale water. They shimmied and grooved to the music, lifting their arms and twisting their bodies haphazardly, as flaccid and helpless as sea anemones. Sometimes Don stopped swimming just to watch. He was transfixed by their movements, the shapes of their bodies, all that loose flesh. He felt like he was peering around the corner into his own old age, which these days felt a hell of a lot closer.

Even if the heart trouble wasn't serious, it was the first whiff of decay.

Beth brought out a bottle of Chardonnay from the fridge and poured a little for each. "So what happened to Jeb?" she asked. "How did it, you know—?"

"End?" Jules said.

So Jules related the story of Jeb, which went something like this: Jeb had stage four liver cancer. Meaning, it had spread. His family gathered. Or what was left of his family, anyway: a son and a daughter, a couple of younger sibs. Jules explained how Jeb's whole body would tense with pain. "Like a hundred amps down his spine," Jules said. After the pain, Jeb would close his eyes and go into one of his long creepy silences.

"Eventually," Jules said. "Jeb went with Sororium." She looked at Don and Beth, who were obviously puzzled. "It's a euthanasia med."

"Wait," Beth said. "You mean Jeb *killed* himself?"

"That legal?" Don said.

"Is now," Jules said. "After ballot measure seventeen or whatever it's called. You just need a prescription. Imagine walking into the pharmacy one day and asking for *that.* Imagine you're the clerk. What do you even *say*?"

Now Jules had their full attention. Don felt a little queasy. Suicide was an impossible thing to fathom. It was like thinking about the universe. In some ways it was hard *not* to think about.

At Jeb's end of life ceremony, everyone waited for Jeb to mix four ounces of milky liquid in a clear plastic cup. Jules said, "Everyone was just sitting around waiting for Jeb to drink this stuff. He couldn't make up his mind on the mixer. At first, he was thinking tonic water. Then it was soda. Eventually, he went with Jack."

"Like a Jack and coke," Don said.

"Don," Beth said.

"Bingo," Jules said. "We're all sitting there in the living room. Jeb says his goodbyes. Of course, everyone's crying—everyone but me and the other nurse, Anne. Then Jeb just picks up the cup and swallows the whole thing in one gulp." Jules paused, like she'd just nailed the punch line. Obviously, Don and Beth were not in the know.

"He's wasn't supposed to," Jules said.

"Supposed to what?" Beth said.

"Supposed to drink the whole thing like that. He was supposed to sip."

"What's the difference?" Don said.

"There are instructions. This one was the sipping kind." Jules shifted in her seat. Don thought her eyes were changing color, from blue to green maybe, or from slightly off blue to a deeper, more mysterious color.

"Anyway," Jules said. "Anne reached for the cup, trying to stop him. That's when Jeb slapped her."

"Ha!" Don said.

"What a jerk," Beth said.

"You think?" Jules said. "I actually thought it was hilarious. I mean, I didn't laugh obviously. But who would have guessed *that* would happen. Who would have guessed *that* would have been his final moment. It was perfect."

"Perfect?" Beth said.

"You know what I mean," Jules said. "Perfectly representative of *life*. Of its basic fucked-up-ness." Her eyes moistened, but she didn't look like she was going to cry. She looked happy. Don watched her from across the table in the sudden bloom of his desire. He wondered if Jules could even see it, the soft, luminous light of youth that followed her, resting on her shoulder, or sometimes drifting off to the corner of the room, hovering at lamp height. Watching her, he became aware of each beat of his heart.

"She's up to something," Beth said to Don that night, after Jules was back in the basement, and they were upstairs with the TV. "I don't know what it is yet, but I can feel it."

Don walked to the window and opened the blinds. The Rodericks' porch lights hung over the street like a pair of eyes.

"I see the way you look at her," Beth said.

"And what?" Don said. "I'm eating dinner and she's sitting across from me. How am I supposed to *not* look at her." He felt a flash of anger, and then, when he glanced at Beth and saw how tired she looked, his anger softened.

"Soo-roar-rium," Don said. "Probably costs a fortune." Since when had a bottle of aspirin gone out of style?

"That whole story was sick," Beth said. "It was like she was getting a rise out of it."

It wasn't just that they were getting old, Don thought. They were both getting so damn *narrow*, so fundamentally intolerant, a couple of prudes. Fast forward two decades and they'd both be as wrung out and withered as…

…he couldn't think that way, it was such a mindfuck. It precipitated the blackest of black moods.

Beth was at the dresser, holding the amethyst pendant that Izzy had given her over Christmas break. She never wore it, she just looked at it, palming it like a talisman. After 60 seconds of intense staring, she put the pendant away and turned off the TV, causing a void of splotchy darkness. Don groped along the wall and climbed under the comforter beside his wife. The room was a swirling blob until his eyes adjusted.

"I bet she's into my boxes," Beth said.

"Stealing stuff?"

"I didn't say that. I just don't want her messing with my boxes."

The basement contained an unfinished storage room by the furnace, the one place Beth had told Jules was "strictly off limits." It was a whole room full of boxes.

Don wasn't even sure what was in the boxes. Internet crap, likely. Half the Visa balance. Before Jules moved in, the boxes piled up by the front door until Beth carried them down to the basement for safekeeping. He'd once stumbled on her sitting on the concrete in the glow of a bare light bulb, just looking at the boxes. He wondered if it was a symptom of some secret unhappiness.

"Tomorrow," Beth said, her voice muffled by her pillow. "Tomorrow after work I'm going down there to check."

The next morning Don drove to the gym. His doctor hadn't said anything about avoiding exercise, and instructed him to just do what he normally did. He imagined a tiny electrical storm firing among the web of arteries crowding his heart. Most of the time he felt okay. Other times, when climbing stairs or during those middle-of-the-night episodes, his heart kicked wildly.

He walked by the basketball court on the way to the pool. A group of kids with Down syndrome were playing, passing listlessly, slow as a game of chess. It made him sad. When the ball bounced over to him, he passed it back. "Here you go, bud," he said. At the side of the pool, Don put on goggles and eased himself into the water. It was freezing. A high school swim team had taken over three of the lanes. He pushed off and fanned his arms out in a breast stroke, which was the only stroke he was any good at. He once tried a sidestroke, until he noticed a lifeguard standing at the lip of the pool, watching him anxiously, one of those red things tucked under her arm.

Two high school swimmers moved into the lane next to Don. They were fast and agile, cutting long freestyle strokes and performing tidy flip turns after each lap, their swim caps bobbing up and down, up and down. Don pushed off once more and tried to keep pace with the lead swimmer. For a moment, they swam in tandem—Don's big round body in one lane and the angular, muscled body of the boy in the lane beside him. Don kept pace for a half lap, feeling great. Then his heart began to flutter, more noticeably with each stroke. When he reached the wall, he pulled himself out of the water and lay by the side of the pool, panting like a dog.

"You okay?" One of the lifeguards had wandered over. "Sir?"

Don realized how he must look, lying on his back with his arms and legs splayed out. "I'm fine," he said. "Not dead yet, anyway." He waved her off. He hauled himself up and walked to the shower, then to the locker room where he changed, and finally to his car, feeling like a swarm of bees was trapped in his ribcage.

When he got home Don went into the kitchen and poured himself a glass of cold water. Beth had left for work. He sat down on the sofa and took several deep breaths. He put his hand over his heart, feeling the wires. The monitor went: *beeeep...sccccbhreeeep...beeeep...sccccbhreeeep*

Should he call the cardiologist? He wandered back into the kitchen to look for the phone number. He was a goddamn walking fax machine. That's when Jules came up the stairs. "That you?" she said.

He unclipped the monitor from his belt and showed it to her, flushed with embarrassment.

Jules took the monitor and pushed a button, silencing it.

"You make it look easy," he said.

"I used to see these all the time," she said. "Ever feel like throwing it against a wall?"

"Every day."

Jules handed the monitor back to Don. "So your diagnosis was what? Tachycardia?"

"Something like that."

Don sat down on the sofa with Jules beside him. "Is your heart racing now?" she asked him. He nodded yes.

Jules scooted closer. "Sometimes it helps just to relax," she said. "Not that I'm an expert or anything." She smelled wonderful.

"Can I feel your pulse?" She took Don's wrist. He felt like he was floating up toward the ceiling.

"Wow," Jules said.

"What?"

"It's just…fast, that's all."

Don looked at her thighs, heart at full gallop.

"Let's try this," Jules said. "Give me your hand."

Jules guided Don's hand onto her own wrist. "See if you can feel my heartbeat. It should be slow. Like sixty beats per minute."

He couldn't feel Jules' heartbeat. He felt only warmth, smooth skin, and then he looked up at her white turtleneck, the slope of her chest. Here it came again, her youth, drifting over the sofa cushions. He wanted to feel its strange light.

Jules lurched back and Don pulled his hand away. He realized he'd touched her right breast. Just shy of the nipple, he guessed.

"Sorry," Don said. "I guess I got a little carried away."

"Yeah, you kind of did." Jules stood up. She went into the kitchen and he heard the ice machine going, the cubes dropping into her glass one by one, clink, clink. "I'm going out," she announced. "I have to run out for something so I'm going out. Not that I have to tell you."

Upstairs Don paced the bedroom. He hadn't even tried to explain himself. He paced and swallowed, a hint of nausea rising up from his stomach. A minute later he heard a car engine start, and when he looked out the window, Jules was backing down the driveway.

Don walked down the steps to the basement. He hadn't been down here since Jules moved in and he felt the need to poke. It was his right, anyway, wasn't it? Sort of like an inspection. Maybe they shouldn't have skipped all the formal lease paperwork. He briefly considered the possibility that Jules was currently driving straight to the nearest police station.

Her bedroom door was open. He sat down on Jules' bed. It had always been a nice bed. It was even nicer now that it smelled like her perfume. In his head he went over the boob touch, his little *oops*, play by play. Even 20 minutes later the really sharp details were lost to the fog of his subconscious. Lost forever, probably.

The silver oxygen tank was propped in the corner. Jules had done a bangup job with the decor—picture frames and white lace curtains over the windows, a nice touch. He paused at her dresser and gazed into a mound of panties. He shuddered to think he'd stooped this low. He closed the drawer and went straight for the bathroom. Surely, in the bathroom, he'd expose some vital flaw. Maybe she was a naughty little girl with a naughty little secret. He swung open the mirror cabinet and, *ha!* Bottles of pills. Not the kind you get at the CVS checkout. Prescription only stuff: Ambien, Vicodin, a bunch of others he didn't recognize. He had a warm memory of a week long Vicodin high following a root canal that went awry. In this spirit, he swallowed a Vicodin with a gulp of sink water, and, feeling instantly better, meandered back through the bedroom, out to the living room, and finally to the rear storage room, where Beth's unopened boxes were stacked with infuriating precision on the concrete.

He tore into one with his hands, ripping apart tape and cardboard. He did the same with another, pulling out dish towels and holiday magnets and a tin of small white candies that smelled like vanilla. The tin looked hand painted—from Sweden probably, or some other absurdly faraway place. He didn't want to imagine what Beth paid for them. Out of spite, he shoved as many of the candies into his mouth as he could before realizing they weren't candies at all, but wax.

Upstairs he plopped down on the sofa in a happy Vicodin delirium. For the next hour, he would not have to form a single coherent thought. Izzy's pendant was on the coffee table. A deep, moody purple. He'd never been a fan of purple—it felt witchy, conjuring tarot cards and trashy Halloween stores and, for some reason, tabloids. He opened the front door and flung the pendant into the yard. For a moment, he just stood there, staring at the invisible spot where the pendant had landed near a tall spruce.

Oh Jesus Christ. What the hell was he thinking? Some things, once done…

Without grabbing his boots, he rushed out. When he got to the tree, he knelt down and dipped his hands into the powder, frantically searching, feeling for something hard. He crawled forward on his knees. The wind gathered the snow, erased his footsteps, gathered, erased. It was hopeless.

When he sat up, there was Beth just 20 feet away, stepping from her car.

"Don?" Beth said. She walked toward him across the pelt of snow. "What are you looking for?"

Don stood up. "You home for lunch?"

"What's going on?"

"I was—" He felt short of breath. "I was about to go for a walk, actually." He zipped up his jacket, but his feet were going numb, and he hopped from foot to foot.

"In your socks?" Beth said. "You were going for a walk in your socks?"

"I forgot my boots."

"Oh. So let me guess. That's why you were crawling. You were crawling across the snow because you forgot your boots. It all makes perfect sense now." She folded her arms over her jacket and looked down at the snow. She bent over, and when she stood up again, she was holding the pendant. "I'm sure there's an explanation for this," she said. "But right now, I'm cold, and I'm not going to stand here while you lie to me again."

Don lay back in the snow. His feet throbbed. He looked up at the sky. The sun was a thin disc bobbing in milky clouds. He remembered a conversation he'd had with Silas before he left for college. It was one of those surreal moments in which Don felt like he was speaking not to his own son, but to an adult who had taken up occupancy in his son's body. Here he was, all grown up, with his own ideas and notions of the world. They sat on the deck, watching grasshoppers zip across the tall grass. It was the first time Don spoke so candidly with his son, the first time he felt unafraid of tarnishing him.

"So what's better? College or after college?" Silas said. "You do think I'm smart, right Dad?"

Of course, Don didn't know what the hell to say. And then this, at the back of his mind: the idea that, in his youth, he'd vastly overestimated the joy life would bring him. Don tried to communicate this to Silas, hoping that, by understanding this now, Silas had a better chance of avoiding the blitz of unhappiness, or even depression. But very quickly he realized this was an impossible thing to communicate to an 18-year-old, all of life ahead, all those glittering possibilities. Don remembered that feeling, a keening nostalgia that seeped up from his gut.

He stood up in the snow, dusted his pants on the front porch, and went into the house. Beth was unloading the dishwasher, slamming stacks of plates into the cabinet. "I knew it," she said to Don. "I want you to go into the basement right now and see what Jules did. Just go down there and look."

From the kitchen table he looked at his wife. She was in a frenzy, and her face was so ugly. He couldn't even look at her.

"It was me," Don said. "I opened your stupid boxes."

Beth looked at him across the marble island. "*You*," she said, "are a son-of-a-bitch liar. You're defending her because you're infatuated with her."

Don wanted to run out of the house, to get in his car and drive to some hamlet in the woods, a place so remote he'd have to chop wood for heat and hunt small animals and not see another human being for the next five to ten years.

"She took the pendant too, didn't she?" Beth brushed away a tear. "People are so cruel. I should have seen this coming." Beth stomped out of the kitchen.

The Vicodin was disappointingly short and he could feel the new mood descending. One of those truly black moods. One of those moods where he was glad he didn't own a gun (though sometimes he wished he did). At the window he watched for the return of Jules. Here she came, pulling into the driveway in her dumpy car. She stepped from the car and whisked across the yard, scarf flapping in the cold.

Don waited until Jules reached the house and then walked down the steps to the basement. He wanted to apologize. At the very least, he felt the need to clear things up.

Jules' bedroom door was still open and the bathroom sink was running. A bar of light seeped under the door. Don sat down on her bed. The room felt small, all squished together.

Jules stepped out of the bathroom, looking surprised.

"You're sitting on my bed," she said.

Don stood up.

"Is that something you normally do? Like, just go sit on people's beds without asking?"

"Um," Don said. What was he trying to say? He couldn't get it out.

Jules' face was full of contempt. Where had the kindness gone? Don crossed his arms over his belly, aware of his own bulk. Sometimes he felt like he was stuffed into an ape suit. They stood facing each other. And Don had to say something, *anything*, but words escaped him, and so he reached over and touched her shoulder with his ape hand. Tenderly, he thought.

"Don't touch me," Jules said. She jerked away, giving him a bitter look. "I'm going to be honest with you," Jules said. "I've always thought you were kind of sweet. And also, I felt bad for you, because of the heart thing. But when I came out of the bathroom and saw you sitting here, I realized you're like all the other guys. Just older."

"All the other guys?" Don said.

"All the other guys who want something from me." Jules leaned against the wall. "I'm leaving. Probably tomorrow, or whenever I can get somebody to help move my stuff. Because if I find you down here again, I'm calling the police."

"What about the lease?" Don said.

"What lease?" Jules stiffened. "And oh, by the way, I can hear you and your wife talking at night. Your voices come down through the heat vents or something. I never took anything. I can't believe you thought I was sneaking upstairs. I think your wife's a psycho bitch. So, in a way, I still feel bad for you. But not bad enough to give you what you want."

For a second, just for a second, Don wondered what it would be like to force her onto the bed, maybe sneak in a kiss or two before she kneed him in the nuts.

Jules left the bedroom and marched across the living room, then into the snowy afternoon, leaving the slider open.

Snowflakes circled the carpet and a cold wind pushed through, roughing the curtains. Don closed his eyes and focused on the black, sparking cloud in his brain. It never ceased to amaze him, how nature made pleasure, and pleasure gave way to need, and need agony, and so on. Or maybe it was the other way around. He looked up at the ceiling and screamed.

Then he walked to Jules' bathroom and turned on the sink and drank from his palm. In the mirror he took stock of himself. Donald Blankenship. 52 years old, *son, husband, father.*

He opened the medicine cabinet and gazed at the pill bottles. So many bottles, red and green and clear yellow ones, and something he hadn't noticed before—all of them carefully ordered by height with their labels turned outward, an obvious labor of love, the tallest on the ends with the shorter ones safe in the middle, a perfect little family.

Michael Stigman

The Holocaust Survivor

After confirming over the phone details of the upcoming visit by the Holocaust survivor, the History and Culture Committee Chair lay her head on her arms and breathed deeply. Her lungs unfurled to draw oxygen that felt, at that moment, unlike any she had breathed in a long time. It was like inhaling hyper-oxygenated air, after breathing oxygen-deprived air, she imagined. In another sense, it was simply relief she felt at having settled the matter of this year's guest speaker.

The Chair had been in hot water for nearly two years over the college's bad experiences with guest speakers she chose. She sensed that it had spread into others' perception of her suitability as a faculty member, and she was two years from a tenure application. Remaining Chair of the History and Culture Committee was part of it, too. While the college's president had tried to make the Committee Chair feel better about these unfortunate experiences, he had also warned her that she should never let this kind of thing happen again. Getting the speaking commitment from the Holocaust survivor was the solution for how to never let that kind of thing happen again.

At their very conservative, religious college, the Committee's last guest speaker had glibly argued against the existence of God or, for that matter, anything beyond the material world. As the President pointed out, the parents of the students who heard him say that didn't pay $100,000 to have their children hear that. In fact, they paid $100,000 so their children wouldn't have to hear it. Just as bad, in the year before that, the guest speaker, in the short time he was in town, had tried to purchase cocaine from an undercover cop on a sting operation that had nothing to do with the guest speaker.

While the Chair beat herself up in the aftermath, she told herself no one could have known either guest would do what he'd done. The first guest was the director of the city's largest art museum, not a well-known atheist philosopher. And although the second guest had once had a publicly acknowledged drug problem, on this occasion he was actually invited to campus to speak on overcoming addiction by putting trust in a higher power.

During late, sleepless nights that the Chair spent torturing herself over these botched events, she had only been able to make sense of it one way. She observed that while the second speaker embraced both a higher power and, as it turned out, addiction, the first rejected both in the same breath, religion being an addiction, the opiate of the masses, etc. The Chair, however, was neither consoled nor absolved by this logic and kept it to herself.

So this time, the Chair reasoned that a Holocaust survivor, despite the certain trauma and horror of his Holocaust experience, was a very good candidate for the speaking engagement. His would most certainly be an inspirational talk, and he was very likely to avoid any of the controversy brought by the previous speakers. As far as denying the existence of God, who'd ever heard of a Holocaust survivor who was also an atheist? Most were Jews, God's people, and the rest had to give someone or something credit for them beating the odds and surviving. God was a safe bet.

As for any unbecoming behavior like that of the cocaine addict/guest speaker, the Chair had Googled him and found absolutely nothing even remotely questionable about him. She'd even contacted two national organizations that had once hosted visits by the Holocaust survivor, and they'd both provided glowing reviews. He'd been inspirational across the board, one said.

Assured by her investigation of the Holocaust survivor, the Chair made arrangements. Like any Holocaust survivor, he would undoubtedly have something significant to say about his experience, humanity's potential for good and evil, and our responsibility for each other. Upon reading his biography, she became fascinated by all that he had endured, and she was sure members of the college community would also find it fascinating, and would thank her for bringing him.

His name was Claude Eiger. He was born in Brudzew, Poland, and held for nearly three years in Stutthof Concentration Camp. At one time, he'd been assigned to a job that required him to remove bodies from the gas chamber. He'd survived a typhus epidemic that many of his fellow camp members did not, and of course, he'd avoided death in the gas chamber or death otherwise. When the Soviets finally surrounded German forces in Poland, the already high death toll among the prisoners continued to rise in tandem with Germany's desperation. In the end, Claude Eiger had survived a greater than 50 percent chance of dying. The Chair couldn't imagine living with that kind of knowledge, of being tormented by the burden of surviving what half a population had not survived.

While preparing for the Holocaust survivor's visit, she corresponded with him through email. She sent the itinerary for travel between his home in New York and the college campus, as well as explanation of the college's expense reimbursement policies, a contract for the honorarium, and a W-9 for taxes imposed on the honorarium with a request that he complete and return the forms to expedite payment. She also included a description of the History and Culture Committee's mission and its previous guest speakers. She told him how excited they all were about his visit.

He seemed pleasant in these email exchanges. He sent back the contract by mail. He did not acknowledge the W-9, but he did ask for a first floor hotel room. She sent the W-9 again with a request that he complete and return it, promised him a first floor hotel room, and again mentioned how excited the campus community was to welcome him and hear him speak. He did not reply.

Just before noon on the day of Claude Eiger's speaking engagement, the Chair arrived to meet him at the airport gate. She held a paper sign with his name on it. When she saw him approach, she was glad she had made the sign, since he looked much older, smaller, and more fragile than he did in the online picture of him she'd seen. She rolled his suitcase for him across the parking lot while he walked with a cane behind her. Coming out of the terminal into the bright, mid-day sun temporarily blinded her, so she looked back toward Mr. Eiger.

"I know you want to kill me right now for moving so slowly," he said, stopping at the edge of the sidewalk. When she objected, he waved it off. "I don't blame you. But you'd move at least this slowly if your hip had been shattered by the butt of a German soldier's rifle."

She tried to recover, saying something about never wanting to rush him and about his graciousness for coming to their modest college to teach them history and culture, but she didn't know how much of this he heard. In the long ride from the airport to the college, she learned that he'd had lunch on the plane, the flight was tolerable ("I've been through much worse"), and yes, he'd been to their city before. She tried to ask him about New York, about family, and about hobbies, but she found it difficult. He didn't seem to catch onto the idea of conversation as a way for fellow travelers to pass time. Besides, she felt strange asking him about life beyond the Holocaust. For example, what about hobbies? Seriously? Do Holocaust survivors want or need hobbies, or was it simply enough to have survived the Holocaust?

And although she'd wanted to dispense with red tape at the outset, she didn't ask him about the W-9 until they arrived at his hotel room. When she did, he asked her to repeat her question, and when he seemed to grasp what she was asking, he said, "I don't usually deal with that sort of shit," as if that were enough. She suggested that she could bring another copy when she returned to take him to the college.

"Sure. Whatever you want," he said.

"Well, Mr. Eiger. It's not that I want to," she said. "In fact, I'd rather not bother you. But they won't give me the check until they have the W-9." She began to apologize, but he cut her off.

"After what's happened to me, it's hard to give attention to insignificant details like this. Something you obviously can't relate to." With that, he got out of the car.

She reminded him of what time she would pick him up for dinner. He nodded and waved at her like he was shooing flies. And with that, she slowly drove off in what felt like a cloud of insignificance.

She had nothing to do until dinner, so she tried to while away the hour or so in her office answering emails and reading through the latest committee meeting minutes. She read two emails from the business office about not receiving the W-9, and she guessed that the same message existed in her voicemail, indicated by the red light on her phone. By email, she thanked them for the reminder but told them she had still not received it from Mr. Eiger.

She did all this with a sort of absence, since she couldn't help thinking instead of Claude Eiger in that small hotel room. She wondered what he was doing there. At his age, maybe he was taking a nap. She pictured him taking off his suit coat to lie on top of the comforter. Or maybe he was watching something on the hotel television. What show did a Holocaust survivor watch on TV? Something important? Did he even know how to spend free time, after spending three years wasting away in a prison camp, free time there having been limited to waiting to see if and when you would die?

The only way she could clearly imagine him was as she had first imagined him when she read his story, in the prison camp. In her mind, he wore the infamous striped prison garb so many pictures showed, and he was led in a line between barracks and work sites. The part that had made the biggest impression on her was his role working in the gas chamber, walking inside after it had been used to kill some of his fellow Poles. Certainly he had been forcefully made to do this, at the point of a gun, perhaps. And then he actually had to do it.

Although it made her sick to follow the thought through, she pictured him at the chamber door, drawing a deep breath for fear of inhaling any lingering poison gas, and then holding that breath as he entered through the chamber door to drag one person at a time out by his ankles. Maybe he had a work partner, and maybe they hoisted the bodies into carts to take to a mass gravesite. She wondered how many of these dead men he recognized while carrying out his ghastly chore; whether the man who slept near the door in his barracks, or someone from the town of Brudzew, maybe. Did he ponder how it could just as easily have been those other men pulling him out by the ankles? What did it mean to survive that room and its greedy fumes, simply because of the timing of your being sent there? You were sent there now instead of then, when standing in that room meant you had no other choice but to submit to that moment's envelope of killing air.

She brought him to the dinner late because, in fact, he had been sleeping and had turned off his hearing aid, which she learned once she and the hotel manager stood over his bed to wake him. Like most old people, he looked dead while sleeping, but he sprang awake with a deep, gasping breath that startled her the same as if he'd roared in her face. After a moment of confusion, he fumbled with the hearing aid, which produced a brief whine as he adjusted it. As they drove, she handed him the W-9 and asked if he would complete it now. "For the honorarium," she reminded him.

"Please," he said. "Just cut me a check for $1,000. No less."

She told him again that they were holding the check until they had the W-9.

He rammed his cane into the car's floorboard. "There will be no W-9. Do you imagine this is easy for me? I have come to tell my story. It's not an easy story to tell, and one I hope you never have to tell. You will give me that check."

He charmed everyone at the dinner, the college president, the handful of faculty members invited, and the small contingent of Honors History students, with whom he shared story after story about his cat, Rupert Murdoch. All at the table thoroughly enjoyed his stories, including the President, who several times had to wipe tears of laughter from the corners of his eyes. Over dessert, the President winked approvingly at the Chair.

She was seated next to Mr. Eiger, and several times as he told these stories, she turned directly toward him, as if to check what she saw against the person she had delivered from the airport to the hotel and, now, to the dinner. She wondered whether what she now saw was a public persona he wore, the one about which the previous hosts had written so gushingly, or whether the difference was her fault. Should she blame herself for a lack of ability in putting him at ease? Had all the pressure she felt and applied to him about the W-9 made her come across as some sort of monster, some sort of monomaniacal bureaucrat oppressing him with her officiousness? Why her?

To a packed house, her introduction of him in the auditorium was an easy sell, and as she read from her prepared version, she thought of him as the person who had thoroughly entertained his hosts and possibly begun the repair of the President's confidence in her as the History and Culture Committee Chair. She felt grateful to Mr. Eiger, and the audience's applause sounded like immense gratitude, like the swell of a rainstorm on a roof at the end of a drought. They were already grateful for his visit, for what they knew he would confide about good and evil in the world, about the survival of hope and struggle against despair. They were grateful that although others had died, he had lived, for reasons they just knew would come to light through the power and wisdom of his words. And he did deliver. By the end of his talk, the Chair was sure that everyone in the auditorium had cried as they listened to him, from the President and faculty, all the way down to the students on academic probation who had come only for extra credit points.

Of course he received a standing ovation. When she rose from her seat on the stage to shake his hand and thank him, he whispered in her ear: "The check, or I will tell everyone how you have mistreated me here."

Afterward, many of the students and faculty hovered around him to thank him and even take pictures with him. She looked for an opportunity to speak privately with the President, but she knew that she wasn't trying very hard, since everything else was going so well and she didn't want to ruin it. Eventually, Mr. Eiger approached her and asked her to take him back to the hotel.

The car exited the campus and began to accelerate down a two-lane highway. As if on cue, Mr. Eiger growled, "Where is my check? Where is it?" He pulled at her elbow, and then he yanked at her purse and started digging through it. She veered to the inside shoulder of the road, but between trying to do this and grab her purse from him, she misjudged the distance to the shoulder. The car began to roll, at an angle, down a small embankment, and before she had even begun to understand that the car would not recover from this error, they bounced down it and came to an abrupt stop at the V in a culvert.

He had not been wearing his seatbelt, which meant he now lay pressed up against her on her side of the car. As soon as they knew the worst was over, he tried to wrap his hands around her neck. She held him back by his wrists and screamed over and over that he should stop, but he would not give up. He was crying, but he did not stop trying to choke her.

They were stuck in her small car, with one door that led up toward the lighted highway. She was tired, and she felt there wasn't enough space or air in the car. She couldn't believe this was happening to her. And although she knew it had never been a question of survival, she thought of the story she would tell about it. It began with her. It included history. And it ended with, "Why me?"

Michelle Donahue

Foam

That morning I was tired from another long night of insomnia and contrived porn. Tired of my parents' goddamn kitchen, our hog farm, the smallness of this life that I'd made for myself. I opened the fridge. My brother, Bill, kept the milk by the beer. The cheap fluorescent light of the fridge sputtered and that light made my pupils widen. In that momentary blindness, I grabbed a beer bottleneck by mistake and my hands were so used to popping the top off with the metal cabinet handle that the beer was open and breathing on the table before my mind could catch up. I gathered a bowl and a box of generic Cheerios and I sat, staring at the open bottle. It was like a bomb, and I was just willing it to explode. Even then I couldn't feel anything.

I hesitated, just a momentary tremor. Funny how quickly people can make such large decisions so fast. I poured the open Shock Top into the bowl and the beer turned those Os soggy, disgusting just like milk would. I shoved spoonfuls into my mouth, and even though those Os polluted the beer it still made me shudder. That first swallow of alcohol was always the best, that instant rush of warmth. I was always chasing that fleeting comfort.

I wanted to paint this, those dissolving Os in beer, the weak dawn light streaming from the window. I wanted to turn this into something beautiful. Back when I was 20 and studying art I would have stopped, run to my easel, but now I spooned beer into my mouth only wishing and realizing how ridiculous I was, trying to be an artist. Father was right; I never should have studied art in college. What a farce, a waste of money. But still, sometimes I liked to try that hat on and view myself as an artist. Sometimes I liked to pretend.

I popped open a second bottle and poured it into my almost empty bowl.

That was when Delilah walked down the stairs. She wore a pink tank top and her pale brown skin burst from it, the slight curve of her lower stomach, angular shoulders, the upper swell of her breasts. She always had great hair, long and thick brown.

"Hey, Carl," she said.

"Where's Bill?" I asked.

"Bill and I had a disagreement." I wondered what that meant. I wondered in the same way that drivers idly ponder what caused a crash on the side of an interstate. As if I were removed and all this was only happening around me.

From the fridge, Delilah extracted a pitcher of orange juice. The Minute Maid kind that's kept frozen and concentrated until someone takes pity on it and chucks it into warm water to thaw. She took in a deep breath, as if trying to breathe in enough air to last her a lifetime. Then she dropped the pitcher. All I remember is the sound of it hitting the floor, that cataclysmic plastic smack, and the flutter of orange liquid splattering the floor like a goddamn Pollock painting. Her lips were hot and the beer spun my head and she was all over me, her slick skin on mine. I remember beginning to feel a flicker of something, some heat stirring in my abdomen as she ripped at each button on my flannel and pushed her tongue so deep into my mouth that I could hardly gasp as she unbuckled my belt.

"Not here," I said. I had only sense enough that we couldn't do this out in the open. So I grabbed the empty bottles with one hand, and Delilah's hand with the other.

In my basement room I slammed the bottles into my trashcan. I didn't think *damn it, I can't sleep with my brother's girl.* I didn't think *damn it, I don't have condoms.* I simply didn't think. This wave of heat was forming inside and I'd forgotten what it was to feel.

When I pulled her on top of me and looked into those brown eyes I thought I knew full well what darkness I was entering. At the time, I thought that promise of heat, that fleeting squeeze was worth it.

"You're better than your brother," she said when we were done, when the mid-morning light peeled through the egress window and I heard Bill up above, rustling. "It's because you're an artist. You really see people. You get them."

I tugged on my white shirt. I tried so hard to feel remorse. I couldn't even feel awkwardness. I had just slept with my brother's girl. Sure they'd only been dating six months or so, but I thought they were the real deal. Thought they would maybe move in together, get married, and so on. Neither of them were that young, not anymore.

But for a few seconds during the sex, I felt something. The hazy warmth from the beer grew stronger, more solid. Sitting in the room with her, with her scent on my skin, I felt a tremor of it still, like passing my finger over a candle flame.

"You give me too much credit," I said. Bill had always been the good brother, following right in Father's farming footsteps. Perhaps I could be better than him in other ways. Delilah smiled and that was enough.

"What if I do?" she asked. Delilah always had unanswerable questions.

I had questions too, like why she was here with me when Bill was up above, but with Delilah I never could ask what was on her mind. She silenced me. The world fell apart and I was left with nothing but her body glowing.

That first time I slept with Delilah was a cold fall day in Iowa. The breeze, a ghost chattering at the nape of my neck, and the frost in the air warned of winter coming. I walked with my back hunched to it, hands thrust deep inside the pockets of my Carhartt jacket. I walked the two miles to the family hog farm, a big time, industrial scale CAFO. Bill always gave me flack for walking. Most of the workers drove their four wheelers or their trucks everywhere. But I preferred walking. Ever since Eleanor, love of my life, cheated on me, I couldn't trust myself behind a wheel. One DUI was enough. So I was yet again the odd one out. The wannabe artist, the inept farmer, the once-binge-drinker, the walker.

I sighed. The breeze blew harder, bringing with it a smell, at once rotting roses and pickled feet. The smell reminds me a little of Mexico, where I was at post in the army. Except here it was more pungent. Welcome to good old Budapest, Iowa, pronounced Bud A Peest, the end, a long e like feet. Not at all like I imagine the Hungarians would bend their tongues to fit the word. We pronounce everything wrong here. Nevada becomes Ne-VAY-da, Madrid, MAH-drid, emphasis on the mah. Now that I've left and returned, the absurdity has sunk in. I didn't think two years of being bored as an IT guy in the army would change me that much. Perhaps it hadn't. Perhaps it just brought me back to the surface, right there beneath the skin, bubbling.

The first time I slept with Delilah was the first day I noticed the pig foam. I was checking on the sows in the gestation crates when I saw that foam, bubbling up beneath the wood slats of the barn floor. Beneath sat large pits that captured all the manure these hogs generated. I figured the foam was just filth. The smell of the place really gnawed into my cranium and made me believe anything. Like a little gray foam was normal. The pigs sprawled—mounded lumps of flesh, all fat, not muscle—in their cold metal confinement crates. I'd lost all ability for compassion. Even then I'd been so hardened by the boring hurt around me that I couldn't look at these creatures as anything but meat.

I left the barn. At this time of day, the CAFO was usually a hive of workers, and among the many bodies was Bill, leaning against a tree.

"Carl," he shouted and walked closer. I wondered if he'd been waiting for me, which would be unusual. Ever since I crashed his car six years ago there'd been this rift between us. That was when I got the DUI and Father gave me the ultimatum that I had to clean up. He pressured me to join the army.

Bill said he forgave me, but we aren't close like we used to be.

"Did you see Delilah leave this morning?" he asked.

"Nope," I said.

"Shit."

"What happened?" I asked.

"She broke up with me. Can you believe it?"

Sadness formed wrinkles in Bill's forehead, but all I cared about was how the darkness clung to Delilah as I pressed my palm to her wet mouth to muffle her screams.

I asked, "What happened?" But Bill shot his hands in his pockets and stalked off. I should have run after him. We weren't the hugging type, but I should have at least given him a manly tap on the back. Tell him to buck up, it's her loss.

"It's her loss," is what Bill told me when I found out that Eleanor was cheating on me. I was saving money to buy a ring to propose. Back then I'd sit in my room, real silent, with the lights down low and imagine Eleanor and I together. Of her in a white dress. I saw us with children, a boy, a girl, both with my nose, a little flat, a little flare at the end. In Budapest, Iowa, in a country home with too many dogs. A sun-washed picket fence. My dreams were simple, predictable.

I had asked Eleanor if she slept with my best friend. I'd wondered for a while. There was one night when she vanished with him at a party for a full 57 minutes. I counted every goddamn second they were gone.

She said she loved him.

And it was the love that tipped me over that edge. Pure sex, I might've been able to handle. But raw love? I didn't stand a chance.

The second time I slept with Delilah was another cool fall day. She came around to the house. Gutsy, because Bill might have been home, but he wasn't. She had a plunging blue top and she leaned so close to me that her goose bumps glistened. Her fingers were pink and white from the early cold and she picked relentlessly at the cuticle of her right thumb.

"Can we go see the pigs?" she asked. "Bill would never take me."

I wanted to, but there were cameras and security protocols, plus Father would be furious. "The public's not allowed in. Safety measures," I said.

She unearthed her cuticle from her nail bed, lifted it with a long fingernail, and pulled, wrenching it from the nearby skin. She maneuvered and pushed until she ripped it straight off. A soft ooh and hot blood dragged down her thumb, one drop forgetting to fight gravity. It stopped at her knuckle and just sat there and glistened.

"Do you have any beer?" she asked.

My face twisted then she laughed, "I meant, root beer. And ice cream." She entered the kitchen. Her hand with the bloody thumb threw the freezer door open to reveal nothing.

"We could buy some," I said.

We peeled from the house and walked to the Kum-N-Go, a 10-minute walk down a back road, the asphalt of it pitted from past salt and snow. I grabbed the ice cream and root beer and I paid for them because I was feeling chivalrous and also desperate. She asked the cashier for a cup and he proffered a red plastic one. The same red cups that held the booze I threw myself at after Eleanor and I split. As I drank more vodka, she'd grow clearer to me. I'd sit alone in bars as I remembered the taste of her. She was on my lips and tongue. This is still the best way I know how to grieve.

Delilah and I walked from the Kum-N-Go to the edge of a cornfield. We sat on a tree stump, the edges of it rotting and threatening to crumble. She extracted an old credit card from her small, red plastic purse, and used it to shuttle the ice cream from the carton to the cup. Then she poured the root beer in. It fizzed, a thick froth of it foaming to the cup's rim. I was mesmerized by the way her fingers scooped the foam and channeled it to her mouth. The way her lips curled as she tasted it, how her eyes closed and she tilted her head back. I pulled out a pack of cigarettes and offered her one. She shook her head. I pressed my lighter's flame to the tip of one and let the smoke of it slide hot down my throat. Delilah licked the foam. She cleaned her fingers from knuckle to tip.

"I'd love to paint you sometime," I said. I thought if I could paint her, then maybe I could be a real artist, maybe I wasn't just a fraud. I was always trying to prove myself different from my family.

"I'd love to see the pigs sometime," she said again, with foam still on her fingers. "I'd just look and I'd never leave your side."

Then she stood, her little red cup falling to the ground and a frayed wedge of ice cream poking from the rim. She leaned over and pulled me into the cornfield.

"I promise, Carl," she whispered into my ear as one hand dove beneath my waistband. Her other hand ruffled through my hair. "You have good hair," she whispered. "Nice and thick." The cornstalks pressed around us.

"There could be rats in here," I said.

"What if I like rats? What if I'm crazy?" she asked.

I dropped my cigarette to the ground. I couldn't resist her body.

"Fuck me," she said. And so I did, right there in the rough brush of corn, in that beautiful fall cold.

After the 12th, or maybe the 15th time I slept with Delilah, Bill and I were at the hog farm and Father said, "You two look like shit." It was a Saturday and I knew Bill had been out drinking the night before. Father was wide awake. He was always at the farm; it was his only real source of pride. Passed on from his father, the farm had grown quickly from a small family farm and now held more than 55,000 weaner pig births a year. If I weren't his son, I would have never been hired to work here. As it was I only did small jobs where I could.

"Didn't sleep much," I said, which was true, but not the reason I looked like shit. I'd been over to Delilah's place and she had a fridge full of beer and it was there so cold and shiny, and the sound of her popping the cap off her own was too much. I had to grab one and she lifted an eyebrow and said "Are you sure you can handle it?" And I said, "No," but I drank it anyway.

"What if I'm too much for you?" she had asked as she unbuckled my belt.

At the farm, Bill looked at Dad and I and said, "I miss her." And for a moment there, I felt sorry for him. Tension flared in the pits of my stomach and I wanted to hug him. I wanted to tell him I was fucked up and I was so, so sorry. I wondered why him and Delilah had split. I wondered if he had done something, or if she was the guilty party.

Dad said, "Why don't you take the day off? Carl can check on the pigs in Barn

4." I was angry that Bill was always the favorite son. That Bill was always the good one. I thought of how I wanted nothing more than a day off so I could gather myself together again. Figure out that next step. All I knew was I didn't want to be some farmer in goddamn Budapest, Iowa.

I clenched my first, slammed it in my overall pocket. I was afraid the smell of the hog barn, where the smell was ripest, like rotten banana peels in battery acid, combined with the hangover would make me barf. But instead of saying *fuck you* or speaking up, I bowed my head and trudged to the barn.

"What if I have secrets?" Delilah had said the night before. I said, "Don't we all?"

I entered Barn 4, the one closest to the entrance. I had to breathe, and my stomach, already unsettled, clenched when the smell hit my nostrils. But a lifetime of smelling this stench had prepared me, and finally my stomach settled. And that's when I noticed that pig foam again, gray bubbles, as solid as clouds. It sprouted from the emptiness between wood slats. I imagined all the shit percolating down beneath the slats.

That winter was a rough one. Mild summer, extreme winter, *The Farmer's Almanac* had said. I didn't want to believe it, but I had to once I was knee deep in one of the bitterest winters I could remember.

After the 78th (92nd?) time I slept with Delilah, we walked together in that harsh cold. It was early April, but the cold continued strong. The snow fell in great sheets and towered in mountains on the sides of the road.

"Reminds me of home," Delilah said. She grew up in California, but she never talked about it. "It's a nice change from the constant flatness."

The wind had calmed and Delilah deemed this suitable walking weather. The cold clung to every bit of exposed skin, but I liked seeing her all bundled up. I imagined peeling one piece of clothing off after another. She withdrew her hand from a glove and ran it through my hair.

"It's getting long," she said. She twirled a lock at the nape of my neck and it tickled. "You should let me cut it." Delilah worked at the only hairdressers in town. Mom said she gave the best haircuts.

"You should let me paint you," I said. I thought maybe, if I kept asking, one day she'd abandon her shyness about her body and agree. I didn't know what she had to be shy about. And I thought maybe her body would inspire some great art in me.

"You should let me visit the pigs," she said. She smiled, but then her face went blank. "I imagine they're lonely."

We ran through this back and forth nearly every time we saw each other. I guess we were both persistent. And we had nothing else to do.

I didn't want to think about the pigs. I hadn't allowed myself to imagine the pigs with the ability to feel such complex emotions. When I was awake late into the night, I'd picture them with a hopeless desire for food or for sex. Somehow these basic drives I could give them. But loneliness, that was too close to my own mental state, that impending sense that the ground beneath me was shifting. That was too intense for a pig. For the bacon I ate on my plate some mornings. I took such pleasure in bacon, crispy and salty. Immediate gratification.

"Can we stop at the Kum-N-Go?" I asked.

"To buy beer?" Delilah said.

"Or something stronger." I wrapped my arm around her waist and both loved and hated that she kept my drinking secret. But secrets were what we were built on. Sometimes I wondered why Bill and Delilah had broken up, but I mostly didn't care. I cared only about the time we spent together.

"You're a mess, you know that?" Delilah said.

"I do," I said. But at least for once, I was a somewhat happy mess.

"What if I like a mess?" She grabbed my hand. Every ridge of her fingers imprinting her onto me. The heat of her creeping through her skin to mine. "What if I'm a mess too?" she asked.

The walk to the Kum N Go was cold but quick. When the doors slid open its heat hit us and I was surprised how cold I had been.

"What sort of day is today?" I asked.

"Bill told me you were a fan of vodka? Perhaps flavored?"

So they had talked about me. I pictured past conversations as they stretched on Bill's bedspread. He could spin stories all day about his poor little brother. He could build himself up. "I paid his bail when he got a DUI," he could say. "I knew Frank on the police force, so they let him off easier." All this is true. I can't really begrudge him. Bill is such a goddamn paragon of good, I can't hate him. But I do.

"Let's visit the pigs," Delilah said.

"Let me paint you," I said again. As she considered this, Delilah ran her hand through my hair, until she said, "OK," and then she shoved a bottle of whipped cream vodka at me. I loved vodka, but not this sickly sweet shit. But I bought it anyway and brought it home.

As the snow began to thaw, I prepared to paint Delilah. I was thrilled by the prospect of it, its intimacy, the long stretches of time where I could just stare at her body. And the mere fact that I could be thrilled excited me, too.

I bought thick paper and charcoal for the initial sketch. I moved the space heater into my room and unearthed a discarded lamp from the basement and brought it to my room for extra light.

Delilah came over on a Sunday. We were guaranteed at least five hours. My family was at church and would be eating at *Big Gs Log Cabin BBQ*, Father's favorite place. I pretended to be sick.

Delilah lurked in my doorway.

"Could you turn around?" she asked. So I did and the door shut and clothing rustled. "Ok," she said.

She wore a blue silk robe, the neckline plunging, providing a peek at her breasts. My body thrummed and my stomach felt weightless, the way it does as you plummet down a roller coaster. It wasn't just attraction, but maybe the artist in me had reemerged and was excited about her body.

"How do you want me?" she asked.

I smiled to reassure her. I couldn't remember the last time I smiled and meant it. My face felt stiff after it. I grabbed her wrist where her pulse fluttered and I guided her to the bed.

"Just relax," I said. She leaned against the wall, propped her left arm on a pillow, her legs outstretched and lightly crossed. "Perfect," I said. I wanted her natural. I kissed her on the forehead, then untied the belt of her robe. Her eyes were wide, but she allowed me to pull the robe from her body. "You okay?" I asked.

"Yeah," she said.

"What if I were naked too?" And then she smiled, the corners of her eyes creasing. I didn't see that real smile often.

"Yeah," she said. So I pulled the clothes from my body and I posed a little for her. Basic training had given me a hard body. The only real thing I'd gained from the army. Delilah laughed and her body eased into its pose, the tension easily filtering out of her. I wished it were that easy to get rid of sadness.

I settled behind my desk. I bent over the paper and started with basic shapes. The angular point of her chin, looping swell of her breasts, the bend of her right knee. I'd forgotten how quickly I could fall into art and think only of shapes and beauty, of light and shadow. I'd forgotten that maybe I was good at this, Father be damned. Maybe I *was* different from him. My body buzzed, part of it sexual, but the real feeling I think came from the art. I thought of nothing but her and the paper and the charcoal in my fingers.

I thought I was in love with her before, but now I was lost in it, fogged not with apathy but with this intensity that threatened to burn me from the inside out. I looked straight into her eyes and she looked into mine and a shiver ran through us at the same time. In that moment, I thought I could see right into her and know her. I forgot about Dad and Eleanor and Bill and hell, even alcohol, and for the first time it was just Delilah and me in the room. My fingers found their own rhythm as I drew dark lines, made shadows, smudged the charcoal with my fingertips.

When I'd finished, I brought the sketch over to the bed for her approval. I wanted to show off. I'd forgotten how easy art was for me. I was surprised by how good I was.

"I'm beautiful," she said, her voice soft and surprised. I'd captured that look of hers, intense and dark.

She kissed me.

That was the best time I slept with Delilah. Was it the 100th time? How simple and clean that would be.

After, when we were all warm and fuzzy, she bit my ear, ran her fingers through my hair and whispered, "Can I cut your hair?" I would've agreed to anything then.

"Sure," I said. It was getting long, and she knew what she was doing. I got her some sharp scissors and she told me to get my hair wet. This was a different kind of intimacy than the sex, than the drawing. My heart was tight and warm and I wanted to open it up and pull Delilah inside.

"Next Sunday, can we visit the pig farm?" she whispered like a love song into my ear. The scissors were cold at the back of my neck.

"Yeah," I said. She caught me that day, in a way she never had before. Even after we had long parted ways, I still felt her heat all about me.

The next Sunday, Delilah and I stood in front of the gate to the hog farm. The day before I'd disabled two of the front cameras, so that no one would see us if we only went into Barn 4, by the entrance. On Sunday there was almost no one there, because everyone was at church. There was only Pascal, a security guard, but we were old friends, and he wouldn't snitch if he caught us.

I thought Delilah would look happy. Ever since I drew her and she cut my hair, I felt a big balloon of happiness swelling inside me. But her face was set.

Father would kill me if he found out I brought a non-employee to the hog farm, so I'd smoked and drank the whole way here. I felt steadier now. I punched in my security code and Delilah leaned her face on my arm as I punched in the numbers. I guess she saw the code and that's how she got in the second time.

I led her to Barn 4, the largest with the most pigs. I felt hot like my skin could make steam, and my heart seized to a fast double beat, a *thrum, thrum* of panic. I ripped off the vodka cap and took another sip.

"I don't want to come in," I said.

"But you will," she said, and so I sucked in a long breath as she opened the door. The smell was a solid wall of fiery shit.

Delilah walked to the closest confinement crate and bent over the sow, just a sprawling stretch of coarse hair, marred hooves, an infected snout. She stood so still. Those dark eyes I loved were so focused on that one pig.

She said, "What if they could talk? What sad stories they would tell." She smoothed the hem of her dress. She always was wearing dresses when other people would wear pants.

I didn't want to think of the pigs. My eyes left her and fell instead on the ridge between wood slats. The gray foam bloomed from it again like a secret yearning to be told. If I had guts enough to touch that pungent froth, if I were stupid enough to reach my naked hand to it, I would've felt its hardness. Nothing like foam, but like a pillow, too firm from sleepless nights. That foam felt singular, unusual, as if, like us, it didn't belong here.

"If they could talk," I said in a whisper.

We stayed in that barn long enough for the smell to lose its power. It's amazing what a person can get used to. Delilah finally broke the silence by saying, "What if I told you I love you?" She turned to me. In the slanted gray light of the barn, her cheeks glistened. I wondered if she'd been crying. "What if I told you I didn't love you?"

"I'd believe you," I said and I was unsure which statement it was that I believed. I pulled her from the barn and closed the door. Here, in front of the barn, the cameras still couldn't reach us. Still we were safe. Thinking about the possibility of Delilah's love was too much happiness all at once.

She said, "What if I said you shouldn't love me? What if I told you I might be pregnant?"

I kissed her, right there outside the pig barn, because I didn't want to think of her heavy *what ifs*. I pressed her bones into mine. She still smelled of the pig barn as I lifted the skirt of her dress, unzipped my jeans. In the darkness of her eyes, the small, undiluted pupil, I saw myself, intense and sad. *What if?* She gasped and my fingers were on her bare thighs and her mouth was mine.

On the walk back to my house, I jittered. I pulled out a cigarette and asked, "Want a smoke?" like I always did. Delilah stopped walking and said, "Yeah." I didn't think much of it at the time, how I'd never seen her smoke. I just thought she wanted to cover the pig stench. She held the cigarette between her lips as I lit the tip.

What if, what if.

That would be the last time I slept with Delilah.

The next day, early Monday, Bill was driving the four wheeler. I sat beside him, which I didn't like because just sitting in something like that made me nervous. I'd been avoiding him because I was afraid he might smell Delilah on me. But I was running late that morning, and needed the ride. As we got closer to the farm I smelled smoke, and then saw flame.

"Shit," Bill yelled. A thick gray cloud billowed in the air. He sped up. He wanted to get the knowing over with. To stare face first at the destruction and face the consequences. I would've slowed down, preferred not to know. To never know. To stay in my bed forever that day.

Bill drove the four wheeler up to the security gates and then killed the engine, jumped out and punched in his ID code. He ran in, but I sat for a second and then lifted my heavy legs and stepped out.

The charred stench of it hit me. Fire flashed ahead. Two fire trucks and an ambulance were already there. Barn 4 was shattered, the roof in shards, the wood splintered, in smolders. Dead sows lay feet up, sprawled on the grass. Some of their stomachs bulged with never to be born piglets. I stared at one sow for a good long while. The way its snout pointed up to the sky, the smashed nostrils and the wrinkled eyes. The snout inflamed, possibly from an infection, possibly from fire. I couldn't stand it. There were bodies everywhere I turned. It smelled eerily like bacon. Long strips of charred pig flesh littered the ground. I walked on tiptoes to avoid it.

Bill had already found Father, who was talking to an EMT. I made my way to them, slowed by the fire, and the smoke, and the pink, pale bodies.

"Any people in or near the barns when it happened?" The EMT asked.

"Not that I know of," Father said. I wanted to pat Father on the shoulder, but I couldn't bring myself to touch him. But Bill did, like the good son he is.

"What happened?" I asked.

"We don't know yet," Father said. Then he slammed his fist to his thighs. "Shit," he said.

But the medics did find someone. The EMT rescued her from the pig grime. I saw her at a distance, on a gurney. Bill did too, and by the time my brain kicked into motion, he was already running to her, already there. I followed, my body sluggish, already too heavy from grief.

Delilah, my beautiful, my sad Delilah. They carried her away in an ambulance. She was already dead, but Bill rode with her anyway. And he cried, not silent man-tears, but great bellows. I stood and watched him. I'd never thought of how much he must've loved her. I loved her with every fiber I had, yet here I was, with no tears, on the destroyed hog farm, while Bill was with the body in the ambulance.

That was a week ago. Now I sit in my room with whipped cream-flavored vodka, almost gone. It's the only way I can bring her back. I've propped the sketch of her on my desk and I'm painting. It would be better if I could have her pose again. The colors won't be quite right, because all I've got is this goddamn beautiful black and white charcoal sketch. I begin with the outline. The dark colors, her face shape, sharp eyes, the shadows falling into her curves.

When I walked away from the pig farm after the explosion, I didn't know how the hurt would come in such waves. I didn't know what that gray pig foam was. Our manure pits didn't vent properly, so methane gas formed in the anaerobic system of pig shit and trapped gas. Methane created the foam, and when the bubbles popped they released great waves of gas. And then, explosion. I didn't know we lost hundreds of pigs that day.

But I knew I'd lost her.

I paint, and even as I do so I wonder if I'm just pretending, or if this is real: this feeling, this painting. I fill in the shadows. The deep waves of her dark hair. I wonder what she was doing there at the hog farm so early in the morning. Perhaps she just snuck in to visit those sad pigs. She was drawn to them. Perhaps she thought her few minutes of company could spare them some loneliness. Perhaps she was lonely. I wonder if it was just bad luck, her being there, so early and alone. I paint the dark areolas of her breasts. The soft creases of her stomach that gathered darkness.

I wonder if she knew exactly what she was doing. Perhaps she was smarter than any of us and knew about the pig foam. I think of her on that last day, taking my offered cigarette.

What if she had a lighter. What if she decided to smoke in that barn and didn't think. It might've been enough to spark an explosion.

What if I'm pregnant?

What if she knew of the foam, and stuck the cigarette in her mouth anyway. What if she thought this was a good, dramatic way to go. I'll never know because I disabled the cameras.

I mix just the right colors for her skin. I create eight hues from pale flesh for the highlights, to deep brown to fade to black for shadows.

Did she know how bright the explosion would burn? How the flame would become a wave and lick the roof off. The pigs rose, perhaps grateful for this freedom and terrified by the slick of heat cracking their skin. When I close my eyes I see pigs in flight, their engorged bodies, pink and on fire, arching through the lightening sky. It must've been like magic. Like hellfire. And it lifted her too and she flew, one girl in a burning blue skirt. Pigs slammed the earth, lost limbs, long strips of flesh. Scattered hooves, crisped tails, hair charred and liberated from skin. The scene almost looked worse a few days later. The pigs imprinted the shape of their bodies into the earth.

I am printed with her. She's in every breath I inhale. I paint her skin, layer the lighter colors upon the darker ones. I try to capture the way the light seemed to shine about her, bouncing from those dark eyes. In this way, I bring her back. Prove to myself that I'm different from my father.

I paint Delilah's lips last. They were such a lovely color, soft pink, coral, peach. Now that I think of it, the color of pigs. I feel sick. I shoot some vodka. My hands tremor, but I focus hard to keep them still as I finish the last little dip in her top lip.

I have paint all over my hands. I run my fingers through my hair, still short, just the way she cut it. When she was alive I didn't care about her mysteries. But now I'm desperate for the answers. I've learned to feel again, but this feeling I have clenching my chest is one I can hardly stand.

I stand back from the painting. It's gorgeous and looks exactly like her, except it's cold and flat, as all paintings are. I slam another gulp of whipped cream vodka. My vision blurs. My stomach churns and I want to let out a goddamn howl. I keep it in. I've captured Delilah's mysterious glint in her eyes. But I don't know what it means.

John Mandelberg

The French Horn

R.'s girlfriend took him up to San Fernando to meet her odd shy half brother. Later R. was to wonder why she had brought him there. Was she as deeply in love with R. as he was with her, and had she decided that R. must meet even the peripheral members of her family, to interlock all of her life with his? Or, on the other hand, was she suspicious of R., and did she want to test him by seeing his reaction to her strange fat half brother Gilberto?

Did she want to remind R. that she was Latina (of Mexican descent) and that her real father's family was Mexican, whereas R. was Anglo (actually of Polish ancestry; at least his grandmothers were Polish)–and that they'd have to overcome this stupid but obvious division?

Or maybe she just wanted to show off to R. how kind and good she was, coming all the way up from Pico Rivera to visit poor reclusive Gilberto and his little elderly aunt, who lived all by themselves in a tiny sunbaked white wooden house. But when they arrived, she only kissed her half brother quickly and perfunctorily, and left R. alone with him while she went to the kitchen to talk Spanish with Gilberto's aunt (to whom she was not actually related). So R. couldn't help feeling that she had arranged this meeting for some concealed purpose.

He shook Gilberto's big limp damp hand, and grinned at him in a friendly way. Gilberto was obese, 15 years older than R.'s girlfriend (who, like R. himself, was 32) and thus already 47 years old. He was pyramidal in shape, with a small head, puzzled moist brown eyes, and narrow shoulders sloping down to immense belly and hips.

Gilberto carefully sat down on a large sagging chair, and R. sat, smiling eagerly, on the edge of a worn-out couch. Gilberto was shy, and said nothing. R. said, "Hey, this is a nice little house. I've never been out to this part of the Valley before. . .I live in Silverlake now." But Gilberto only nodded, courteous and diffident.

R. could hear his girlfriend shouting from the kitchen, repeating the same Spanish phrases over and over, because the old aunt was nearly deaf.

"So–I hear you have a job," R. said. "Where do you work?"

Gilberto muttered something, scarcely audible.

"Marco's? Mardo's? What's that?"

R.'s girlfriend shouted from the kitchen, "It's a restaurant, a steak house! He's a cook's helper!"

"A cook's helper! Hey, that's great!" R. enthused. "You a good cook?"

"Yeah," Gilberto shrugged, without vanity.

And R. began to feel an expansive affection for this enormous gentle man, and not only because he felt so much jubilant love for his girlfriend that it overflowed toward everyone around her.

"Well, what else do you like to do? Hobbies?" R. persisted, amused. "What do you do for fun?"

Gilberto cleared his throat. "I like music TV. . . "

"Got a girlfriend?"

"Naw. . ." said Gilberto.

"What? No girlfriend? Come on, man, you're still young!" R. said. Already he seemed to look down fondly on Gilberto from heights of joy.

Then R.'s girlfriend called out from the kitchen, "He plays the trumpet!"

"Do you?" R. laughed happily. "Do you really play the trumpet?"

"He learned to play all by himself," R.'s girlfriend said, coming out of the kitchen with her lovely blue dress swishing, folding her arms and smiling merrily. "Don't you still have your trumpet, Gilberto? Yes, you still have it, don't you? Pues, ándale, let's see it, 'mano!"

Gilberto pushed himself up out of the chair, then walked unhurriedly to his bedroom. His half sister followed him, so R. followed her, and stood in the doorway of a small room with a very worn wood floor. The room, where Gilberto had lived almost his entire life, seemed poignantly empty. There was a bed with a tattered gray blanket. On the wall was a large carved crucifix which R., himself a waned Catholic, noted with nostalgic respect, and a photo of a once-famous blonde TV actress, cut from a faded magazine, and a small shelf. To R. the room had an ancient simplicity worthy of the old Spanish missions, which seemed to express the gravity and dignity of Gilberto's whole inoffensive life. It smelled heavily of body odor and damp wool, but also of a sweet flower that was blooming just outside the hazy window.

On the single wooden shelf were Gilberto's few possessions: a catcher's mitt, three photographs tacked to a piece of wood, and a dusty trumpet. Gilberto took down the trumpet, worked the keys, and played a few rusty notes. "I don't play much no more," he said.

"You're out of shape?" his half sister teased him.

"Yeah. . . out of shape," he agreed solemnly. He played a few more notes, making cracking and farting sounds, then launched into an old rock 'n' roll song.

"Hey, that's pretty good!" R. cheered, and he and his girlfriend clapped and shouted, "Yay! Viva Gilberto!" But Gilberto wordlessly put the trumpet back on its shelf.

"You should play in a mariachi band!" R. said.

But his girlfriend shook her head seriously and said, lecturing him a little, "With all the new people coming into this neighborhood from Mexico, the mariachis are really a big business now. They're very competitive, there are a lot of bands and the musicians are really, really good–a lot of them were professional musicians in Mexico. . ." So R. felt embarrassed.

Then she smiled at Gilberto and said, "Gilberto's more of an old rock'n'roller anyway, aren't you, Gilberto? Eh?" But Gilberto was quiet.

"I should sell you my old French horn, Gilberto," R. said. "Yeah! I should!"

"*You* have a French horn?" R.'s girlfriend said, and burst into laughter.

"Yeah, I do. I do! Really! I have a French horn. You don't believe me?"

When R. was in his mid-20s, feeling harried and lonely, he impulsively bought an old used French horn at a music store. He had played keyboard instruments as a teenager, but had always loved the sound of French horns, as well as their glittering beauty as objects, and had always wished he could play one. Feeling mournful for the passing of his earliest youth and the narrowing of his possibilities, as only an American man in his twenties can, he vowed to learn to play the French horn. He purchased an instruction book along with the instrument, and tried to produce music. But he had not expected such difficulty. He could read music already, but the idea of using the same key for a vast number of different notes was too confusing for him.

Since then, he had kept it in its battered brown case, moving it from one apartment to the next, keeping it in one closet or another. It was an antique, made before the second world war. Occasionally he opened its case to remind himself of its hard swirls of dark brass and its big graceful tarnished bell. More often, he only thought of it, as a secretly innocent dream or as a refuge of serenity and concentration that he might be able to recover sometime in the future. But right at this moment, in the presence of this woman who brought him so much pleasure and contentment, he realized he didn't need or want the French horn anymore.

"You know what a French horn is, don't you, Gilberto?" R. asked.

"No. . . yeah. . . I seen them, I don't know," Gilberto said. His eyes widened and brightened a little.

"Sure! The horn that's curved around–like this–you've seen them. Do you want to buy one?"

Gilberto was intrigued. He seemed to revive out of his perpetual half-stupor. He smiled, he gave a quick childish laugh. But then he said, "Naw. . ."

"Why not?"

"I don't have enough money."

"I'll sell it to you cheap!" R. cried. "Don't worry, man! I'll bring it over here and show you. You think I'm joking? No, this is for real, man! I mean it, I'll bring it right here to your house!"

R.'s girlfriend watched Gilberto, laughing fondly, but then she said, "Come on, don't tease him."

"I'm not teasing him! I mean it!" R. insisted.

R. and his girlfriend said goodbye to Gilberto and the old aunt, and went out the door. The meager front yard was mostly straggly half-dead early summer grass and gray-brown Valley dirt, but along the house, Easter lilies were blooming extravagantly in a long uneven row, their glistening white blossoms giving off exquisite perfume. This was what R. had smelled in Gilberto's room. R.'s girlfriend bent down in her beautiful soft blue dress and picked three of the lilies, then held them to her face. She asked, "Did you like Gilberto?"

"Oh, he's a great guy, he's the sweetest guy I've ever met," R. said.

His girlfriend kissed him and said, "I knew you'd like him, I just knew that you would." They drove back, and the perfume of the lilies filled the car for the whole trip.

R. and his girlfriend both worked at the headquarters of one of the public utilities in downtown Los Angeles–that's how they met–but R. sometimes had to attend operations meetings in various locations. He had a meeting scheduled in the West Valley in two weeks, so he put the French horn in the trunk of his car.

After the meeting, he drove east to San Fernando, and found the back street and the old wooden house where Gilberto and his aunt lived. He had heard that Gilberto worked at the restaurant from 5 p.m. to 10 p.m. every evening, and he expected that Gilberto would be home in mid-afternoon.

R. knocked on the door. The aunt opened it, but she didn't seem to remember him. He shouted, "Gilberto? Is Gilberto home? Está en casa Gilberto?" Finally she let him inside. He set the heavy case containing the French horn on the floor, and sat on the edge of the dilapidated couch as he had done before. He could hear Gilberto in the nearby bathroom. The toilet flushed, and Gilberto came slowly into the living room.

"Well, here I am!" R. proclaimed. "Here's the French horn!" He opened the case, and the whole brass spiral and wide bell gleamed upon the moth-eaten velvet lining in the dim room.

Gilberto was amazed, but he hesitated before reaching for the horn distrustfully. "Go on, try it out!" R. urged, delighted to share the excitement. "Put in the mouthpiece! It's a little smaller than the trumpet mouthpiece, I think, but you'll get used to it. No, no–you're supposed to hold it pointing down–stick your hand in the end–that's right. . ."

Gilberto took a gigantic apprehensive breath, then blasted out a loud tone of pure brassy magnificence. He let out a low laugh, took another breath, played again.

"See?" R. shouted. "You're good at it! You're a natural!"

Gilberto played a few more notes, soaring up, blaring low, then he withdrew his lips from the horn. His face had warmed and reddened, his eyes shone, he seemed thrilled.

Even the deaf old aunt had heard it, and she came hobbling over to yell at Gilberto in Spanish, evidently asking him what the hell was that? "Es un French horn, tía," Gilberto said to her. He sat hugging the horn on his massive lap, breathless, desirous, hypnotized. All of his timid childishness seemed to fall away as he suddenly, so late in his miniature life, wanted something so desperately.

R. planned to give him the horn, but R. had also decided that he must ask Gilberto to pay for it. To give Gilberto charity would mean that Gilberto needed charity, and this would make Gilberto worthy of pity, R. thought. But R. had conceived strong admiration and respect for Gilberto and did not want to pity him. So he said, "How about it, Gilberto? Thirty dollars?" R. himself had paid $155 for it six years ago.

But Gilberto's smile fell and he lowered his head. "Naw . . ." he said slowly.

"OK, OK. . .make it fifteen? Twelve? Twelve dollars! Is it a deal?"

Gilberto counted out tightly folded dollar bills from a coffee can. R. recalled that his girlfriend had told him that her half brother had been making minimum wage all his life, and that he signed over all his paychecks to his aunt.

"That French horn's going to change your life," R. said. "Really! It's magic. You take that horn outside and blow it, and the ladies will come running. You're going to get yourself a girlfriend with that horn–you think I'm lying?"

"Naw. . ." Gilberto said bashfully.

R. said goodbye, feeling buoyant. He felt he had brought a transforming pleasure into Gilberto's life, a pleasure exactly suited to that life, just as his own happiness, brought to him by Gilberto's half sister, had been perfect for his own life.

R. was actually shy himself; he himself had long felt like a loser, more or less comfortable inside his own small territory but also constricted there. She had broken open his boundaries with her own blast of music. Thus he was repaying her by giving a different joy to a different life, which was also bound, but in a different way, to hers. All this delighted him.

As he came out the front door of the house, he looked to the row of white lilies. But they had all already faded; the gorgeous flowers of two weeks ago were now withered strips of gray membrane.

Some weeks passed when R. and his girlfriend weren't able to see each other. But she told him on the phone, "Oh, my brother visited Gilberto and he says Gilberto really loves that French horn! He plays it beautifully, he plays it all the time! And you know what? He got a girlfriend from that horn! He took it to Las Palmas Park where the mariachis practice, and he just played it and these ladies came over to talk to him. Now he goes there every Sunday to play the horn and talk to this lady there! I think it's really good for him!"

R. always had a terrible memory for names and faces. But Gilberto made a very strong impression on him. Whenever he heard anything about San Fernando, or about French horns, or met any Mexican-American man who was heavy or plump, he remembered Gilberto and thought about him.

And after he broke up with his girlfriend, after gradually and painfully disengaging from her because she wanted too much organization and he wanted too much impulse, or because he analyzed things too much and she was too impatient, or because she was just too much one way and he was too much another way–then when he sometimes thought of her, he thought of Gilberto too.

Then when he thought of Gilberto, and Gilberto's humble mild life in that bare simple room of that tiny old house in San Fernando, R. also thought of his French horn. Though R. still felt satisfied and proud that he had given–or at least effectively given–the French horn to Gilberto, he now also wished that he still had the French horn. He wished he still had the youthful potential to learn how to play it. He wished he still had available to him, just in case he could ever find time for it, an object that would let him master a discipline of beauty, an object that would make him happy in himself. But the French horn was no longer in his closet, because Gilberto had it.

Some years later when R. was 37, he brought a woman he'd recently met to dinner at a new restaurant that had just opened near her apartment in Studio City. The tables were crowded, the steaks and salsa were pretty good, and the chef was walking around accepting congratulations. And though R. so often could not identify acquaintances and co-workers from even a year ago, he saw this huge dark-complexioned chef moving ponderously among the tables, and thought instantly–Gilberto!

"Oh my God," he said to his companion, "I know that guy! That's Gilberto!"

R. burst out laughing. He felt that his French horn must've worked a miracle! Gilberto, metamorphosed by the horn, taken up by some smart woman with ambition, had become cook, head cook, chef, and now ran his own restaurant!

R. waited, grinning, for Gilberto to reach his table. Then he clasped the chef's big damp hand and said, "You remember me?"

"Sure!" Gilberto said warmly. "How are you?"

"I'm great! Are you still playing the French horn?"

"Oh. . .well. . ." the chef shrugged. He had changed so much; he had lost weight, hardened his face, focused his attention. But now when his small brown eyes flickered uneasily, showing confusion and timidity, he looked just like Gilberto again.

"But look at you! Everything's turned out so good for you!" R. laughed in disbelief.

"Yeah. . .I'm a very, very lucky man," Gilberto said. He waved and moved on.

"That's amazing," R. said to his companion. He was so emotional that he almost lost interest in her. He said, "That guy was so shy and lost and out of it, he was working for minimum wage at a steak house when he was already in his forties. He was such a loser! And you know why he's been successful?"

"Why?" she asked.

"Because of my French horn! I sold him my French horn for twelve dollars!"

"And that changed his life?" she asked skeptically.

"Looks like it!" R. laughed.

After that, thinking often about Gilberto with amusement and wonder, he began to think about his old girlfriend. By now the pain of breaking up with her had faded, and he was able to ponder objectively–what happened to all the joy he had felt back then? Where did it go? Had it all been useless, because it ended?

It pleased him to think that the joy of those days had not been fruitless after all, because the generosity and love it had inspired in him had been preserved in his gift of the French horn to Gilberto. Maybe she had even foreseen this, maybe this was why she had brought R. to meet Gilberto on that day when those white lilies were blooming. It was Gilberto who had been transformed by R.'s happiness, not, in the end, R.'s girlfriend or R. himself–and that was fitting, and good.

So it was Gilberto who stayed in his mind, not the girlfriend. R. went back to that restaurant, alone this time, to try to see Gilberto and talk to him. After eating, R. went to the kitchen door and peered in, then asked a waiter to get the chef. And big Gilberto came to the door, breathless, harried and beaming. "How are you doing?" R. exclaimed.

"Oh–just great!"

"That's good! Boy, I'm glad to see you so successful," R. told him, nodding and smiling fondly. "You see your sister much?"

"Oh man, I'm so busy I don't have time to see *anybody*."

"Well. . .but you're doing all right?" R. said.

"Oh, fantastic!"

"You still got the French horn?"

"Oh–" said the big chef, backing away into the kitchen, waving robustly, "I got everything I ever had!"

After that, seeing that Gilberto hardly remembered him anymore and probably had given up the French horn and everything else from his old life, R. did not try to renew the acquaintanceship. But Gilberto became a private legend for him, and an example of fabulous redemption. Then R. was turning 40 and, having lost jobs and girlfriends, and struggling with car loans and credit card debts, suspected he was not doing so well in life. But he thought, well, Gilberto was still a dishwasher when he was forty.

Suffering from painful kidney stones, R. was heading for a regular appointment at his urologist's office in Eagle Rock when he saw a familiar-looking woman in the lobby of the medical building. He thought she was his old girlfriend, Gilberto's half sister.

Hesitantly, distrusting his memory, he approached her and then turned away, deciding it wasn't her after all. But then he heard his name called, and looked back to see her smiling, surprised and amused. "How are you?" she said warmly. She was 40 by then too, she had cut her hair very short and her neck was pudgy and thick. But she still looked very pretty to R.

She said she was now married, owned a house in Eagle Rock and had two sons, one of whom unfortunately kept getting ear infections. Her eyes looked sad about that. She'd just hurried into the medical building to pick up a copy of her son's blood test to bring to some other doctor. R. expressed sympathetic interest, then told her about his job problems, etc. But then, to bring back an atmosphere of happiness between them, he said, "Hey, I saw Gilberto at his own restaurant! I was so surprised–but he's doing great! It's wonderful! I knew it was all because of my French horn!"

She looked at him, smiling a little sadly, and said, "What restaurant?"

"Gilberto's restaurant! In Studio City, in the Valley!"

She shook her head. "Gilberto doesn't have a restaurant. He died."

R. was dumbfounded. For a moment, he thought she was joking. He said, "What?"

"Gilberto passed away, it was over four years ago," she said. "He was walking home from work in the dark one night, and some car hit him and he had to get surgery, and he died during the surgery."

R. said, stunned, "I–I can't believe that. I thought I just saw him at this restaurant. I talked to him–" But even as he attempted to argue, he remembered the chef's conversation and gestures, and realized he had made an idiotic mistake, not just from stupidity but from longing.

"Gilberto could never have his own restaurant!" she laughed. "He could barely keep his job washing dishes. He was retarded."

"But–but I could've sworn that was him," R. said dismally. "I asked him about the French horn and he–oh, man . . ."

"You and your memory for faces," she said with mock exasperation. "I remember how you'd get people's names wrong at work. I'm surprised you recognize yourself in the mirror!"

"But–who was it, then?" R. said. He felt despair.

"It must've been some other fat Mexican," she said wickedly and laughed. Then she made a long apologetic sigh. "I'm sorry," she said more seriously. "I was so sad when I heard. He was a sweet man in his way. He lived very simply and didn't really need anything." She looked at her watch and gasped, "Oh jeez, I have to get going." She stepped closer to him as if she might kiss him on the cheek, but she just patted his arm.

"How old was he when he died?" R. asked.

"Oh, I guess he was. . .fifty-one."

"That's–that's terrible," R. said gruffly.

"Well, that's what God wanted for him. He had a beautiful life."

R. struggled to think of something else to say about Gilberto before she could hurry off. "He loved that French horn – I could tell," R. said. "Did he play it much?"

She shrugged, starting to pull away. "I didn't go out there very often, but I guess he probably gave it up after a while. He didn't have much energy for anything."

"What happened to it then?"

"I guess his old aunt still has it, she still lives in the same house. Hey, if you want to buy it back, they're going to have a yard sale there."

"Really?" R. said.

"Yeah," she called as she strode off, "the aunt is getting too old to be by herself, I hear the other nephews are taking her back to Mexico. Go up there sometime and see."

So on Saturday, R. drove to San Fernando. Meeting Gilberto had left a strong imprint at least in his spatial memory, and he still knew where the little old white wooden house was. He found it, and parked at the curb. It was a warm winter day. He walked up through green uncut rain-fed grass and weeds to the front door and knocked. There was mail in the mailbox, and the house did not look vacant. But no-one answered.

The next Saturday he didn't go, but on the Saturday after that, he drove to San Fernando again. This time the little yard of the old wooden house was filled with tables of worn household objects and heaps of old clothing spread out on blankets. The neighbors were picking through it, murmuring in Spanish, while a scowling stocky man with calloused hands sat on a rusty patio chair, watching.

R. glanced around, and quickly saw and grabbed the French horn. He bought it for 60 dollars. Someone else had already taken the trumpet. As he counted out money to the stocky grim-looking man, R. wanted to ask him if he was related to Gilberto. But the man looked in a bad mood, so R. said nothing, except, "Thanks."

R. took the French horn back to his apartment. He sat on his couch and opened the case on the floor. Once again he gazed at the dark brass tubing in its intricate coils, the splendid flared bell, the round brass buttons of the valves, the three tarnished keys that he had never figured out how to use properly. His kidney stone ached, and he decided not to risk taking a deep breath to play a note.

R. started thinking about one of his Polish grandmothers. She and her sister were stepchildren of a skilled mechanic and labor union leader. The stepfather was sent to prison in 1930 when Marshal Pilsudski and the "Cleanliness" regime turned against the unions, and the sisters divided up the modest family china. One sister stayed in Poland, saw her husband and son killed by the Nazis, endured immeasurable suffering, fell gravely ill. But when she finally came to America after the war, her teacups were unscratched. R's grandmother emigrated earlier, and lived placidly for decades in Illinois, but her teacups were chipped and cracked in the first wild American dishwashers. The tea set, when reunited, formed a strange riddle that both symbolized and mocked the hollowed-out family.

R. looked at the French horn. Older than either he or Gilberto, it still gleamed sumptuously, exactly as it had before. Gilberto had left no visible mark or influence on it, nor had R. himself. Nor was there any sign upon it from the auras of emotion and mythology that his thoughts had wrapped around it, first when he possessed it himself and then when he only remembered it. It was a musical instrument, and could've been classified in a higher category than other material things. But it was as mute and enigmatic now as all those silent objects finally are to us, when they keep mysteriously existing after we no longer desire them, or after we are dead.

Nicholas Maistros

Full of Life Now

I once told Walt that, on occasion, I fantasized about killing him. This was when I was young and Walt was an old man.

We were riding in his buggy along the Delaware and watching the ferries when I said it. I was holding the reins. Walt told me with his laugh that I'd caught him off guard and, simultaneously, that it was about time. Then he said, his voice trembling from the jostles of the cab, "Tell me, dear boy, how you've planned to rid of me."

I told him that, well, just now I thought about pushing him off the buggy and watching him roll on down to the water, to which he laughed again and leaned against the edge of the cab, facing me, a boot heel—the one belonging to his good leg—propped against the brace. *He's magnificent,* I thought, *perched and rocking there in the sunlight, the length of him somehow not fitting the buggy, his overcoat flapping over the side, his perpetually amused brow which turned up even for the sun, his white hair flowing from beneath his floppy hat. He's a living monument.* "And why would you want to do a thing like that?"

"Because you keep calling me *dear boy,*" I said.

He wanted to hear more, so I told him asphyxiation was a possibility. Either by pillow in the night, or maybe, in the middle of a meal, I'd get up, ostensibly to go fetch some more bread. Then I'd strike from behind, wrap his long white beard around his neck and pull and pull until he fell dead into his soup. He seemed to like this idea the best and took me into the embrace we reserved for public outings, one of his arms draped across my shoulders, the other clutching my lapel.

"*Boy* is something we can alter, but I'm afraid *dear* has to stay put. What do you say to *my dear fellow*? Will that so seize you with homicidal fervor?"

I said that that would do, and we continued about our ride, both of us thinking I was only fooling.

Shortly after I came to live with Walt, I stopped sleeping. Walt said it was because I was too defiant, afraid to give myself over. "What, you suppose you won't be you again when you wake?" I should calm myself, he said, allow my inner pathways to open up. I should drift, he said.

But lying there next to him, with all the bedclothes and the pillows and the room so quiet, excepting intervals of passing trains and Walt's light snores—so pleased did he seem with his sleep—I found it difficult to breathe and had to stand up, permit my head to clear. Sometimes he would stir, and I would whisper an apology. Sometimes he would say something to me, or about me: "Poor boy. Poor, restive boy." Usually he stayed asleep.

And I paced the floor, alive and cluttered with manuscripts and memory. I paced in my bare feet, tripping over something—a boot? a satchel?—seeking out the cracks and grains in the floorboards, listening for their creaks, as if I needed, in the absence of the sound of my own breath, to make some physical noise, as if I needed convincing that yes, I am alive and awake and here in these, his, quarters—and I watched Walt, the rise and fall of him, in his peaceful sleep, and I wondered how he, a poet, a poet of such magnitude, could locate such rest. How uncanny it was that all the images that came to be scribbled onto his pages, all those proclamations and sentiments and stories, could leave him be for long enough and completely enough to allow for such sleep. And how I, not a poet, not in the slightest, couldn't keep from turning over ideas all through the night, grotesque and half-formed ideas that refused to find language or assume figures of any kind, only sudden pieces of figures, sudden faces or simply mouths, saying something I couldn't quite hear but which echoed nonetheless.

Mrs. Suzanne Pendergast had me go around back to make my deliveries, something I always attributed to her accent, which spoke of a higher civility than most from our town. I think she was from Boston originally, but I can't recall—that area at least, with an eye for form and perhaps a knack for interactions with servants of various sorts.

What I knew of Mrs. Pendergast I'd learned not from her but from the store. A widow, though not very old, certain Camden women would say of her with a click of their tongues, a young widow, her husband lost to the war. Moved here with an invalid sister 10 years before and hadn't much acclimated herself. Well-off, it seemed, thankfully, though who knew where her money came from—perhaps a wealthy uncle had passed, or perhaps she'd received a healthy sum from an unknown benefactor for being her sister's caretaker—that is, if she was indeed her sister—until recently, of course, when that horrible woman was sent off somewhere, an institution of some kind, quite the mystery.

Never was Mrs. Pendergast seen at assemblies or festivals or other social functions. Suffice it to say that she was a bit shapeless, a familiar figure but one with only as much depth as was offered by speculation and stories. There were never more than the usual pleasantries of business exchange as I set her bags on the countertop and bid her good day. But one Thursday afternoon, when I was about to take my leave, she said, "Have you a moment, Mr. Duckett?"

I was at first nervous that she'd say something about my tardiness; I'd taken too long at my last drop-off and ridden Mr. O'Shaunessy's mule as fast as I could. Perhaps she'd seen my sweating; perhaps she'd found it distasteful, my handling food and all.

"I've just made a cake," she said. "Would you care to try it? I'd like to have an opinion. Foods are your trade, after all." She cut two slices from a pound cake and carried them out of the room saying, "We'll have our cake in the parlor." It took me a moment to fully recognize this as an invitation.

The first thing I noticed upon entering the parlor were the windows. Tall windows that nearly made up the fourth wall of the room. It was a milky overcast day, which was perhaps why Mrs. Pendergast had those heavy curtains drawn. It was easy to become gloomy on days like that. Walt adored days like that. He said they made one feel transported and strangely unified, all of us in this new place and attempting to go about our appointments as though things were normal. I would tell him that I liked days like that, too.

The second thing I noticed was the birdcage, which hung from a planter hook in the ceiling. The bird inside was still, and it made no sound. I wondered whether it was stuffed.

Mrs. Pendergast had me sit next to her. She set her plate down and sat with her elbow propped against the back of the sofa and her fingers curled under her chin. She watched as I took a bite. It was crumby, and, worried the crumbs would scatter beyond the plate on my lap, I hunched over and bobbed my head down and up, down and up, wiping the corners of my mouth until I finished chewing. She must have taken my bobbing for an acknowledgement of her achievement, because she said, "Good. Good."

She asked me questions about my life, my work. She asked about my Aunt Hettie, what my favorite subject had been in school. The sciences, I told her, though I hadn't really enjoyed any subject. There were some passages from Darwin and Wallace I remember liking, but really, that felt little like science to me.

"Oh? I would have thought it was writing," she said.

"I liked reading all right, but when it came to writing, I couldn't get what I was thinking out on paper. The teacher would say, 'You need focus. You need a plan.' But then making a plan was just as difficult for me as the writing." Something was overcoming me as I spoke. "I'd have to make plans for plans." I felt like somebody else talking, somebody from the store. I was enjoying myself.

"Have you ever tried writing creatively?" she asked me.

"I'm no poet," I said, with a rush that felt oddly like pride.

What was it about Mrs. Pendergast that allowed me to open up as I was? Perhaps it was simply that sitting there, for the first time, after years of delivering her dry goods, I realized that Mrs. Pendergast was pretty. Older, yes, and maybe a bit severe, but there was a sensibility behind her eyes, behind the parting of her lips and the glistening bottoms of her front teeth, suggesting a magnificent smile that would never actually come, behind the tilt of her head as she listened, as though she weren't sure what would come next but she knew for certain it would amuse her.

And she wouldn't laugh if amused, either. She would close her lips tight, as though she tasted something sweetly sour, and she would look up slightly above me for a moment, picturing, savoring, before coming back down. That was it, yes. A gracefulness. A largeness of life and feeling tightly restrained with elegance, with refinement. I found that I wanted to come up with a story or a remark, some unexpected thing that would force her to put her hand over her teeth.

"You should try it," she said, and there was something in the quality of her voice, in her gaze, not dreamy, not *oh, wouldn't it be nice?* It was direct, certain. She was speaking of what she truly saw. "I'm sure you have some lovely lyrics in you."

But before I could demur, and then tell her that perhaps she was right, she said, "You board with that mysterious Mr. Whitman, don't you?"

And with that, whatever summit I'd been scaling felt merely a fiction. I could suddenly see the parlor filled with people, mingling and dropping crumbs onto the floors, Mrs. Pendergast bouncing about between them like a small dog snatching their crumbs where they fell, ears pricked to all that human business. I saw the curtains pulled and the daylight entering.

"Yes, ma'am." I took another bite of cake. Mrs. Pendergast hadn't touched hers.

"A curious arrangement," she said. It was a forwardness I wasn't prepared for. "I had assumed it was because you were a writer as well, a writer-in-training."

"No, ma'am." I was saying *ma'am* again, as I had before the invitation beyond her kitchen. "But I do help him with his transcriptions and correspondences and so forth."

This seemed to relieve her, make her think, *ah*. "That is very dear of you, helping an older gentleman like that." I expected her to ask what I was receiving in return, but she continued with something else, what I began to suspect was the true reason I'd been asked to sample her cake. "I should like to meet him. I am such an admirer of his poetry." She leaned forward, her chin tucking itself into one shoulder, to conceal, it appeared, a jolt of gaiety. "To be frank, his poems do frighten me somewhat."

"They frighten many, ma'am."

She stiffened again, having recovered from her excitement. "But I suppose that is what we come to expect from poets. The double-life of the writer, as they say."

I set my plate of crumbs down on the end table. I let the fork fall a bit too hard against the porcelain, hoping it would signal to her that I should be going. This double-life she spoke of. What was to say that I, who was no writer, no poet, did not enjoy that other, imaginary life? What was keeping me up at night, after all, and keeping a part of me always at the back of my thoughts, if it wasn't my own second life? And for that matter, where was Walt's second life? As far as I could tell, there was but one. The man, the poet. Both were present that morning in the way he first looked at me from up in his open window as I left Aunt Hettie's for work, in the way he lifted a shaky hand to the air and said, "There he goes, my lovely boy, off to enlighten the masses."

"So it's settled," Mrs. Pendergast said. "We shall meet."

"Meet, ma'am?"

"Myself and Mr. Whitman." She took the plate I'd eaten off of, having to lean close to me. I held my breath, but later wished that I had taken in her smell, as though this would have given me some essential information about her, or perhaps, and this has just now occurred to me, to have experienced Mrs. Pendergast in a way Walt hadn't yet. For as comfortable as I had been with her, talking, I was now sitting straight at the edge of the cushion, my hands pressed flat against my thighs. I could hear movement. A scrambling somewhere in the room. Mrs. Pendergast didn't react to it, and I thought it must only be me who heard it.

Mrs. Pendergast stood. "The only question is how you will arrange it."

She looked down at me, waiting. I could not seem to keep my eyes on her, first craning back to meet her eyes, then staring straight ahead, then, realizing I was staring at the waistline of her skirt, across to the doorway, to Mrs. Pendergast's imaginary guests, coats draped over their arms, waving goodbye, an imaginary grin beneath a mustache.

And that scrambling, that shuffling. What was it?

I looked back up at her. "Mr. O'Shaunessy's store?" I suggested.

She thought. "Well, but I suppose that just isn't very—what's the word I'm looking for?—suitable. Mr. Duckett, this is a little embarrassing for me to admit, but I've been considering this, my meeting Mr. Whitman, for some time now. Nearly since his arrival last year. Everyone found him to be so perplexing, maybe a little eccentric. All these questions people had. I'm sure you remember. And I suppose there are still questions floating about Camden, but I never once had a question. Can you believe that?"

I could not.

"I never had a single question about our Mr. Whitman. Perhaps it was because I'd so closely read his lyrics. Perhaps it was because it wasn't long ago that I was myself new to Camden—and to be quite honest, I still feel, well, unacquainted. But never did I question Mr. Whitman."

I knew what she was to say next. I'd said the same thing to my Aunt Hettie, to one of my old school chums when he'd asked where I'd been these past months and why he'd seen me driving that old man around in a buggy.

"It's as if I already know him," she said. "Intimately."

My old school chum screwed his face up when I'd said this, told me I needed to go about with more *young* people, and I burned with embarrassment.

"So you see," Mrs. Pendergast continued, "the setting has to be one that matches the picture I've held for so long in my head." There was movement just behind her. It miraculously matched the shuffling sound in my head. The bird was alive.

I told Mrs. Pendergast that Walt would meet her the next morning, at the pier. She quite liked the idea.

It wasn't until I was on my way back to the store that I remembered what Mrs. Pendergast had said about my trying to write creatively. And, though the suggestion had been but a tactic to win some hidden objective, all of a sudden I had an objective of my own, a thing that would hone all of my restless, anxious energies. I would put them forth into a poem.

Walt was quiet over dinner. He sat hunched over his plate, and at times he sat back, looked off to a corner of the room, digging something out of his teeth and thinking. His mind was on his work. I knew he'd write after dinner, but I asked him nonetheless. "Are you going to write tonight?" And he looked at me, almost startled, pulled suddenly from his second life.

It was one of the things that brought us into this arrangement, the discussions we'd had about his work. Walt would watch me as I read over his latest lines, or perhaps a poem he'd long discarded and happened to find in his scrambling through the stacks. It was difficult to focus, knowing how intent Walt was upon me, sitting back and forth in his chair, resting his chin, crossing his arms, crossing his legs—but it was also wonderful, thrilling, those quiet, intense moments between two men, the writer and the reader. When I finished—or when I'd finally found I had something to say—I'd look up at him. He barely seemed to contain himself in that chair; I expected him to jump up, do something wild, snatch the papers from my hand and fling them out the window. What a feeling that was, making Walt Whitman squirm.

I told Aunt Hettie about those early moments when Walt entrusted me with his work and the discussions that would follow, the way he would look at me—how I stumbled and stuttered through those conversations, how impossible it was to grasp what he was doing on those pages—when I'd accidentally said something poignant. The way it would almost irritate me, that it should come as such a surprise to Walt, and to myself. The way I would balloon with delight.

When I related Walt's invitation to move into his house across the street, Aunt Hettie, who'd always scolded me for descending to the level of my friends at school, or the people at the store—"Don't do that, don't pretend you're one of them. You're not"—took me by the shoulders and said that now I would become something.

And here I was sitting across from the man, my head swirling with snippets and phrases that might, would, become a poem, my poem, and Walt had forgotten I was there.

"Do you know Mrs. Pendergast?" I asked.

"Mm."

"Her husband was killed in the war."

"Yes, I do remember something about that."

"Did you ever meet him? During the war? An officer named Pendergast?"

Walt sat back again, sucked at his teeth. I couldn't tell if he'd returned to where he'd been, to his work, or if he was now seeing all that he'd seen, all those years ago, those soldiers, those men he'd adored—why did I ask about the war?—when I was only an infant. Perhaps it was the same thing, his work, his war, and on his face the same look, the one that recalled the first lines he'd ever shown me. *You are asking me questions and I hear you, I answer that I cannot answer, you must find out for yourself.*

Walt pushed his chair out and walked around the table, his one foot dragging. He put a hand on my shoulder. He stood tall behind me, and I felt the fact of my size in that chair. "How are you going to do away with me tonight?"

I looked up at him, over my shoulder. There were his eyes, crinkled, affectionate, alive with the thought of his own death, with the power he thought I might have in me to kill him. "I have something in mind," I said. "It's still taking shape. I mustn't hurry it."

"May you give a hint?"

His other hand was on me now. He bent down, and I felt the tickles of his beard against my cheek. I leaned into him and whispered, "It'll be the thing you least suspect."

He embraced me, tightly. Then he went to work.

I paced again that night as Walt slept, but the room felt different. It was still Walt's room. These were still his piles of books and pages and photographs, still his wardrobe strewn about, his dust floating, invading my sinuses, but as I paced and fitfully considered my poem—*Once I have my opening line*—I came to feel the room doing for me what it had always done for him. And with a glee that I had to suppress in order not to giggle and wake him, the thought came: *It's as much my room as his.* And then, even more remarkable, as only thoughts in the middle of the night can be, and stranger still as it seemed to come in the voice of the room itself, if a room can have a voice: *I belong to no one.*

I couldn't write about the ferry. Not those children playing on the deck. Not the woman pacing the docks and staring up at the ship as we departed. This was Walt's territory. I needed to find something, some place he hadn't yet been. Which was why I'd hopped the ferry in the first place.

The woman on the docks with a hand to her forehead, cupping out the sun and looking—for whom?—didn't resemble Mrs. Pendergast, but the image of her there, looking, inspired her nonetheless. Mrs. Pendergast had already been here, and had already gone. Part of me had expected to see her at my arrival, still waiting at the pier, perhaps leaning back against the railing with an elbow, trying to appear nonchalant, trying not to evoke the distress she harbored. If she had been there, I'm not sure what I would have done. Hid? Relayed some made-up message excusing Walt's absence? Acted surprised that he hadn't come and then told the woman, with a shift that suggested something more toward the inevitable, *Can't expect much else from Mr. Whitman.* But she wasn't there.

That should be my beginning, I thought. Something about Mrs. Pendergast. Something about the hope she'd felt, the gravity attached to the moment of their meeting, and her gradual realization. *Everyone who passes must surely know that I stand here waiting for a man who isn't coming. It's a very particular look I must have, one that despite itself strikes the looker's intuition with dreadful clarity: this woman actually thought something magical would happen to her today.*

It was a good start, I felt. But the image of Mrs. Pendergast alone again in that dark parlor, cleaning out her birdcage, ended that possibility for me.

Of course, I shouldn't have felt any guilt. It had been too much to ask of me. This was the only way to close the matter, and who was I to Mrs. Pendergast anyway? I didn't have the power to make her feel whatever disappointment she might have felt—that was her own doing. And who's to say she had herself shown up? Perhaps she'd had second thoughts. Perhaps I was making a trauma out of nothing.

I focused instead on my poem, still watching the children playing on the deck from my bench. One of them fell too hard and was rubbing his knee. The others didn't notice him and played on. The Delaware was opening before them and washing beneath them, and they didn't notice that either.

Walt had been here too.

The only thing Walt could not touch, the only thing beyond him, was the future. His health was failing him. He'd already been left partially crippled from one stroke, though at times you wouldn't suspect it, the way he moved, the way he spoke, as if tapping into something besides pure physical strength; something else was fueling him, making him more alive now than ever. Or was it that he was so alive to me? That the passions he'd introduced to me were a thing more than the man himself, the living poet. My poet.

While we joked about his ailments, and about my murdering him, I never told Walt how much, at times, I truly wanted him to die. How I was convinced that, should he die before I was to leave him, or he leave me, should he die now, right now, I would be the one to say the final goodbye. The one to tearfully help him into whatever came next, those mystical places he wrote so often about. I would be the one to mourn him.

Could it be that Walt feared the same thing? Feared that according to every human law he spoke and wrote of, we were to eventually end our engagement—it was already decided for us, by us, by him—and that he would have to endure the transition alone? Is that why he so wanted me to kill him?

The ferry arrived at Gloucester.

All right now, I said to myself. Something that Walt cannot touch. Something that will outlive him. Some new technology. That's it! A thing that will develop beyond Walt's comprehension. A thing not of the earth, but of man, of an evolving man.

We walked in a loose unit, those of us who'd decided that Gloucester was our destination, in no general hurry, as though the whole group of us were on the same aimless errand, silently deciphering our own poems, taking in the rhythms of our collective steps—all of us strangers, and yet all of us familiar. But when we scattered at the entrance to a street whose name I didn't know, I thought how silly it was to imagine anyone else in the same state as I.

It exhilarated me, as I climbed the steep hill of that nameless street, an incline not unlike Camden's riverside—and yet this was not Camden; these businesses, this tailor, this post office, these gentlemen leaving this tobacco shop, all warped mirror images of the people and bustle of the town I was from—to know that mine was a singular purpose, that I was the only poet here.

With that thought, and upon seeing a pretty young woman seated at a bench, the Delaware receding behind her, the both of them being photographed, I knew what it was that would outlast Walt. It was right there, the figure under the tarp with his camera, his hand reaching out to give the pretty young woman her direction, his words caught and muffled, though the woman responded to him with exuberant nods. It was what that photographer saw, and what his camera saw.

There was a lifetime of photographs to be taken—they were being taken now—a lifetime of images, beautiful images that Walt would never see, that I would see, that I would write about.

When he'd first shown me his room on Mickle Street, I'd asked, "Why all the pictures?" They were everywhere. Some framed, most loose and poking their corners out from under various stacks and mounds of things. Walt's eye here, a bent elbow there, the bone of his strong nose, his lips, sometimes obscured by facial hair, sometimes visible and looking about to speak, Walts of different ages, complexions, moods. In reply, Walt asked me if I'd ever had my picture taken. No, I said—I didn't even think there was a picture of my Aunt Hettie anywhere in the house. "Well," Walt said. "That's something we must do."

He'd arranged the date with a local photographer. The portrait was to be of the both of us. The studio, as the photographer called it, took up one of the two rooms of his residence. The time of day was integral, the photographer told us, for the sun had to come through at just the right moment for the proper exposure. He had his camera set on three legs next to the window, pointing at what looked to be a small stage, something fit for a play. An empty straw-bottom chair sat slightly turned before a large mural of a seascape, whitecaps and a ship with sails and a lighthouse. Before the mural was a small, freestanding railing with flowerpots covering each of its ends. It was as though this were a terrace in some other land, in some other time.

Walt sat in the chair, and I was thankful for that; he would have towered over me had it been the other way around. But that was not his reason for sitting. Though no one seemed to be speaking much, aside from Walt asking how the gadget worked, it occurred to me that they had orchestrated this beforehand, Walt and the photographer. Walt seated, me at his side, both of us in our most respectable attire—Walt had purchased for me a new top hat to wear, the fun he had setting this one atop my head, then this one, until he was satisfied. "Rest your hand there, Mr. Duckett, on the back of Mr. Whitman's chair." And as I did, Walt gave a slight nod to the photographer, and then the photographer set about his work behind the lens. Looking back, I believe that to be the moment of my full reckoning of what Walt and I were to become. All I could think, as the camera clicked and whirred to life, was, *I'm being photographed with him.*

When Walt gave a copy of the photograph to Aunt Hettie, she looked at it, and for a moment, with great fear, I thought that she must know, must be able to see in the picture what I knew was there. But then she looked up at the old man with eyes that seemed to want for tears. "Now I have proof of your great friendship. I'm going to show it to all the ladies at the factory."

I was now walking a dirt road, away from town. I still needed my first line. I could see the shape of the poem, I could see what it wanted to be, and the reaction on Walt's face when he read it and realized that this was what I'd had in store for him. But what was my first line?

As quickly as it had seized me to write about photography, I knew that I could not. It wouldn't be his, not like those people on the ferry, not like the lonely woman on the pier, but it wouldn't be mine either. It would still have been something Walt had introduced to me. *Have you ever been photographed?* It would be a response to him, a rebuttal, as much of him as I wanted it to be separate from him, beyond him. When I first saw that photograph of the two of us, I now remembered, there it was, the edge of the backdrop along the side of the image, where the seascape was affixed to the wall.

That's when I realized my error with Mrs. Pendergast.

I'd misjudged her. I too easily made her into the sad, tragic heroine alone at the pier. She may have been disappointed, but she wouldn't have abandoned all prospects. She'd been waiting far too long to give up after this initial pitfall. She was resourceful. She would find another way. She might even—and this possibility became more and more the actuality as I constructed it—have gained the strength, the courage to walk right from the pier all the way up to Mickle Street.

Right up to Walt's door, to knock until he stirred from his sleep, fumbled into some clothes, and when he answered, she looked—yes, this had indeed happened—she looked up at his tall, imposing figure and demanded to know why he hadn't shown himself. Walt was confused at first, and then, I knew—for what else would he do if met with such a surprise, such directness from a woman he'd never met—he laughed, he laughed that laugh he had.

While I was wandering, they were becoming acquainted. They were discovering each other, or rather, since Mrs. Pendergast had been so convinced of their astral union, rediscovering each other. They were making plans. I could already see her caged bird in Walt's bedroom. Except Walt would likely see some terrible metaphor in the birdcage and let the thing fly freely throughout the house, leaving splotches of filthy white all over his papers and manuscripts. He'd jokingly call the bird his editor.

My time was running out.

I had never myself been here, but I knew where I was. This was Timber Creek. This was where Walt would go, alone, when he was overwhelmed with memory. This was where he sorted them, all those things he'd never confessed to me. And here I was now, somehow thinking this would be the place of my inspiration. A place we hadn't even shared.

Once, while Walt was in his corner, at work, not long after I'd moved into his quarters, I noticed that he was looking at me. At first, I'd only felt it, something pulling me out of my reading, something keeping me from finishing the next sentence.

Then I saw his eyes, lifted from his own manuscript. It startled me, for his eyes were not welcoming anything, not requesting a conversation, nor were they appreciative, *here's this boy I've admired, sitting in my room, reading the book I gave him to read.* They were hard, concerted, unaware even that I had noticed. He was studying me, and gradually, as he went back to work only to look up again a moment later, I came to realize: Walt was writing about me.

I tried to continue reading, but I found that I was reading the same passages over and over without catching a lick of meaning. *He's doing it now,* I kept thinking. *He's looking at me now. He's writing about me now.* I'd enjoyed my life in Camden—and actually, after the fact, I almost wished I could go back to my simple existence before—just another schoolboy, then just another young man waiting for that special girl, a merchant's assistant, nothing special. But here I was, in this old man's room, this old man from across the street of whom I'd been so curious, whose book I'd been so enraptured by, as were so many others, and he was looking at me. He was writing about me.

That night was the first night I couldn't sleep. Walt was snoring, having exhausted himself from his writing, and all I could think about was what he must have written. Eventually, after an amalgam of almost-images left all their echoes upon me—was it my face he wrote about? my body? something deeper?—I climbed from the bed. I tiptoed around to his side, where his chair was, his desk, his writing corner.

For the longest while—who can tell the length of time in the dead of night?—I stood listening to Walt, convincing myself he was too far into his sleep to stir. Then, slowly—it was excruciating how slow, buzzing as I was with excitement and nervousness and terror—I sifted through his papers, through the several stacks there about his desk, his chair. My hands shook. The sounds of the paper flapping and folding in my grip were loud enough, I was certain, to shock Walt from wherever he was, but I continued. I held pages to the moonlight, looking for my name, whether it be my actual name or whatever Walt had decided was my true name. He'd seen me, I knew it. He'd seen through me, and he recorded, with his illustrious powers, precisely what he saw, precisely what I needed to know.

This is it! The ink here has smeared. It's fresh. I can almost feel the warmth from his frantic swipes, his mind having always worked so much faster than his hand; I can feel it coming off the page. I turned it in the light. There was a train coming. I had to read quickly, faster than my excitement would already encourage, for what if the train would rouse him?

And so I read. But I did not find myself. I only found Walt. Rewritten lines from long-ago drafts. *I dream in my dream all the dreams of the other dreamers, and I become the other dreamers.* The train passed. Walt still slept. And I stayed up the rest of the night, reading everything I could find, finding nothing.

Isn't that why I'd come to Timber Creek? In search of something that was my own and never his, wouldn't I always come to this? Walt was the actor and the actress, the voter, the politician. Walt was the emigrant, the exile, the criminal, the judge, the stammerer, the well-formed, the wasted and the feeble. He had been everything in dreams, in the dream that was his book, all that was, all that will be. Walt was even me as I was now, in my attempts to thwart him. He was his own timid swimmer, and so was I.

It was late when I returned home that night. I stopped outside for a moment, expecting to see something ridiculous up in the window, Walt and Mrs. Pendergast dancing in circles to some song he was crooning, Mrs. Pendergast clapping and clapping.

When I reached his bedroom, I did not find Mrs. Pendergast there, or any evidence she had ever been. There was only Walt, crouched before the fireplace, looking so misshapen I almost didn't think it was him, how crumpled he seemed in that position, made even smaller by the large trembling shadow he cast on the wall. He was holding a manuscript, and he was crying.

"Walt?"

He didn't look up. I almost wondered whether I'd called out to him.

Then he said, "My dear boy. Where have you been off to all day?" *Off to enlighten the masses.*

I crossed the room, stepping over his scatterings of objects, all those photographs, all those Walts, one of the two of us somewhere. I knelt next to the old man. He kept his eyes on the fire. He looked terrible. Those eyes should only ever appear benevolent, loving. That face should never tighten like this, should never twitch as it was before these flames. His sounds should only be snores and laughter and the voice of his poetry. He looked terrible, and he looked beautiful. He looked very old, and very, very young.

"I need your help, I'm afraid," he said. I looked at the manuscript he was holding against his chest. "I can't do it myself."

"Are you sure?" I said. I wanted to know what on those pages had so offended him, what secrets his writing had let slip. But at the same time, I knew that my helping him would marry me to them, whatever those lines were. They would never make it into his book, never make it to any reader. This is where they would stay, in this moment, at my hand. And with that knowledge came not the least of the exultation I'd hoped for.

He handed me the manuscript. I held it for a moment. I memorized the feeling of it, its weight, its dimensions, the sharp lines of its edges along my fingers. The sense of that object still comes to me, whether I seek it or not. After Walt nodded to me, I set the thing down in the fire.

Walt watched the fire take it, transform it, and he seemed to gather himself. Something had lifted or passed or found its rightful place. Just like that, he'd returned to the Walt I'd known. Then he looked at me. He reached out a hand and placed it on my knee. Our foreheads were nearly touching.

"I will tell you," he said to me, "about a period in my life of which no one knows. Not now. Not tomorrow. But someday before long. I want to tell you the whole story."

We remained there until the fire went cold. I told him about how I'd tried to kill him that day, and how I'd failed, and he laughed and laughed, and, though I knew even then that Walt would never tell me what he'd promised to tell me, all I could think was, *He's mine. He's still mine.*

Anthony Spaeth

Jim and Nancy

Jim thought he'd buy a little house for him and Nancy and so they got in the realtor's Cadillac and went to have a look. The neighborhood she drove them to was south of town, down near the U of H. She called it Lawndale, but it was really just the Short East End. The lots were on the small side. Not everyone had mowed their grass. Still, it was two exits inside the loop and a bike trail ran along the bayou. There were plans to bring the rail there, she assured them.

The place they liked the best was just a pillbox on a half-lot, not much more than that. Two bedrooms down, a den, a galley kitchen and a bath. But the attic had been finished out. It ran the whole length of the house. Jim had to pull himself through a scuttle hole in the hallway to get up there, but once he did he was impressed. The ceiling was 10 feet high at the ridge beam and angled downward toward the eaves. A giant picture window faced the street. Jim's eyes turned toward the antique glass. The waves and bubbles in the panes gave the world outside a liquid sort of look, like the neighborhood was boiling hot.

The realtor'd worn a dress and so she excused herself and said she'd have to stay downstairs, but Nancy followed him up there. Jim offered her a hand, but she ignored him. She braced her arms beside the hole and lifted herself through, just as he had. The two of them stood there, side by side. They looked around the attic the way that people do. Jim ran his hands along a seam in the drywall—there had been a lot of settlement, he noted. Nancy bounced on the floorboards to show how badly they creaked. She tried the light, a naked bulb that pulled on with a thin white string. It worked just fine.

The window casing was as tall as Jim was and as wide as he could reach. He measured it that way, standing up against it. Nancy reached over his shoulder and rapped her knuckles on one of the panes. The glass rattled in the muntins like a snare. She tried the sash, but it wouldn't budge. Someone had nailed it to the casing. Jim pointed out the nailheads in the wood.

They were close. Nancy gave him a sly look. Her chin ticked toward the scuttle hole and she cast her voice that way. "Bet it gets pretty hot up here in July," she said.

"The ac'll run all summer," said Jim, playing along. "God knows what the bills are."

Nancy cupped her hand around his ear and whispered to him, "The light's not bad up here." Her breath smelled like mint gum.

Jim imagined how the attic would look with all their stuff in it. His drafting table on one side. Nancy's canvases running down the other. All his hand tools. All her dirty rags and easels. They hadn't been looking for something like this, not specifically, but now that they were here it was just perfect.

Jim was a finish carpenter by day. A few weeks after they'd moved in, as he was driving home from a job, something caught his eye along the curbside. It was Big Trash Day for the whole East End. Stuff was stacked along the curb in front of almost every house. Mostly it was tree limbs and old box springs, couches, busted lawn mowers, stuff like that. Things no one could use. But someone must've died on Forest Hill, because furniture was piled all over the corner lot at Alta Vista. Still mostly junk. A TV stand on wheels. A chipped-up secretary without the top. But Jim slowed down, just to have a look. And there, right in the middle of all this jumble, was a naked figure, lying on its side. The mannequin's knees were bent at right angles and so were its elbows, sort of like a fetus. Its skin was pink and smooth as milk. It was an old-fashioned display dummy, the kind they used to put in storefronts once upon a time. From the way its arms and legs were set, Jim could tell it was supposed to be sitting in a chair even though there wasn't one around.

He leaned toward the passenger window of his truck and gently eased two wheels up on the curb to get as far out of the traffic as he could. The mannequin wasn't polystyrene or fiberglass. He could tell that from where he was sitting. Little brown chinks dotted the enamel, especially at the elbows. Underneath the paint, there was some kind of wood. He was pretty sure.

So he hopped down to the street. When he got to the mannequin, he toed its rib cage (or what would have been its rib cage if it had ribs) with his boot. Seemed solid. Had all the pieces to it. He rolled it on its back and it lay there with its arms and legs sticking up. The face had all the features of a man—broad lips, recesses for the eyes, a slightly hooked nose—but still looked absolutely blank.

Jim got it by the forearms and hauled it to its feet. They were standing there knee-to-knee, their weights balanced against one another like they were on a teeter totter. It was two hundred pounds at least. More than that. Really heavy stuff. Its hands were open with the broad palms turned toward its face. All the joints were locked in place. From the way it held its arms, Jim thought it was probably meant to be reading from a book. Or maybe a newspaper. He imagined it relaxing in a bathrobe in a display window, maybe 1930s.

He licked his thumb and rubbed at a bare spots on the mannequin's cheek. The wood grain underneath came right up. It was really fine, mid-brown. Tighter bands than boxwood or cherry. Not dark enough to be mahogany. Some kind of ironwood maybe. Something hard and dense.

Jim thought about that. He doubted they made wooden mannequins anymore. Certainly none like this. It was worth something maybe. Or maybe it was just a project for him to fiddle with. He picked the dummy up and carried it fireman-style to his truck. When he dumped it in the bed, it weighed heavy on the struts. The bed sank down and didn't come back up. He threw a drop cloth over the mannequin because it looked so odd and naked there, kind of like a dead body. To some extent that made the problem worse. But the drive home wasn't far and he was innocent in any case.

He beat Nancy home that night. When Jim saw she wasn't there yet, he hoisted the mannequin out of the back of his truck and carried it inside, walking up the front stairs as quickly as he could, grunting with the effort. When he got to the trap door, he had to hold the mannequin's whole weight above his head while he worked its limbs through the opening. Sweat rolled down his cheeks and the veins stood out on his forearms and biceps. His arms shook with the effort. Actually shook. It nearly broke his goddamn back to do it. Still, he pushed it through the hole, and once he did he let it roll over on its back, grinding on the old oak runners.

He didn't have a plan for it. Not really. There wasn't much to do with a wooden mannequin, now that he thought about it. It was way too big to fit on the day bed he'd put up in the attic. The only thing strong enough to hold it upright was his drafting chair. So what he did was he slid his table over by the window, where the evening sun was hitting. Then he moved the chair into place behind the table and gut-wrenched the mannequin into the seat. It fit right in, actually. The size and angles were all perfect for its frozen joints. It sat there, ramrod straight, staring at the palms of its hands. But it did look mostly human.

He couldn't just leave it there with its empty hands like that. It didn't make any sense, compositionally. So what he did was he went and found himself one of Nancy's cookbooks, the one from Better Homes & Gardens. It was a great big book, maybe sixteen inches tall. When he slid the checkerboard cover into the dummy's hands, it stuck right there. The thumbs held the bookboards open to just about the middle page. You couldn't get more right.

Jim took a step back and stared at what he'd done. He found the string for the overhead bulb and pulled the cord. The studio went dark. Or mostly dark. The only light left in the room was the evening sun and the bulb of his drafting lamp. He angled the hood down toward the cookbook. Lit that way, the mannequin caught a nice mixture of amber and shadow. It hid the details and emphasized the overall shape. From out front it could've passed for a man. Maybe.

Nancy's Subaru had a mushy clutch and so he heard her coming from way down the street. He hid himself just beside the attic window. When she parked and got out of her car, she was holding two small plastic bags, one in each hand, and also her keys. She had to kick the car door closed behind her. But she did it gracefully, extending her leg in a neat arabesque. She'd trained to be a dancer and it still showed through at strange moments just like this. The car door didn't slam behind her, it simply clicked. A perfect use of just the right amount of force.

He couldn't tell whether Nancy'd seen the mannequin or not. She didn't exactly look up at the window, though she might have glanced that way. He took a step back anyway. When he got to the scuttle hole, he put his feet on the rungs and hurried downstairs, looking for someplace to hide. There was the little pantry off the hall. That was the first hiding place that presented itself. So Jim stowed himself behind the spice rack with the handle of the vacuum jammed against his back and pulled the door to. He was breathing heavily and he had to fight to control the sound.

The house had clapboard walls, paper thin. No insulation. Even in the pantry, Jim could hear Nancy jangling her keys out front. She was talking to herself. He couldn't quite tell about what. She sounded a little pissy, so she was probably having an internal argument with one of her professors.

The bolt turned. He heard it slide.

The front door creaked open.

Nancy rustled through the doorway with her plastic sacks.

"Hey Jim?" she called down the hallway. "Little help here, babe?"

She waited just inside the threshold for a second. "Jim?" she said again, a little louder. And then he heard her creak-creaking slowly down the hall.

There was a gap at the hinge of the pantry door. Once Nancy'd come about halfway down the hall, he could see her through the crack. She stopped right outside the kitchen, just below the scuttle hole, and turned up her pointed chin. She wore her bangs long and they fell back from her face.

"C'mon down, babe! I brought dinner!"

She stared up at the dim light coming from the attic for a few seconds. Her face turned a little cloudy. She kicked the bottom rung of the ladder and then turned away.

When Nancy came into the kitchen, she was only three feet from the pantry. Maybe 40 inches. She put the sacks down on the countertop. There was this prickly feeling running up and down Jim's neck while he stood there listening. He had to concentrate on staying still. If he twitched, he'd bump the spice rack on the door and all the little jars would rattle. If he breathed too loud, she'd hear him.

He watched through the crack as Nancy went over to the scuttle hole again. This time she put her hands on one of the ladder's rungs. "Come on, Jim! It's dinner time!" she said. She used her sing-song voice. "I got us some Chi-NEEE-eese."

He could have burst through the door right then and really scared her. Made her shit a brick. But something held him back. For one thing, she hated being startled. She'd really blow a gasket once the fright had passed. There'd be a fight and then she'd sulk, maybe for the whole evening. And then the next day she'd tell all her friends how weird he was. And what a doofus. It really wasn't worth it.

Also, standing there in the pantry, spying on her, staring at her back, he felt a little bit protective of her. And a little guilty. She'd brought him dinner, after all. She'd thought of him on her way home. She'd done something nice for him. Gone out of her way even though she really didn't have the money. And here he was with a mannequin sitting at his desk upstairs, trying to get her to piss in her pants. His nerve gave way. Or else he thought the better of it. It was a mixture.

He watched her slowly climbing into the attic. She was wearing those three-quarter kind of pants, Capris, and flat-soled slippers. She went up cautiously, one rung at a time. Her head disappeared through the scuttle hole and then her shoulders and her hips. Her shoes came off the last rung with a little scuffing sound and then she was gone.

Nothing. Silence for a moment. Creak. . . creak. . . creak. . . . . creak. He heard her walking on the old boards. He could tell she was moving carefully.

When he turned the cut-glass knob on the pantry door, he pulled up on it to take the weight off the hinges. It still squeaked, but just a little bit. Nothing she would hear from up there. He slid his boots across the floorboards to keep them quiet. Quiet as he could. When he turned to look back down the hall, all he could see was the little cone of orange light coming from the scuttle hole above. Nancy was still up there somewhere. Silent. Not moving anymore.

He opened the back door and quietly let himself outside. The evening air was steamy. Thick. Houston weather just at the edge of a summer night. There weren't any stars. Too many clouds or too much haze. From trying not to breathe too loudly, he found his heart was really pounding.

He crept down the back steps, careful as a cat, and then cut through the side yard, keeping to the shadows below the eaves. When he reached the front porch, he thought about things for a second. What he should do. What he could do. Whether he should sneak back in. Maybe slide into bed and pretend that he'd been sleeping there the whole time. But that would never work. Besides, she might have already looked into the bedroom. It opened to the hall. So instead he took a running start and bounded up the front steps as loudly as he could. The wooden stairs were hollow and they boomed under his weight. It shook the whole house.

The front door was still standing part-way open when he got there. Nancy's keys were hanging in the cylinder. He pushed the lock rail. The door swung in until it hit the doorstop, the hallway dark and empty except for the light coming down from the attic.

"Honey?" he called. Or tried to call. Barely a whisper came out.

Nothing.

"Nance?" he said, a little louder this time. There was something false about his voice, he thought. Maybe only he could hear it.

He pulled the door closed behind him and walked slowly down the hall toward the attic ladder. When he looked up through the scuttle hole, he half-expected to see Nancy's face framed there in the trap, scowling down at him. Or laughing. Or maybe even screaming in one of her wild rages. But there was nothing there. Just empty space. He could make out the rafters above in the orange light.

"Nancy?" he asked.

No answer.

"Hey Nancy," he tried again, "smells like you brought dinner."

He got hold of one of the ladder's rungs and pulled himself up a little bit. Then a little further. When his head came through the trap, he was pointed toward Nancy's half of the studio. Her canvases were leaned against the wall there, frame-side out. Jars of brushes lined her shelves. She had about a dozen tackle boxes spattered with dried paint and a wooden stool that matched them, Jackson Pollock.

Jim's eyes slowly adjusted to the hot spot in the darkness, the lamplight by the window. The checkered cookbook was sitting on the floor there, beside the mannequin's feet. And all Nancy's clothes were piled beside it, her bra and panties on the top. There she was, too. She was sitting naked in the mannequin's lap, still as a stone. She'd tucked herself away in there. Her eyes were closed. Her head was turned to one side. Her back was slightly bowed. Her lips were open and her teeth were clenched. The big wooden hands were cupped around her breasts. It looked as though she were in ecstasy. The very moment of it. Frozen in it. He hadn't seen her so in years.

She let him look at her a while, just like that. And then she turned her head, glanced at him scornfully, and wriggled free. He thought that she would laugh at him, or say something cruel, or mock him for thinking he could fool her, but she didn't. She just walked right by him and let herself downstairs.

After a while, Jim came down the ladder with her clothes tucked under his arm in a messy bundle. He didn't know what else to do.

In the morning, Jim played possum in bed until Nancy left for class. When he heard her car door slam, he got up and made himself a pot of coffee, extra black. He'd just come off a job—a custom banister for the Jones Hall Jonses, their place in River Oaks. He'd carved the caps himself. Turned every newel. He'd even bent the rails using his own steamer. And Freddie Jones herself had actually hobbled down the stairs to stroke the glossy finish and give him his retainage. She'd said she loved it. She absolutely did. She'd never seen such attention to detail. He was a credit to his people. And she would surely tell her friends.

He had 65,000 dollars in the bank now. It was more money than he'd ever had in his entire life by a factor of about ten. He didn't have to hang cabinets or install counter tops right now. Not for weeks. Not for months if he didn't want to. And so his mind was on the mannequin. It had been since the night before.

Jim had a certain theory about woodwork and drawing and all art for that matter. He liked to get started early in the morning, with the night oils still on his skin and the stink of his ammonia. He preferred an empty stomach, too. When he was getting ready to work on something special, what he'd do was wake up early, drink a whole pot of coffee and take a thorough, cleansing shit. He always wore the shirt he'd slept in. The process helped him keep his head clear. It helped him focus on his work.

What he wanted first was to see the wood underneath the mannequin's enamel. He couldn't tell enough just from the chips. He wanted to see all of it. The face.

The arms. The hands. The chest. If they were all the same wood and what sort. So he put on an old pair of shorts—still stiff with varnish from the Jones's job—and then went outside to get his tools from the back of the truck. There was some 220 grit and some 500 in the job box along with a few scraps of coarser paper. He got that and his palm sander, then went back for the Dremmel and a light extension cord. It was supposed to be 95 by noon that day, or something crazy like that, and so he hauled a big jug of water upstairs with him. He'd need a wet towel for the final sanding.

The mannequin was hard to work with because of its odd shape. It wanted to move, no matter how he placed it on the floor. The best thing he could do was set it down on all fours and jam some shop rags under the knees and elbows to keep it from rocking.

He started sanding on the shoulders, which were big, obvious surfaces, and worked at them slowly with his Bosch. The enamel came off easier than he would've thought. It actually flaked off, like bits of rust. And the wood underneath was so hard he really didn't have to worry about taking too much away. After the paint came off, the sander barely left a dent. But what surprised him most was the grain. The sapwood was gold and tan, but there were bright green layers in the heartwood, almost the color of pea soup. Even though the lumber in the mannequin had been dried and cured for at least 70 years, it still retained its oil.

Lignum vitae, he thought. The whole goddamn thing was lignum vitae. Great big solid chunks of it. You couldn't find them in that size. Not anywhere these days. He did the math. If you cut the mannequin in slices, it would come out to about thirty board feet. Maybe $1,700 worth. But the torso was one huge piece all by itself. He'd never seen a piece of lignum vitae that wide and deep. It would have run the diameter of the whole tree, the biggest tree there was. It almost didn't seem possible. He wondered if he was mistaken. But he wasn't.

It took him eight straight hours of solid work to get the mannequin sanded down to bare wood. Some things—the fingers, the crevices between the toes—he had to do with a nail file. He worked the inner ears with a fine wheel on the Dremel. That alone took 20 minutes. But, when he was finished, the mannequin was actually magnificent. It had features you couldn't really see when they were covered up with paint—a cleft chin and a heart-shaped indentation in its upper lip. It had little Asiatic creases in the inner corner of the eyelids. Although the surfaces of the eyes were blank, without pupil, the eyebrows above them were carved right into the wood, hair by hair.

When Nancy came home that evening, she started screaming just as soon as she walked in the front door. "Goddamnit, Jim!" she yowled from downstairs. "What the fuck?!"

He'd taped a transparent plastic drop cloth over the trap door and he could see her murky image through it as she climbed the ladder toward him. She punched the thin mil plastic, ripping up the tape along one side. "Jesus Christ, is it even worse up here?" she sputtered. Her hands were covered in fine dust and there was a little powder on her face.

"Who do you think's going to clean this up?" she asked. "What were you thinking?"

And she went on. It was unnecessary to fight about it now. He was already through with what he'd done. She couldn't go back in time and stop him. But, when Nancy took a breath, Jim pointed to the mannequin. He'd rubbed it twice with linseed oil. The surface of the wood glowed yellow, like an incandescent bulb. The growth rings in the heartwood were as thin as dollar bills. He turned her toward it, physically, taking her by the shoulders. He showed her the tightness of the grain, holding a scrap of oak beside it so she could compare. He said, "I know you're pissed, Nance, but you can't find pieces of wood like this anywhere on earth. Not this size. They don't exist."

Nancy swatted at the sawdust in her hair. She seethed. She said she didn't care.

"This wood is denser than rock, Nance. It has a special oil in it that keeps it from decaying. If you took this dummy out to sea and threw him in, he'd sink straight to the bottom. And he'd stay right there, without ever rotting, for about a thousand years."

Nancy bugged her eyes in mock surprise and then she turned her back on him. She said that she was moving out.

They mended easily. They'd made a virtue of necessity. But when, on the following day, Jim asked Nancy to pose for him, at first she resisted. The truth is she would have fought the idea of posing for him even if all that stuff—the fight over him trying to scare her, the fight over the dust—had never happened. She liked to be begged to do things. That's what he thought.

She said, "It's creepy, Jim. It's creepy that you want me to do that. Don't you get it?"

"Just think of it as modeling."

"I don't model for you, Jim. I'm your partner."

"Lots of women model for their lovers. That Freud guy's screwed everyone he's painted. Even the guys."

Not his best argument, perhaps. But in the end he struck a bargain with her. There was another project for the Jones Hall Joneses. He could take it if he wanted. They had a lodge near Vail and they'd asked him to design a mantle for it. A unique mantle, carved entirely by hand. There were no plans or specs for it. He could do whatever he liked. Within reason. Just like with the banister. But to do it of course he would have to see the lodge first, see its walls and fireplace, see it in its native setting. Freddie Jones had said she'd send him up there for a weekend in her jet. He could take a friend along with him if he wanted. It had to be finished before ski season. That was the only condition.

"I'll take you with me if you like. It'll only take a day at most to draw you."

So, in exchange for a trip to Vail, Nancy agreed that she would pose for him. She also agreed that she wouldn't tell a soul about it until he was all through. She wouldn't ask why he wanted to draw her. What the project was. What the purpose was. None of that.

And it was actually Nancy who woke him up the next day to get started. She'd already brewed a big pot of coffee for him, extra black. She had her own routines when it came to art and she respected others' processes. She tapped him on his shoulder and handed him his large white mug. He lay there on the pillow, blinking.

"Vail, here I come," she said with that big slanted grin of hers. She was already naked.

He drank his coffee while still in bed. After a while, he followed her upstairs.

When he was drawing with a model, Jim almost never said anything aloud. He used gestures more than words. Her lips open like this. He showed her. Her teeth clenched like this. He showed her that. Her head turned. No, no, not quite that much. Too much. Yes, like that. Now hold it there. Chin out.

Jim drew Nancy in charcoal first, then in pencil. He started all over again from scratch at least half-a-dozen times. As he worked, he jotted notes along the margins of his sheets of watercolor paper. Stray thoughts. Colors. Measurements. Equations. Exploded joints. When he finished with a drawing, he rolled it up in a tube and put a rubber band around it. He marked each sheet on the exposed corner with his broad architectural script. Concept # 1, #5, #10 w/ Cutaway + Dimensions.

The top of Jim's drafting table was turned away from Nancy. He never showed her what he'd drawn. He never asked for her opinions. He never even invited her to look. He measured every inch of her body with seamstress's tape, from heel to forehead, sometimes more than once. Then he measured the mannequin in the same way.

Nancy lay still and watched him work. She was calm and patient with him, hour after hour. She did as she was asked and nothing else. And this impressed Jim more than anything she'd ever done—that she actually kept her half of the bargain, that she bore it all so well. It took all day, and finally, when he saw her eyes were growing dull, he raised his hand and said, "Babe, you look hungry. Go and get yourself some dinner."

But, even after Nancy had put on her robe and gone downstairs, Jim remained there in the attic. He was still, but his hands were tingling. There was a sort of excited pressure behind his eyes. He couldn't wait for the next morning. He couldn't wait for Nancy to head off to class where she couldn't break his train of thought. The last thing that he wanted was to speak with her. He would need his coping saw, he thought. He would need his joiner and his router and his dozuki-nokogiri. He'd need at least three dozen sheets of ultra-fine chrome oxide and a can of tung oil. He made and remade his mental list of things he needed for the job. He unrolled each of his drawings and pinned them to the sloping walls and stood there looking at them, thinking.

Jim didn't go downstairs at all that night, but instead slept curled up on the day bed, sweating in the awful heat. By the time that the first light came in through the upstairs window, Nancy was already easing her car down the gravel drive. He watched her from the window, her neck turned chin-over-shoulder as she backed toward the street. She'd left the coffee maker on for him. He could hear it bubbling and hissing. But he didn't even bother with it. His stomach was still empty from the day before.

Jim worked all that second day and then a third day and then part of the fourth. Nancy brought him food occasionally, resting it just inside the trap door and taking back his empty plates. But mostly she stayed clear of him. She kept the volume on the t.v. low. She went to class without saying goodbye and came home at night without calling for him. She waited until he'd finished. All the way. Until he called down to her and told her he was through.

When she came up through the trap, he didn't know quite what to say to her, so instead of speaking he opened his arms toward what he'd done with a kind of joking flourish. She stood up from the hole and slowly walked over to it. She looked at it up close. She ran her nails along the finish as if searching for a crack. She was impressed. Not as much as he, but still she was impressed. She didn't say it aloud. She said it with a look.

"How do you know if it will fit?" she asked him.

If you go to Vail today and you take the road toward Minturn, you can still find the old ski lodge that was once owned by the Jones Hall Joneses. It's high up on a private mountain, near a private lift. They call it the Brass Tavern now. It says so on a little mailbox on the highway, though it is not a tavern or an inn. The neighbors think someone from Silicon Valley owns it. Mostly, it stays empty.

The walls of the lodge are made from giant river stones—brownish, purple and gray—real load-bearing masonry construction, not simply a veneer. When you go inside the front door, there is a vaulted living room, two stories high. Rough-hewn timbers carry the span above. The walls are covered in the trophy heads from floor to ceiling—deer and moose and bison, dozens of them, staring with their hard wet eyes.

A stone hearth juts from the middle of the far wall and, just above it, there is a sleek wooden mantle. It looks as though it were built especially for this place. The sanding on the mantle's frieze is so fine it shines like polished glass even from across the room. The wood is tan, but green in spots. The joints are hidden; they follow the bends and bows within the grain of the wood. You can't find a seam in the finish, not even with a razor.

Carved at one end of the mantle are two figures. They rise up from the corbel and extend above the shelf. The woman is seated on the man's thighs. Her back is pressed against his chest, her lap is pressed against his lap. Her breasts are hidden in his hands. Her eyes are closed. Her jaw is clenched. Her head is turned aside in ecstasy. She bares her vicious teeth.

But behind her the man's face is blank. His eyes have no pupils in them and his mouth is a flat line with just a trace of philtrum. He is beneath the woman but not attached to her, present there but also someplace else. He takes nothing from her. He gives her nothing back. He does not share in her emotion or her bliss. He exists there, just like that, without expression. And he will exist there, just like that, touching her but not a part of her, for another thousand years and maybe after that.

Jacob M. Appel

The Current Occupant

Idiot that he was—and every time Lewinter dozed off, his wife woke him to remind him of his infernal stupidity—he'd bought a house from a mail order catalog. An *online* catalog, but still! "Who buys a house from a catalog?" griped Isabelle. "What *century* do you live in?"

They'd ch ecked into the nearest vacant motel, a tumbledown motor lodge 20 minutes over the New Hampshire line. Their room smelled vaguely of wet dog and disinfectant. Behind the headboard, the plumbing yowled and keened. The mattress felt like one colossal iron spring. Even if Isabelle hadn't poked his shoulder every 30 seconds, he'd have tossed fitfully until daybreak. What a difference 24 hours made! On Friday night, they'd been driving up from the city, greased in cheer, anticipating their first peek at the summer refuge of their golden years. They'd stayed at a bed & breakfast whose cornmeal scones earned superlatives as far south as West 96th Street. And nary a word of complaint from Isabelle about his means of procuring the house. She'd been just as pleased as he'd been for the discount, and the expediency, of a readymade dwelling. Who needed the carpenter ants and stress that came with renovated farmsteads? But that was before she'd eyed the level concrete slab where their prefabricated paradise was to have been deposited three weeks earlier, before he'd phoned the manufacturer and asked a question equally slapstick and infuriating: How in heaven's name can you deliver a *house* to the wrong address?

"Are you *sure* you gave them the correct location?" asked Isabelle.

She used the same tone she inflicted on the dog when he nibbled on their bedspread.

"Yes, I'm sure. It's their mistake."

But Lewinter was only 99.9 percent sure, not 100 percent. He'd filled in the location over the Internet alongside his bank's SWIFT code. Who could say he hadn't plugged in the wrong town or acceded to the wrong auto-correction? Not that it mattered. The bottom line was that they'd have to locate the structure in Hager's Corners themselves, and then hire a transport outfit on their own dime to haul it back to Hager's Notch, to the 28 lakefront acres they'd inherited years earlier from Isabelle's bachelor uncle. After a decade of shelling out taxes for the unused parcel, the moment had finally come to milk some pleasure from the property.

"What if we can't find it?" pressed Isabelle. "Or what if they just abandoned it by the side of the highway and it's become a hangout for crystal meth addicts?"

"In three whole weeks?" asked Lewinter. He stumbled out of bed and groped his way into the bathroom, leaving the door ajar as he urinated.

"The Hindenburg burned in fifteen seconds," called Isabelle.

She'd taught high school history for two years before their oldest daughter was born, which had armed her with an arsenal of marginally-apropos rejoinders.

"I'll keep that in mind," said Lewinter, retracing his steps, "if I ever buy a Zeppelin."

"All I'm saying is a lot can happen in three weeks."

He kissed the exposed flesh above her collar bone. How familiar she was—her body, her henna bangs, the contours of her cynicism. How familiar, and for all her barbs, how comforting. After 37 years of marriage and three children, he knew exactly what came next: "Half a million men died in *one* week during the Battle of the Marne...."

"And the Nazis flattened Rotterdam in three hours," countered Lewinter. When they argued, they parroted an old time stand-up routine. Like Burns & Allen with hangovers. "I know all about it," he said. "Now let's get some sleep."

At daybreak the next morning, they checked out of the motel and set off for the tiny blemish on the map that was Hager's Corners. Lewinter had arranged coverage for his patients only through Sunday, and he was scheduled to extract cataracts starting at 7 a.m. on Monday morning, so he wanted the house locating and schlepping finished quickly. In his fantasies, they tracked down the dwelling and arrived back in Manhattan early enough for a twilight jog around Central Park. His goal was to shed another 15 pounds by Memorial Day. "So I can fit into my bikini," he quipped to their Armenian doorman, but his real fear was the leaden arteries that had felled so many of his contemporaries at the hospital. He'd turned 64 that February, the same age that his own father had died, and every twinge in his chest unsettled him.

Isabelle uttered hardly a word as they climbed through the rolling greenery, past the ramshackle dairy farms and single-stoplight hamlets of southeastern Vermont. Her Automobile Association tour book, from which she'd quoted relentlessly the previous day, lay untouched atop the dashboard of the Oldsmobile. Lewinter reached for his wife's hand. She drew hers into her lap. Soon enough, he recognized, her seething would explode into outright fury.

"Hager's Corners," he ventured. "Isn't that where *Our Town* takes place?"

"That's *Grover's* Corners," said Isabelle, clipped and icy.

"I thought Martians landed in Grover's Corners. Didn't Orson Welles get fired for reporting that Martians had landed in Grover's Corners, New Jersey?"

Isabelle's shoulders stiffened. "Grover's *Mill.* And Welles wasn't fired."

"Okay. Welles wasn't fired."

"And how could you be so irresponsible?" demanded Isabelle. "Didn't I tell you we should use a broker like everybody else? Why do you do everything ass-backwards?"

Lewinter kept his eyes focused on the vehicle ahead, a tandem trailer towing a powerboat, its wheels struggling with the high-grade turns. He said nothing. Once Isabelle generalized from a particular fault to "everything," his best defense was to hunker down and let her blows land where they might. "Ass-goddam-backwards," she repeated. "Uncle Harry was generous enough to leave us some of the most beautiful land on the planet, and all you have to do is go to a realtor and buy a house, and you can't even get that right."

Isabelle's logic, of course, was convoluted: A home purchased through a realtor would have come attached to its own property. Using her uncle's land required either relocating an existing house or erecting one from scratch. Lewinter chose not to mention these inconsistencies, nor did he point out that her "generous" uncle—a man whose psychiatric affliction, while never formally diagnosed, was instantly apparent to all who met him—had died intestate, leaving the property to them by default *after a tedious sojourn in probate court*. Instead, he heeded the GPS device and eased onto a steep, shingly lane shadowed with conifers.

"And what about Frank?" she continued—her voice rising in volume and pitch. "How can you expect anything of him when you're too lazy to call a real estate agent? Did it never once cross your mind that you have some iota of fatherly duty to set a good example?"

That was what was really eating at Isabelle, he knew. Their youngest had left college to spend a year on a desert retreat in Nevada, studying the art of traditional drum carving. The boy wasn't asking them for money, and on the telephone he sounded genuinely happy, if a bit clueless, but the uncertainty surrounding his future was unwinding his mother, minute by minute.

"I do the best I can," said Lewinter.

"The best you can? Is that all you have to say?"

Fortunately, according to the GPS device, they'd reached their destination. To Lewinter's relief, the timber-frame ranch house stood only 20 yards away, beckoning them across a lupine-tufted meadow. One solitary poplar towered adjacent to the dusty drive, its gnarled branches speckled with starlings. In the distance, the slate-blue peaks of the White Mountains melted into the horizon. Someone—maybe the manufacturer—had done the kindness of furnishing the post-and-beam porch with a rocking chair. Not even the airbrushed photos in the catalogue had prepared Lewinter for the perfection of the structure.

"Here we are," he announced. "Home sweet home."

And he'd already eased the Oldsmobile into the drive when he caught sight of a clothesline connecting the poplar to the porch rail, and then a buxom, gray-haired woman hanging garments from a basket.

"I'll take care of this," said Lewinter. "I'm sure it's a misunderstanding."

"Or a crystal meth den," rejoined Isabelle. "Or a brothel."

But now she wore a faint smirk—her exaggeration a sign that her anger was fading.

They'd parked halfway up the drive; their approach scattered the starlings. Outside, the air hung damp under the early morning sun. The gray-haired laundress stashed her basket on the porch and approached them. She wore a jonquil above her left ear and carried herself with an aura of proprietorship; she was clearly *living* in their house.

"Sorry to bother you," said Lewinter, "but I'm afraid there's been a mix-up."

Even as the words left his mouth, he was swept with the unsettling realization that he knew the soft-featured woman who stood arms akimbo between him and his dwelling.

"Allen Lewinter," she declared. "As I live and breathe."

"Kitty Canaday?"

That elicited a broad smile from the laundress. "I don't think anyone's called me Kitty in a couple of centuries," she said. "And I'm Catherine *Conrad* now."

"You're married?"

Lewinter heard the surprise in his own voice—although there was no earthly reason why Kitty Canaday, whom he hadn't laid eyes upon since college, shouldn't have married. How could he have expected otherwise? Yet somehow she'd remained frozen in his mind as the 22-year-old coed who'd urged him to postpone medical school for the joys of communal living in the North Woods of Maine.

"Divorced," replied Kitty. "But I kept Phil's name so I could tell people I got something out of the relationship."

"Was it *that* bad?"

Kitty shrugged. "We had our ups and downs," she said. "Who doesn't? But in our case, we ended on a down note…."

Lewinter sensed his wife's eyes boring into the back of his skull. "This is my wife, Isabelle," he said rapidly. "Kitty and I were up at Cornell together."

"It's a pleasure to meet you," said Kitty.

Isabelle cleared her throat. "For the love of God, Allen. I didn't drive six hours for a college reunion." Her smirk had evaporated and her voice sizzled. "You work this out," she added—without even acknowledging Kitty. "I'm waiting in the car." Moments later, the door of the Oldsmobile shattered the alpine calm.

"I'm sorry," apologized Lewinter. "She's been on edge all weekend."

He regretted the words as soon as he said them: Why should his wife's mood be any business of Kitty's? More unsettling was how easily he'd betrayed Isabelle, even in this minor way, to a woman he hadn't seen in 42 years. *And* he'd been relieved to learn her marriage had failed. There was no denying it.

Schadenfreude, he assured himself. Nothing more.

"What I've actually come about is…."

Kitty waited patiently, her eyes poised on the verge of laughter, as though anticipating the punchline of a joke she'd already heard.

"Our house," said Lewinter. "This is our house."

And now Kitty—Catherine—did laugh. Her delight quivered over her breasts and hips like an earthquake cascading through cranberry sauce.

"I don't see what's so funny," snapped Lewinter, as he'd done countless times before, lounging on the Arts Quad at Cornell while they argued over politics and war. Kitty might have been the only person on earth who'd ever found the Tet Offensive amusing. "Isabelle and I bought this house through a catalogue and it seems to have been…mis-delivered."

"That explains a lot," said Kitty, matter-of-fact. "I was wondering where it came from."

Lewinter resisted the urge to ask her how she'd ended up living in their house. Isabelle was right—this *wasn't* a college reunion. Why his ex-flame was squatting on his hard-earned timbers shouldn't be his concern. "So anyway," he said. "We'd like to have it back."

His request carried across the meadow. Behind him—he dared not turn—he felt the full bloom of Isabelle's rage. Overhead, a lone hawk glided on the currents.

Kitty shook her head. "You're out of luck."

"Excuse me?"

"I don't mean to cause you any trouble, Allen," said Kitty, "but I'm afraid it's my house now. You see, I've lived on this land for 15 years—in a lovely old farmhouse dating from Ethan Allen's days—and then last month I went to visit my sister in Phoenix, and I came home to this…." She waved her fleshy arm, embracing the house in its arc. "My neighbor says your people tore through the old place with a wrecking ball and carried the debris away in dumpsters."

"You can't be serious? Why didn't anybody stop them?"

"Vermont folks mind their own business," said Kitty. "That's what I like about them. Usually." She retrieved her plastic basket from the porch. "I was upset at first….especially about losing my stuff…but I'm adjusting. Telling myself to think of this as a long-overdue spring cleaning. You can laugh at me, if you like, but I believe in signs and omens. Deeply. If the universe wants me to live in a modern house, instead of a colonial one, who am I to question? And now that you're here, I'm *certain* there's meaning in all of this…."

"It *is* a strange coincidence," conceded Lewinter.

"I don't believe in coincidences. Things happen for reasons."

She rested the laundry basket on her hip, her face aglow. Was she flirting? And what did it matter if she were? "Again, I am sorry for the inconvenience. If you have no place to go, you're welcome to stay. For as long as you need. Your wife too…."

The situation left Lewinter flummoxed. "That's all right," he stammered. "We have to get back to New York…."

"We're both very lucky, you know," said Kitty.

"Lucky?"

"A lot of people would have sued you over what happened. *Most* people. Honestly, anybody else but me," she said. "So we should both consider it a blessing that the universe delivered your house to my doorstep, so to speak."

Before he'd had a chance to respond, or even reflect, an automobile horn bugled across the landscape like a battle cry. Kitty grinned. "So good to see you," she said, and she returned to stringing clothes, leaving Lewinter to savor his good fortune.

Isabelle found nothing in the situation to feel grateful about. Once she'd learned how Kitty Canaday had come to occupy the dwelling, she gave Lewinter the silent treatment from the Massachusetts Turnpike to the Cross Bronx Expressway—three solid hours of frost. Several times, he attempted to distract her with remarks about the countryside, and the volume of city-bound traffic, and their daughter's upcoming baby shower, but she glowered at him and scowled. When they reached the Manhattan tolls, his wife slammed her tour book against the front of the glove box. "Aren't you going to say something?"

"What do you want me to say?"

Lewinter, road-soaked and drowsy, fought back his own irritation; if Isabelle had found herself in Kitty's shoes, she'd have sued his pants off.

"You could begin by apologizing," said Isabelle.

He inched the Oldsmobile through the toll plaza. Dusk was descending. Once he'd garaged the car, it would be too late for a jog.

"Okay, I'm sorry. I didn't mean to upset you."

His wife hissed air between her clenched teeth. "Dammit, Allen. You don't even know what you're sorry for."

That was true. But nothing unusual.

"I'm sorry I bought a house from a catalog," he said. "It was lazy and shortsighted and I wish I could take it back."

"You're *so* missing the point. How naive do you think I am? Do you really think this is about some lousy house in the country?"

"Isn't it?"

"This is about that—that *woman*," but the word could easily have been *whore* or *slut*. "Do you actually expect me to believe that if anybody else had commandeered our house, you'd have shrugged your shoulders and walked away?"

"Kitty didn't *commandeer* anything," answered Lewinter—maybe too quickly. "It was an honest mistake."

"Like hell it was," cried Isabelle. "I can't believe you let her keep the house. *Our* house."

"What did you want me to do? Haul it away on my shoulders? I'll phone the dealer in the morning and tell them what happened. I'm sure they'll want to avoid litigation—Kitty might not plan to sue, but they don't know that. If we're lucky, they'll refund our money *and* let her keep the house."

"What if they won't refund our money?"

"They will. Trust me, Isabelle. It's all going to work out," he promised—his own confidence increasing as he spoke. "And next time, I'll call a realtor."

He ducked out of the operating suite several times the following morning to phone the home manufacturer, as planned, but nobody at Modular Miracles answered. On his lunch break, he sent them an email message that instantly bounced back: "Mailbox full."

"Why don't you try Brazil?" jibed Isabelle that evening. "Or Argentina? They're probably sitting on a tropical beach somewhere, courtesy of the Lewinter retirement fund, laughing their asses off at the guy who bought a mail-order house."

"I'll try again tomorrow. If that fails, I'll send them a certified letter."

"To where? Buenos Aires?"

Lewinter refused to let her gripes under his skin. All he wanted for his future—far more than a retirement home in New England—was a small measure of harmony. As the week progressed, and Isabelle's frustration mounted, he even considered asking for advice from a medical professional, but the only psychiatrist he knew at the hospital was reedy, bespectacled Dr. Blauvelt who seemed no match for the challenge of a misdelivered dwelling. Instead, at Isabelle's insistence, he called the Better Business Bureau. His complaint, he discovered, was one among dozens. Modular Miracles had filed for liquidation in bankruptcy court and folded up shop.

I'll tell Isabelle next week, he promised himself. *After the baby shower.* Rachel's daughter would be their first grandchild and he didn't want to ruin it. But duplicity, even on a small scale, defied Lewinter's nature. Climbing into bed beside his wife that night, the television tuned to a documentary about aerial warfare, he couldn't hold back.

"I have bad news," he confessed. "You were right and I was wrong."

Isabelle muted the television. "Not the first time and not the last," she said. "So which was it? Brazil or Argentina?"

"They filed for bankruptcy," explained Lewinter.

Now Isabelle's expression sharpened. "You're serious?"

"It's not as awful as it sounds. I spoke to a lawyer at the attorney general's office. We can add our names to the list of creditors. We'll get something back…."

"Like hell, we'll get something back." Isabelle pounded a fist into his pillow. Her glasses, braced atop her head, had bunched her hair into stray loops, and her flared nostrils lent her a flavor of madness. "Fuck your list of creditors. It's *our* goddamn house and *we* paid for it and we're going to take it back—even if we have to throw that *woman* of yours out a window. Am I making myself clear?"

Lewinter suppressed the urge to say, "That woman's name is Kitty." Which wasn't even true anymore. "We can't just *take* the house," he pleaded. "Be rational, Isabelle. Even if it was the right thing to do, nobody is going to move a house while someone's inside it."

"Then chase her out. Get a court order." Isabelle folded her arms across her chest. "I swear to God, Allen, it's either me or her. As far as I'm concerned, letting that woman live in my house is no different than cheating. It's like having an affair, but without sex." She switched off the bedside lamp and slid down under the covers. Lewinter wondered if she was aware how ridiculous she sounded—how *unmoored.* "I don't want to fight," she said, her tone more conciliatory. "I just want my house back."

Isabelle drew her sleep mask over her eyes. She'd left the muted television playing; the bombing of Cambodia flickered over them both. Even fighting gravity, his wife's face remained stunning—she'd started with more natural gifts than Kitty, appearance-wise, and nobody could argue that she hadn't aged gracefully. Not that he'd chosen between them. Not directly. Kitty and her fantasies of the Maine Woods had receded into distant memory, a youthful indulgence, before his medical school roommate fixed him up with his own fiancée's cousin. *I'm lots of things,* Isabelle had warned on their second date, swizzling her cocktail with vigor. *But easy-going is not one of them. If you want easy-going and down-to-earth, buy yourself a basset hound.* Lewinter's retort had been: *At least you're self-aware.* They'd both been dead right.

Lewinter did not get a court order the following morning. Instead, since it was a Friday, he presided over his weekly journal club for the ophthalmology residents, then headed across town to his Lexington Avenue office to see private patients. By the time he arrived, both of his daughters had already phoned multiple times. This was Isabelle's version of calling in the cavalry. Lauren proved easy enough to placate with vague promises, but Rachel—who shared her mother's temperament—demanded concrete action. "Put yourself in Mom's shoes," she urged, more a command than a suggestion. "You run into some ex-girlfriend after God-knows-how-many years, and suddenly you want to give her a *house.* How is she supposed to feel?"

"I'm not *giving* her the house," Lewinter protested.

"Then what *are* you doing?"

A long silence followed. One of Lewinter's receptionists had left the door to the examination suite ajar; in the waiting area, two women debated whether "hysterical blindness" actually existed. Lewinter coiled the phone cord in his fingers. "I'm trying to do the right thing," he said. "I *have* put myself in your mother's shoes. But I've also tried to imagine what Kitty Canaday must be going through. Suppose you came home one day and everything you ever owned was gone.... If some grossly irresponsible developer had knocked down your 18th century farmhouse and replaced it with a house off a truck."

Lewinter believed he sounded reasonable and compassionate. He also recognized that reason and compassion were no match for the women of his family.

"You're not married to Kit-Kat Canaday," replied Rachel.

The Romanian nurse practitioner poked her head into Lewinter's office; he shooed her away. "I don't need you reminding me who I'm married to," he said. "And I honestly don't understand what the urgency is. It's not like we were going to move into the place tomorrow anyway. I've already added our claim to the list of creditors. What's the problem with letting the process work itself through?"

"My baby shower, for starters," his daughter objected. "Mom promised me she'd help with the centerpieces—and now we have less than a week and she's too stressed to get out of bed. It's bad enough that you're letting Frank waste his life away…."

"Your brother is a grown adult—"

Rachel cut him off again, but he was no longer listening. What was the point? His daughter hadn't gone skinny-dipping in Lake Cayuga with Kitty Canaday at daybreak on an August morning, nor had she wrapped an arm around the shaking Kitty at her grandmother's funeral, after a nine-hour, snow-blind overnight drive from Ithaca to Conway, New Hampshire. Nothing he said would convince the girl to let Kitty remain in the house. And the reality of the matter was that Rachel and Isabelle probably had it right: If he'd found anyone other than Kitty freeloading on his property, sob-story or no sob-story, he'd have fought them for the structure, pine-floorboard-by-goddam-pine-floorboard. But you can never love another human being the way you love your college sweetheart at 22—and not wanting to throw a former paramour onto the street, or out a window, did not constitute adultery. *It just didn't.*

His NP appeared at the office door again, pointing at her watch. Daciana knew that she'd end up paying for his time on the phone with her own precious minutes after five o'clock. No doubt, the waiting room was already a zoo. He heard the two women who'd been debating hysterical blindness now squabbling over the meaning of the adage hanging above the water cooler: "In the land of the blind, the one-eyed man is king." That seemed a fitting motto for life, reflected Lewinter. Not just for ophthalmology, but for all occasions.

"Frank doesn't even *play* the drums," Rachel was saying. "Mom's not overreacting. You're *under*reacting. Like you always do."

"I'll discuss this with your mother tonight," answered Lewinter—and he hung up, denying his daughter an opportunity to object.

Isabelle did manage to order the centerpieces that afternoon. Lewinter hardly had time to change into his dungarees before she insisted on showing him photos on her laptop. What did he think of the European-themed flower displays: an Eiffel Tower sculpted from hydrangeas, a Parthenon replica in anemone and fleabane? Rachel's mother balanced the computer atop their bedspread and clicked through the various floral replicas. She seemed calmer, but a tinge disinhibited—a sure sign she'd doubled down on her Valium.

"Very imaginative," said Lewinter. "You've outdone yourself."

"She will be an international child, after all. Almost an E.U. citizen."

That *almost* was so quintessentially Isabelle—the same *almost* that had defined Frank's admission to Princeton and Lauren's qualification for Olympic swimming. In this case, Rachel's husband, a copyright attorney, had inherited his mother's Swiss citizenship.

"What are you thinking?" asked Isabelle. "You don't like them, do you?"

Lewinter chose not to point out that she'd purchased the centerpieces *over the Internet.* Was that really any different from buying a house? Well, maybe. But the dealer could still go belly-up and ruin Rachel's shower—so it wasn't *that* different. Personally, he didn't see the need for centerpieces at all. They were hosting a baby shower, not a state dinner. But marriage is about choosing battles, not winning them. "I *do* like them," said Lewinter. "Even more important, I'm sure your daughter is going to like them."

"Which is your favorite?" Isabelle pressed—elbows braced on the bedspread, stockings scissoring the air. She pointed at the laptop screen. "This one? Or this one? Or this one?" Her words lapped into one another, her vowels loose and liquid. Now he was certain that she'd downed a second Valium. "Come on, Allen. What's your favorite?"

"I think they're all brilliant," he said.

"Liar," Isabelle retorted—but with a smile. "My favorite is the Coliseum. They've used azaleas for the arcades and forsythia for the pilasters."

To Lewinter, the floral cylinder on the screen looked like a Bundt cake. At the same time, he was thrilled—and relieved—to find Isabelle in good spirits. If kitsch landmarks distracted his wife from Kitty and the house, he wouldn't complain. And then—without warning—she asked, "Are you happy?"

That was the medication speaking, transforming Isabelle from mordant to maudlin. On two Percocets, she'd want to cuddle. On three, she'd weep for hours.

"Happy enough," said Lewinter. Which was true. Wasn't it? He had a secure marriage, three healthy children, a steady income. For the son of refugees, who'd arrived from Antwerp with 15 Belgian francs between them, this was nothing to sneeze at. He could easily have ended up like Isabelle's hard-drinking baby brother, unemployed and unemployable at 57, or like his own younger sister, divorced from the same sponger twice.

"Do you know what would make me happy?" asked Isabelle.

"I'm afraid to ask…."

She tugged his arm, pulling her down beside him on the bed. "Do you remember how we were sitting here last month, talking about the house—arguing about upholstery and color schemes? Do you remember how *good* everything was?" She nuzzled his shoulder. "I'm sorry we've been fighting," she said. "I want things to be good again."

"Me too."

Isabelle locked her bony fingers around his large ones. "I wish I could explain why this house is so important to me. It just is. Even if I am being unreasonable, can you *please* get a court order and force your friend to move out? For me?"

Lewinter heard the desperation in his wife's voice, a far harder sentiment to resist than suspicion or rage. And he was struck by how old she looked: beautiful, unquestionably, but beautiful *for a woman of a certain age*—an age at which healthy people keeled over without warning from all varieties of illness. He placed his free hand over hers.

"How about a compromise?" he offered. "Why don't I go talk to her?"

She eyed him warily. "To what end?"

"I honestly don't know," he confessed. "Maybe we can work something out. And if I can't convince her, I'll get a court order."

"Promise?"

Lewinter nodded decisively and stood up. "Promise. I'll leave first thing in the morning."

He reached for the phone to cancel his Saturday squash match. He felt himself running on autopilot. On impulse, he asked, "Do you want to come with me?"

Isabelle frowned. "Not a good idea. If I see that woman again, I'll end up in jail."

The overnight doorman was still on duty the next morning when Lewinter retrieved the Oldsmobile from the garage and retraced their route back to Hager's Corners. Isabelle remained asleep. He'd pecked her on the forehead, but she'd merely rolled over and clutched a pillow to her nightgown. On the interstate, traffic remained sparse: drawbar trailers hauling swap bodies, 18 wheelers, a station wagon crowned with a pair of bicycles. When he crossed into Vermont and paused for a complimentary cup of coffee at the welcome center, it was hardly ten o'clock. The notion struck Lewinter that Kitty might be out for the morning, or even away for the entire weekend. His plan to negotiate a deal could prove a fool's errand. He wasn't even sure what he'd be negotiating. Maybe he just wanted to see her a second time. Remarkably, Isabelle hadn't expressed an iota of jealousy about the trip. She knew her husband too well: he was as incapable of sleeping with Kitty as he was capable of giving her his house.

Maybe it was Isabelle's absence, or his own anxiety, but the last leg of the journey took considerably longer than he'd recalled. The distance between towns—if you could even call them towns—seemed best measured in eons, not miles. A wall of Jersey barriers narrowed the highway to one shoulderless lane. Lewinter rolled down his window, soaking in the wood-smoked air of the countryside. On the radio, the Everly Brothers crooned "Bye, Bye Love." Soon came the signs for the turnoff, then the white clapboard church and Ye Olde

Syrup Shoppe and the low-slung grammar school with the farmers' market in its parking lot. Countless places where Kitty might squander a Saturday morning. *How absurd to think she'd be home,* Lewinter reflected. Even in college, Kitty had her calendar booked with small-scale adventures. He was already chastising himself for his poor foresight as he approached Kitty's address when he spotted his former girlfriend knee-deep in the verdant scruff on the opposite side of the lane. She sported a pith helmet; binoculars dangled around her neck. Lewinter parked at the head of the drive.

"I had a premonition you'd come back," she called.

Kitty shuffled toward him; perspiration matted her blouse to her chest. How natural—almost feral—she looked in her habitat. What a mystery, Lewinter thought, that he'd been able to love a woman like this and also Isabelle.

"Warblers are passing through this week," explained Kitty. "Some marsh birds too. A friend spotted a pair of bitterns down at Bragdon Pond."

"I didn't know you were a birdwatcher."

Kitty's eyes gleamed. "I wasn't. A lot happens in forty years."

They stood face to face. Lewinter found himself at a loss—aware that Kitty must be assessing him too, judging his soft belly and hirsute ears. "You had a premonition?"

Kitty met his question with a laugh. "Why don't I tell you about it over a cold drink?" she proposed. "I have lemonade and beer. My neighbor also left me a pear strudel."

"Lemonade is fine."

He followed her into the house. *His* house, he reminded himself, although it didn't feel like his house. In fact, it didn't *feel* like anybody's house: except for a few cartons stacked in the foyer, and a threadbare sofa beached in the living room, the place stood largely devoid of furniture and personal effects. No photographs, no knickknacks. In the kitchen, which did contain a refrigerator and a folding table, the curtain rods ran naked above bare panes.

The kitchen contained only one chair.

"Sit down, please," instructed Kitty.

She retrieved a pitcher of lemonade from the refrigerator and poured him a glass.

"My neighbors have been extremely generous," she observed. "I was afraid I'd have to dip into my savings, but not a day goes by without someone dropping off a used appliance or a box of utensils. It's uncanny what Vermonters have collecting dust."

Lewinter surveyed the wallpaper, the countertops—pink granite, Isabelle's preference. How fresh and sterile everything seemed. An African violet on the windowsill offered the sole hint of a permanent human presence. He sipped his lemonade.

"I know what you're thinking," said Kitty. "Please don't feel that way. What's done is done. And it's quite liberating, really."

"You take life as it comes, don't you?"

"What else can I do? I try to look at the upside. No more dry rot. No more carpenter ants. I practically had a menagerie of ants and millipedes and beetles in that old place…."

Kitty leaned her rump against the counter, between empty sockets carved to house Lewinter's future oven and dishwasher. It was easy to picture her at home in her colonial farmhouse, stoking coals in winter, churning her own butter. "How did you end up here?" Lewinter asked, because he enjoyed the mellow rhythms of her voice, but also to delay the start of their 'negotiations' over the house.

That seemed to be the question she'd wanted. She launched into a narrative of her life—from her six months spent in the Maine wilderness, which proved far colder than any of her confederates had imagined, through her two decades with Phil Sheeler, to her fifteen years in Hager's Corners, where she still worked part-time in the county athenaeum. Along the way, she'd managed a food pantry in Portsmouth, New Hampshire, and a women's health clinic in Lowell, Massachusetts. Her ex-husband, who'd died shortly after their divorce, had paid his bills installing septic tanks. "But Phil was a potter," said Kitty. "You name your medium and he could spin you a flawless vessel. It was a remarkable gift. I wish I still had some photographs to show you…."

Kitty appeared as though she might laugh—or weep—he couldn't tell. "It sounds like you've led an exciting life," said Lewinter. It was something to say.

"I have, I suppose. And you?"

He'd known it was only a matter of time before she asked about him, before he had to shift their conversation toward less pleasant matters. "Exciting enough," he said. "What's that Chinese curse? May you live in interesting times."

Kitty retrieved his empty glass. "So they say. I believe the actual expression in Mandarin is: 'Better to live as a dog in an era of peace than a man in times of trouble.'"

He considered inquiring if she spoke Mandarin, whether this were another of the developments he'd missed over four decades. But he didn't. It was already three o'clock and he could picture himself returning to Isabelle empty-handed. "I hate to change the subject," he said, "But we need to talk about the house. We have to figure something out."

Kitty nodded.

"Is that why you've come back?"

"We're planning to retire here," he said. "To be blunt, Isabelle wants me to get a court order to put you on the street."

"And will you?"

Lewinter was amazed at how calm she remained in the face of his threat, as though they were discussing strangers. She washed his glass in the sink and set it on a dishrag to dry.

"What choice do I have?"

Kitty turned to face him again. "We all have choices."

"Such as…."

Her eyes locked on his—gentle, yet intense—the sort of expression one might wear when explaining death to a young child. He didn't dare look away.

"You could stay here," she said. "With me."

Her words settled over the room like a blanket.

"I told you I had a premonition," she said. "You came all this way for a reason, Allen. If all you wanted was to give me notice, you could have phoned…or sent your lawyers…."

Kitty stepped toward him. "It's not the Maine Woods," she said. "But it's close. Just warmer." And she flashed him a smile.

Her visage was soft, welcoming. He realized that he was smiling too.

"I should be going," he said.

Lewinter stood up. "I'm sorry."

"Nothing to be sorry about," said Kitty. She was already Caroline Conrad once again—kindly, yet stoic. "I'll pack you some strudel for the road."

Lewinter returned home after dark that evening. Again, too late for a jog. Isabelle was waiting for him in their bedroom, still wearing her bathrobe. Another of her military documentaries blazed fiercely on the television.

"Well?" she asked.

He stepped into the bathroom and splashed cold water on his face. His lower back ached from 12 hours behind the wheel.

"Well?" Isabelle asked again.

He shook his head. "I'll call a lawyer tomorrow," he said.

And he did.

He phoned the attorney who'd handled both of his sister's divorces, who in turn referred him to a family lawyer in Burlington, Vermont, who ultimately recommended a property expert with offices in Manchester and Rutland. Everybody sympathized. They promised rapid action: it turned out the property expert had a longstanding relationship with a transport firm that could relocate the structure quickly for a modest fee. "You're looking at a week, 10 days, tops," pledged the lawyer. "Open and shut." Not once did Lewinter mention his prior connection with Kitty.

By the following Sunday, loading his Oldsmobile with floral landmarks for the baby shower, Lewinter had assurances that the matter would be settled that afternoon. In his mind, he pictured Kitty Canaday standing on her lawn, possibly holding a plastic basket containing her few remaining possessions, watching his outfit hook her new house to a rig. How disappointed Kitty looked—but how calm, how dignified. He watched helplessly as she shuffled into her van and set out to seek her fortunes on a neighbor's couch. In Lewinter's own vehicle, Isabelle shouted into her phone, shredding the caterer for his ineptitude. "What do I need with an ice cream cake?" his wife raged. "My daughter can't tolerate dairy. Am I making myself clear? Do you want her to have a miscarriage?"

Lewinter could easily envision Kitty laughing at Isabelle's frustration; he bit his own lip to stifle a guffaw.

"You'll be happy to know we got a court order," he informed Isabelle. "They'll have the house back in Hager's Notch by dinner."

"Is now really the time?" she demanded. "Jesus, Allen. What is wrong with you? You're about to have a granddaughter. Get your priorities straight."

Isabelle punched numbers into her phone again, while Lewinter imagined Kitty, unfazed, knocking on the neighboring farmhouse. He wanted to call after her. He experienced a yearning to tell her that he'd been wrong. *Both times*, he'd been wrong. But she'd retreated into her neighbors' dimly-lit vestibule, and already his urge was lifting, evaporating in a sweat of snags and consequences. Once they reached the baby shower, Lewinter told himself, he'd have a vodka gimlet, or possibly two, and dance with each of his daughters, and soon this impulse, like so many others, would pass harmlessly into the night.

Eric Severn

Bones

When I was 21, I went through a dark period of sexual frustration. My dick didn't work. I was young and terribly horny, but I was useless. I lived in west Seattle—a tiny apartment on Stevens next to an industrial park. My front room window overlooked a fenced-in concrete lot where big cranes moved metal. I heard it at night. Clang, clang, clang. It was a repulsive sound. I worked in a bakery on Alki Ave called The Bulging Croissant, run by a man named Roman who was never there. I heard he was Greek. I worked with Justin and Rachael. They were one and two years older than me, respectively. They were coupled and I liked them. I liked my job. To be a baker is good, physical work that ends in a satisfying aesthetic creation. I wasn't an artist, but still, I enjoyed it.

One morning I had been flipping through the newest Victoria's Secret catalogue, trying to get erect and staring out the window of my tiny apartment. It was spring and everything outside was copulating: birds, insects, even the taxis seemed anxious to mount exhaust pipes. I was studying some blonde in a purple teddy, my junk still refusing to rise, burrowed, like some mournful hedgehog, when Justin and Rachael knocked on the door. I had been expecting them. It was Friday and we had a routine: when the three of us had a day off together, we'd go for a drive. We'd cram into my old Datsun truck—a real shitbox but a shitbox that refused to die—and take the ferry out to Bremerton. We'd drive the 101 and smoke marijuana while sun and slow moving fog braided fir trees. Sometimes we'd drive north. It didn't matter. We just drove.

They knocked again and I slid the catalogue beneath my couch. "Come in," I coughed. Rachael and Justin came in and stood before me like statues stumbling down from Olympus. They were both tall and unreasonably attractive people. His hair, gold and so full of body, elicited crooning from females everywhere. His teeth white and his face ever so symmetrical. Rachael stood next him, dizzying in her tight jeans and V-neck T. Her auburn hair brushed the knolls of her chest. To look at them, together, was sometimes a painful thing.

I said good morning. Justin said it's afternoon. Whatever, I said. It was spring and I thought I could smell all of spring's perversity on the couple that had just walked in—floral and fish smells from a warm wind sloughing off the Sound.

"Details in regards to last night," Justin said to me.

"Justin." Rachael hit her boyfriend on the side. "It's none of your business."

"That's right," I said. "None of your business."

"It's absolutely my business. I set them up." He looked back at me.

I shrugged. "It was fine."

I stood up and got my jacket. My tiny apartment felt cramped and I wanted out, wanted to be on the water, skimming across Puget Sound, the wind in my hair and merging with the distances.

"What do you mean by *fine*?" Justin said. We stood in the hallway now. I locked the door.

"She's a nice attractive woman and we had a fine time. That's what I mean by fine."

Down the stairs and into the parking garage. Justin behind me, yapping, "Details, details, details." And Rachael's voice, easy, understanding: "He doesn't want to talk about it."

I said nothing until we crowded around the shitbox. "We went out to dinner," I revealed while unlocking the doors. "We talked. She had to work the next morning. She went home early. There, our entire night."

"That's it? No physical contact? Devin, you're withholding."

We crammed into the shitbox and I had to work the gas pedal. The familiar smell of must and dirt from the interior brimmed up around us. The truck wheezed, threatened to expire but then revived. I turned to Justin, hands resting on the steering wheel. He knew Lindsay. A friend of his from the last bakery where he'd worked. He kept telling me that I *had* to meet her, that we were the same in so many ways. He was always telling me that I needed to meet a woman, at least go on a few dates. I was glad I had a friend like Justin, a friend to get me out of my slump, but everything was self-serving for him. He wanted to write the lives around him so he could take the credit. He knew me, yes, but he also didn't know me. He was too self-obsessed to sympathize with another man's plight in any real way.

Rachael was different. Large, hazel eyes that seemed to sympathize with the world. Some people only see in others a projection of themselves. Not Rachael, though, at least I didn't think so.

"Justin," she said. "Not everything is physical."

"But it is." He stomped the floorboards with conviction. "It is."

"We kissed," I said. "On my doorstop. Thank you." The engine fired and I snaked through the parking garage, the outside world taking us in.

We drove up to Port Angeles. It was a slow, sunny drive, and once the shitbox got going it purred brilliantly. We got stoned and Justin finally dropped the Lindsey talk, and I was relieved, for I felt him getting close to my secret. I didn't want to have to explain it.

Rachael scanned the open fields as we drove. "I could live out here," she said. "Buy some property. Open a bakery. Exist."

"Hell yes," Justin said, window down and breathing it all in.

"What about you, Devin?" Rachael turned toward me. "Five, ten years down the road. What do you see?"

I shrugged. I didn't know. There was something about the future that scared me then, trying to imagine myself in it, living a life, a real one with real responsibilities. "We've got the present," I said, trying to sound sagacious. "That's it."

We bounced along the 101 in contemplation, and then I had to piss. I pulled off on the side of the road, squeezed into the bike lane. Down into the woods and out of sight, I unzipped. Cars hummed past. Not until I made my way back to the truck did I notice the first skeleton. Under a tree and picked clean, the bones of a deer. It was uncanny, how perfectly placed they looked, as if the deer had just lain down to sleep and then never woke. I crouched there and looked at a skull. The sound of birds and trees drifted against each other in the wind. It was when I stood up that I realized there were more, all around me, not all in such a perfect position, many of them scattered, picked apart by animals. I took a few steps back. It was a strange, peaceful sight, all those bones resting against the forest floor. I sat there and took it in, trying to account for it.

Back at the truck, I got Justin and Rachael, grabbed a joint out of the glove box and led them down into the woods. "Look at this." I spun around, pointing at the bones. "Look at all those."

Sun twisted through the trees, mottled rib cages and the dirt beneath.

"Fucked up," Justin said.

"Eerie," Rachael said.

I lit the joint and then we stood there, smoking. I walked over to one of the skeletons beneath the tree and found a smaller one curled up next to it. Mother and child, it looked like. Rachael and Justin came and stood next to me.

"What do you think it is?" Rachael asked.

"I don't know," I whispered. I didn't know why I was whispering, but it seemed right. Justin handed me the joint. I inhaled.

"Maybe we shouldn't be here," I said. "Maybe it's like a place where people shouldn't go. What if we're interfering?"

Justin scoffed. "Interfering with what?"

"I don't know," I whispered. I leaned down and brushed pine needles from a leg bone.

We drove back to the ferry and smoked more weed. I was getting tired of being stoned. I was stoned all of the time back then. It was like my head had grown roots, projected upward, into the fog. I was in a constant state of watching my life without living in it, as if hovering above and looking down on my actions. I watched myself watch myself until I began to wonder if there was a self to watch. We drove and drove and then there was the ferry waiting like Noah's great ark. We boarded. Justin and Rachael went up to the deck but I refused.

"What's the matter with you?" Justin said.

"Nothing," I said. "I just don't want to get out. I'd rather sit here." They left me there and I thought about the bones. It was captivating, the mystery of them, how they seemed off limits, almost sacred. The way the sun had played on the well-ordered skeletons seemed somehow intentional and full of purpose.

I shivered and listened to the drone of a talk show seeping out from the windows of the car next to me. I drifted off and then jumped at the sound of Rachael rapping on the window. She smiled in at me, motioned to unlock the door and climbed into the cab.

"Hey," she said, folding her arms across her chest.

"Hey."

She pulled her hair up into a lose bun.

I asked her where Justin was and she nodded upward and said he was eating. She lowered her voice. "So, like, what did you guys talk about? How did it go?"

She meant Lindsey. How did it go? We ate dinner at Sunfish, a seafood place on the boardwalk, and talked about the problem of really getting to know another person, as in, is it ever really possible to truly know someone, inside and out. We both thought it wasn't, but that somehow made it seem more possible, like we were communicating right then something about one another in the very act of saying we couldn't really communicate anything about our real selves. She had blond hair and green eyes. I liked her.

"So?" Rachael said.

"I'd see her again, I guess."

She kicked off her sandals and put her feet on the dashboard. She gave me a probing look. "You're always so, I don't know, detached. What's with you, Devin?"

My mind formed a big question mark. It was easier to talk to Rachael than it was Justin, but still I couldn't explain how things were with me. I had gone to a therapist when it first started happening. His name was Chad and his practice was on the 14th floor of a towering building made of mirrors. He was short and bald, a sloping forehead like George Washington. When I followed him into his office, he let me choose between three chairs. I thought it was a test.

"Which one should I take?"

"Anyone you want." His voice low, soothing. "Wherever you're comfortable."

I looked at the chairs. "I'll stand," I said.

"If that's what works for you."

I stood the entire session, clutching my water glass. This was before my job at the bakery, before Rachael and Justin. I was fresh from Iowa and had arrived in Seattle bright-eyed and ready to find myself. I marveled at the buildings and considered my place among them. So long to Mom and Dad. So long to limitless rows of golden corn and sweet Midwestern comfort. I was twenty and out in the world searching for the kernel of the real.

He watched me, and I spoke shyly: "I'm worried about my place in the world. I'm nervous. Like all the time."

He asked if I could explain the feeling in more detail. The thoughts associated with it.

I shrugged. "Like I'm missing something, some deeper connection with things, with the stuff of existence," but I was too embarrassed to explain why I was really there. At the time I worked at the co-op in West Seattle, slicing meats and stuffing sausage in the Deli. I was dating a checker named Abby—black hair, cut in a bob and brushing her shoulders when she walked. Her bedroom was comfortable and clean and smelled like the rose water she was always spraying. Beeswax candles flickered yellow against the wall while we lay on her futon, but my pecker was feckless. Nothing like this had ever happened before. I didn't understand it. And it wasn't that I didn't want her. I did. But all I could do was get a half-chubby while she straddled me, nearly naked. I'd finger her black bra, feeling that if I went any further I would violate some truth.

Finally I gave up. I quit Abby and spent a few lonely nights at a strip club just to make sure I still functioned. After blowing a hundred clams on lap dances, I found I did, though only with strippers, apparently. But I couldn't bring myself to tell any of this to Chad.

So he sat there in his chair, giving me a steady look, pointer fingers jammed up into his lips. He offered some breathing techniques and asked if I had trouble sleeping. Of course I did.

"I see," he said.

He told me to get big, thick curtains and turn off all electrical appliances in my room before going to bed. When I left his office, he leaned back in his chair and gave me a thoughtful nod. "I think you need a spiritual buoy," he said.

I stood in the doorway, wanting to leave.

"Something that you can believe in. Not something religious, but something spiritual."

I slung my backpack over my shoulder. He asked if I understood what he meant. I didn't but I said I did. That was it for me and Chad. I never went back.

I turned to Rachael. The afternoon was cold and her breath fogged the interior of the shitbox. "You and Justin," I said, "you've been together what, two years?"

"Almost."

"Is it the way you imagined it? Better? Worse?"

The ferry horn sounded, a voice boomed over the loud speakers and Justin opened the door. He told Rachael to scoot over and then climbed in. "What are you guys talking about?" he asked.

"Nothing," I said.

I drove the couple home and then idled in their driveway. Justin hit me on the arm and said to call Lindsey. Said if I don't I'll grow old and be alone forever. I told him to fuck off. I watched them walk up to their door, Justin's hand on Rachael's ass.

That night I turned off all the lights in my apartment and thought about things:

I thought about Lindsey. She had texted me hours earlier, when I was in the shower. *Dinner was fun,* she wrote, *we should do it again.* I hovered over my phone, trying to think of a response. What did she mean by "fun?" What did she mean by "again?" As in we should do the exact same thing. Or we should do that and other things. Go back to her place or back to my place. And then what? What if she took my pants off and found I was incapable, which I probably would be because I liked her. I had ideas about her, who she was and wasn't.

I crawled into bed. Lying there in the dark, perspiring slightly, I thought of Lindsey and tried to get hard but couldn't. I imagined her in the most degrading poses, but still, it was impossible. Time passed. Outside my window traffic simmered. I heard metal clank. Clang, clang, clang. A breeze slapped the window and my mind moved to Justin and Rachael. I wondered if they were fucking, or if they had just finished and now were lying together, in the quiet of their apartment, thinking their separate thoughts.

I had the next three days off and I didn't leave my building. I sat in the front room and tried to think about nothing. I ate only what was in the fridge—mayonnaise and tortillas—and I didn't get stoned. I sat there and tried to feel the world move through me, tried to imagine that all the Eastern thought was right and that transition, becoming and change were the rule, that we aren't what we feel. I tried to get hard. This was only possible when I let the most ghastly and deplorable women into my mind, but then Lindsey, the silk of her hair, the idea of her and I, two unknowables knowing each other, walking down on Alki Beach, thinking of this I trembled, became limp. Three days of this. Mayonnaise. Tortillas. Eastern thought.

Then the night before I went back to work, I couldn't sleep. I hovered at my computer. I started googling key words. *Olympic Peninsula. Rituals. Sacrifice. Animals. Deer. Bones. Sacred.* At first nothing, but then as I clawed my way into the recesses of the web, articles appeared, message boards unfolded, until, finding a short, cryptic post about a cult outside of Port Orchard, I stumbled upon a link to a news story. My apartment was dark. It was almost 3 a.m. I leaned into the light of my computer and read. It was a story about a slain goat just north of Port Townsend, discovered by two teenagers walking through the woods. The goat, spread prostrate on a stump, was gutted down the middle, testicles removed. A tight ring of candles circled the stump. The surrounding trees were carved with strange markings. The authorities never found who was responsible, but there was speculation, rumors. A local cult. A ritual sacrifice.

I sat back on the couch and tried to imagine it. I saw the trees under broken moonlight. I saw hooded men tying knots in heavy line. I saw the goat bucking to free itself, its tongue thick and pink and loose in its mouth. I had the feeling that I was peering into something I shouldn't be, some recondite world beyond my knowing. I shut my computer and then texted Lindsey: *Are you awake?* Five minutes later, my phone buzzed. I brought it up close to my face and squinted at the words. *I dreamt I was floating down a river. Why aren't you asleep?* If I tried hard enough, I could almost smell her skin, warm and underneath clean sheets. Slowly, I keyed in the words *Go back to sleep. Sorry I woke you.*

5 a.m., the next day at work, Justin and I groping with the mixer, flour dust erupting before us. We had 80 rosemary twists to make. A few feet off, Rachael stood at the pastry case, loading it with the croissants I had made earlier that morning. ABBA's "Sweet Dreams" flowed from the small stereo above the brick oven. Rachael sang along. Through the bakery's window, Puget Sound was a black mirror gathering up the city lights.

"Lindsey," Justin said, "wants to see you again." Flour clung to his brow. He looked menacing next to the glow of the oven.

"How do you know?"

"Ran into her on the beach."

"The beach?" I worked a tray of pesto rolls into the oven, sweating against the heat.

"Sprawled out on a blanket, reading."

"Reading what?"

Justin heaved another bag of flour over his shoulder, grunted, and then set it down on the floor. "Who cares?" he said.

"I do."

He ripped it open and poured it into the mixer. "She asked about you. She wants to know why you're being evasive."

"I texted her. I'm not being *evasive*. Was that her word or is that your word?"

Justin brushed flour-crusted hair from his forehead and peered into the oven. "You're going to burn those," he said. "They're too far back."

I looked in the oven. "No they're not. They're perfect."

Justin glared at me. I glared back. "She wants to see you," he said. "Christ, what are you afraid of?"

I skirted, avoided the subject and told him I had been doing research.

"Research?"

The bones, I explained, and then detailed what I found online. "I think it's maybe a special place."

Justin looked confused. Flour whirled about us as I tumbled out a mound of dough from the mixer. We started beating it with our fists, grunting slightly.

"Devin," he finally said, "I'm worried about you. You're getting weird."

"I'm not," I said. "That place was weird."

Justin rolled his eyes. We slapped the dough with rosemary filling. Sprinkled goat cheese on it. We folded and cut strips. We twisted and braided and arranged perfect rows on a baking sheet.

Rachael came humming through the kitchen, carrying a croissant. "You make this?" She looked at me. A red bandana held her hair back.

I nodded.

"It's flawless," she said. "Beautiful."

I picked it up and twisted it in the glare of the oven. It was a perfect, textbook croissant.

"Nice job," Justin said.

I felt the weight of it in my hand, the fragile, flaky dough. I said, "Maybe we shouldn't sell this. Maybe we should put it on display."

"That's ridiculous," Justin said. "We bake pastries. People eat them."

I handed it back to Rachael and watched her load it in the case with the other croissants, but an hour later, when Justin was on his break and Rachael was working the ovens, I pulled it out of the case. I didn't know what I intended to do with it. Hiding the croissant under my chef's jacket, I went into the dry storage room and shut the door. I sat on a 20-pound bag of flour and stared at the pastry. Through the walls I could hear the ovens creaking in the kitchen. I could smell the vanilla in dark, plastic jugs. I felt some unnamable frustration well up in me, and then I dug my fingers deep into the hollows of the croissant. It crumbled into my lap and I was sitting there like that when Rachael walked in.

She turned on the light and I startled, stuttered out some words: "I was going to get high," I said.

"In the dark?" Her eyes moved to my hand, my lap full of crumbs. "Is that a croissant?"

"No."

She took a few steps closer and uncurled my fingers from what was left of it. Her hands were warm. "Is that the croissant you didn't want to sell?"

I felt ridiculous, like a child. "You've got to destroy it to preserve it." I tried to smile, tried to make a joke of the thing. "You've never heard that expression."

"Devin, it's a croissant. It's not some artifact." She took what was left of it from my palm and threw it in the trash. "What's getting at you?"

I didn't know.

She sat down on the bag next to me and we were quiet for a minute. She pulled out a small pipe and filled it with marijuana.

I took a few deep breaths. "Do you have a spiritual buoy?"

She took a hit and then handed me the pipe. The dark red walls of the dry storage swallowed up most of the light. "I don't know what that is," she said.

"I think it's like a belief or something to keep you connected with things, you know, like when you feel lost or whatever. Like a beacon."

She put her hand on my shoulder. She seemed to think about this, to weigh it. "No," she finally said. "I don't think so. I don't think anyone does. Not really anyway." She stood up and grabbed a bag of hazelnuts. "I think we all just have to figure things out as we go." She reached for the light switch. "On or off?" she asked.

That night Lindsey texted me again. One word: *Well?* It sent me into a panic and I closed myself in the bathroom and took an hour-long shower. When I got out, I stood in the kitchen in a towel.

I returned to the phone. *Well.*

Well, I thought. *Well well well.* I thumbed the words into my phone and waited. I hit send.

You're being difficult, she wrote back.

Life is difficult.

I know.

I crawled into bed with my phone and a joint. I stared at the screen, then up at the ceiling. I heard the machines outside my window, the sounds of industry and construction. *Are we afraid of each other?* I thumbed the letters slowly and watched the words take shape and then deleted them. *What scares you most?* I hit send. I took a deep hit of marijuana.

Maybe that everything is much simpler than we want to believe it is.

I didn't understand. *Explain.*

Nothing to explain. It's all right there, in front of us, no explanation needed.

I texted back. *How is that scary?*

It isn't what we want to believe.

It isn't?

There was a long pause. I finished my joint and then she wrote back: *I don't know. You tell me.*

I stared at my phone for a long time, and then turned it off and went to bed. I dreamt I was the sacrificial deer. From above I saw my body spread upon the cold dirt, surrendering my bones to the quiet earth.

A week later Justin and Rachael wanted to take another drive. I told them I was sick even though I wasn't. It was a Saturday and I lay in bed until noon, listening to the traffic outside. Then I got up and found a pair of jeans on the floor and a sweatshirt crumpled on the couch. In the parking garage, I climbed into the shitbox and drove to the ferry terminal. I stood on the deck alone and felt all right. It was good to breathe in the open air, to not have to answer any questions.

Outside of Bremerton, I headed north on the 101. The day wrapped around me clear and blue. I drove past Sequim, searching for some familiar sign, something I recognized. I hunched over the wheel, blew past a lavender farm and then pulled to the side of the road near a dense tangle of fir trees. I hopped out of the shitbox and took a few steps into the woods, but knew I had it wrong. Back in the truck, I drove further north. A mile or two later, it cropped up, the little incline, the familiar potholes and a massive hemlock. I pumped the brakes. The shitbox rattled to a stop. The engine ticked while I sat in the car.

Outside, the sun beat against the road and it was still and warm. I pushed down the embankment and then made my way into the trees. There was the smell of dirt and sap. In the cool carriage of the underbrush, I paced back and forth until I found a rib, knuckling from the dirt. Next to it were more, picked over by animals. I made small loops, spiraling outward, counting skeletons as I went. But it was hard to know which bones belonged to which. I got to 10 and then crouched down and ran a finger along the smooth white surface of a skull.

Above a breeze brushed tree limbs together and carried with it a sweet stench. I put the sleeve of my sweatshirt over my mouth and followed the smell. It grew stronger, like soured milk and sugar. Behind a tree I saw the deer, half decomposed, picked clean from the haunches down, ribs fingering out of matted fur. The head twisted upward toward the sky and I could tell the neck was broken. I crouched at its side and looked into its black eye. The trees around me drooped with moss.

For a moment I just stood there, looking at it, unable to guess how it had died. I reached into my pocket for my phone. I used the camera and let the deer fill the frame, its decomposing hindquarters at one end and its peaceful expression at the other. Each picture I took was from a different angle. For some I crouched on the forest floor, got close and held my breath, trying not to gag.

In the dirt, next to a stump, I sat down and scrolled through the images. Each one showed the deer's eye, as if it were in communion with the camera. The one I texted Lindsey showed the deer from above, looking down on it like some omniscient god.

I stood there waiting in the forest. A minute later, she texted back. *That's a little weird and very gross,* she wrote.

I didn't respond when another came: *Where are you?*

In the woods.

Do you always send girls pictures of dead things?

Sorry? I wrote back.

A minute passed and then she responded. *It's kind of beautiful.*

The deer? I wrote.

Death.

I stood up and took a thick leaf from a branch. Folded into a square, I placed it over the deer's eye. I felt strange then, flooded with a feeling I didn't understand, like I was being carried away in some overwhelming current. There were no cars on the road, and the only sound was that of the wind, sifting easily through the trees. As I made my way back to my truck, I stooped down and picked up a skull. It was pale-brown and rough in my hand. I felt protective and impulsive. I raised it up over my head and threw it hard at a tree. It burst into brittle, white chips that scattered the forest floor. In the sunlight, a small plume of dust hung in the air where it had collided with the soft bark. I left then, drove to the ferry without music or marijuana, listening the whole time to the hum of the road.

Over the next two weeks, she texted me. I texted her back. I made plans with her and broke them, twice. *Dinner, soon,* I wrote. *Yes, please,* she wrote back. Then the night of I sent her an explanation: *Exotic stomach flu. Out of nowhere. Possibly the plague.* She offered to bring me soup, but I refused to expose her to my ailment. We settled for a walk on the beach, days later, but then I feigned a twisted ankle. *Can't walk,* I wrote. S*tuck hobbling around my apartment. But. But, but, but, I do want to see you. I do.*

We settled into vagaries. We wrote lines like mystics. Aphorisms. *Moon,* she texted, and I looked out the window and there it was, slivered and cresting the clouds. Later that night, when the rain came, I texted *listen* and imagined her lying in her bed while the thrum of spring showers played against her windows. The next morning, she wrote, *Life is just beyond the Plexiglas.* I accidently locked myself out of my apartment and wrote, *Trying to get inside.* She wrote, *You're a shadow.* I wrote, *We all are.*

Another week passed. I read articles about animal sacrifices and thought about the bones, at night, under the moon and clouds and the sound of trees swaying in the wind. I read how sacrifices were about appeasing mythological gods or spirits, to keep them from getting jealous of those who walk the earth. I read about human sacrifices, too, how for some distant cultures, it was an honor to be the sacrificed, a blessing. The days I didn't have to work, I read late into the night and then sat on my couch in the dark and listened to the sound of metal and cranes and machinery next door. Clang. Clang. Clang.

Then, toward the end of the week, I ran out of weed. I texted Justin, asked if I could buy some from him. He texted back: *Word. Whenever.* So I got in the shitbox and drove over to their house. They lived in a basement level apartment with windows that looked out eye-level onto a small, grass yard. It was one in the morning. I parked across the street, saw the warm glow of their bedroom light. I had only been over a couple of times, but I knew the layout, knew what room was what. I sat there in the truck for a minute with the heater on. A thick fog dewed the windows.

Outside, the wet grass sucked at my shoes. I got to their door and stood there. For some reason I didn't knock. I couldn't. Instead I slipped under the shadow of a hedge by their window and peered into their bedroom. On a low futon, they both sat there, watching a movie. They didn't look happy. But they didn't look sad either. They just looked, I don't know, like nothing. Two bodies, staring into space. With my coat pulled tight around my chest, I stayed there for half an hour, staring in. Eventually, they turned the movie off and the lights with it. I don't know if it was Justin or Rachael, but one of them cracked the window slightly. I waited, and then crawled across the yard and pressed my ear up to the screen. At first, I though I heard them having sex, noises from Rachael, soft sighs of pleasure. I kept listening until I realized they weren't having sex. She was crying. They were fighting about something, but I couldn't tell what. I pushed myself closer to the screen, but I couldn't make out their voices. I stayed there until they fell asleep, and then went home and stayed up until the sun rose.

Two days later, at work, and Justin and I trim croissant dough into neat triangles. Scones and olive rosemary bread, done. We'd been there since three in the morning. It was five. Flour hardened beneath my fingernails. Rachael was out across the bakery, at a steel table in the kitchen, where the prepping got done, where pastry fillings, pestos and glazes were blended and mixed. I looked at her and then looked back at Justin. "Hey," I said. "Can I ask you something?"

"What?" he said. We were stoned. We used our palms and fists and weight to loosen the dough. Justin grabbed a wood rolling pin and rubbed it down with flour. "What?" he said again.

"What do you think about when you're, you know, having sex with Rachael?"

He squinted at me. "Are you serious?"

"I think so."

He pumped cream into the middle of each pastry and sighed. "I don't know, man. I don't think about anything. We just fuck. It's in the moment, you know." He gave me a quizzical look. "Are you a virgin?"

"No," I said.

We threw the dough in the oven and I watched it rise. I felt Justin studying me. "Do you want to fuck Rachael?" he asked.

"Of course not," I said.

Justin wiped the pastry cream from his hands on his apron. "It's okay if you do," he said. "A lot of guys do. I mean, it's not *okay*. You can't *fuck* her. But it's okay if you *want* to."

"I don't."

"It's natural, man. That's all I'm saying. It wouldn't mean anything if you did want to other than that you wanted to."

"But I don't."

Justin seemed to think about this for a minute. "Whatever, man. I'm gonna smoke."

I followed him into the dry storage and we smoked. We didn't turn on the lights so there was only the dim glow of the lit joint. Justin flicked the lighter and his face filled with shadows. "You still thinking about those bones?"

"No." I took the joint. "Well, maybe. I don't know. I guess."

"It's nothing," he said. "Just bones."

"It's something," I said. "I can feel it."

Justin flipped on the light. Everything became vivid, the bright green labels on the cans of olives, the deep, wooded brown of bulk hazelnuts.

"Cults," Justin said. "That still what you think? Or religious rituals or whatever."

"You make it sound ridiculous."

He flicked the lighter a few more times. "Maybe it is. Maybe you're being ridiculous."

"Fuck off," I said.

He stuffed the lighter in his pocket, watching me. "Let's get back to work," he said.

Sometime later the following week. It was around midnight. There was a full moon. I could see it out my window. I was eating shredded cheese by the fistful out of a bag. I heard a knock at the door. I froze and it came again. I crawled across the carpet and hovered at the door. More knocking and I heard three voices. Giggling. Female voices. I ran into the front room and looked around. I wasn't sure what to do. Where to go. I stood there thinking and panicking. More knocking. I didn't move. Finally they just walked in. I stood there.

I saw Justin first, then Rachael, then Lindsey.

"It's a full moon," Justin said. "We're going to go look at the bones. See if something weird happens."

I sensed mockery in his tone and sneered.

"Come with us," Rachael said. "We came to get you."

Lindsey poked her head out from behind them and waved. I coughed. I felt cheated. Justin grinned.

"We finally meet in person again," Lindsey said. She was wearing a blue dress, just above the thighs, and tights.

I didn't say anything.

"Well," she said. "Are you going to come?"

We took her car, an old VW Jetta, blue and pocked with dents. Justin and Rachael sat in the back. A drizzle earlier that day and the streets were wet as we made our way to the ferry. The moon was buried behind clouds but then the clouds broke. Sure, in part I decided to go because of Lindsey, because even though I had been avoiding her, I wanted to see her. But I also went because I was curious. I couldn't help it. I wanted to see the place under the cover of darkness.

We idled at a stoplight. Lindsey and I turned to each other. In the back, Justin and Rachael were quiet, watching us. "So," Lindsey said. "Deer bones?"

"Easy," Justin said. "He's protective."

Rachael hushed Justin and I hard-eyed him in the rearview mirror.

"What'd they tell you," I snapped without meaning to.

She leaned over toward me. Her dress was low cut and I could see her white bra. "Nothing," she smiled. "They said you would tell me. That you know more about it."

"Green light," Rachael said, and we lurched forward.

On the ferry, we huddled in the car, listening to AM radio. Then we docked and spilled out into Bremerton with the other cars until we hit the 101. Corridored by trees, it was impossibly dark.

"Spooky out here at night," Rachael said.

Justin rolled down his window and howled into the dark and then pulled his head back into the car. "Historically," he said, "Washington has had the highest number of serial killers."

"Shut up," Rachael said.

"It's true," he said. "I just think it's something we should be aware of, while we're out here, at night."

I saw him flash a smile in the rearview mirror. I felt Lindsey's hand creep next to mine. She kept her eyes on the road. "Do you get afraid of things?" she asked. "Like, you know, the woods and stuff?"

I shrugged. "I don't think so."

"The known or the unknown, what scares you more?"

"He's a man who fears the known," Justin said. "That's my hunch."

"That's not true," I said, but maybe it was. I couldn't tell.

A tangle of shadows crawled across the road as we tunneled north on the 101.

"Where the hell is it?" Justin pressed his face against the window.

"Further north," I said.

"We passed Seqium like twenty minutes ago," Rachael said.

Justin leaned in over my seat. "Why don't you use Google maps and look for the closest sacred burial site."

Lindsey looked at me, gripped the steering wheel. "Sacred burial site?"

"Pull over up here," I said. "I think this is it."

Lindsey eased to the side of the road and we all got out and stood in the dark. The air was damp, heavy with the smell of Puget Sound and soil. "Is this really the best idea?" Lindsey said. "This feels really creepy?"

Justin elbowed me. He whispered into my ear. "Protect her, man."

I told him to shut up and walked up the road a few steps and then came back. "This isn't it."

Lindsey shivered. "I don't like highways at night."

We crammed back in the car and drove for 10 minutes. The road dipped down into a familiar dell, plaited with tracts of moonlight. We were close. "Here," I said.

"Where?" Lindsey downshifted, nudged the breaks.

"I don't know. Anywhere along the road."

She pulled into a wide swath of bike lane. Again we piled out of the car. Again we stood there for a minute, uncertain. Justin flashed a Maglite on and off. "I came prepared," he said. I ignored him, opened my phone for light and started walking in the direction from which we came. We had overshot, but after about

20 yards, we were at a pullout, the heavy bough of a hemlock I swore I recognized, stretching out and above the highway.

Somewhere leaves rustled. "Quiet," I whispered.

"What," Lindsey whispered.

Rachael started to giggle.

"This is it," I said. "I'm sure of it."

We followed Justin down into the woods, the yellow dome of his flashlight bouncing off the trees. The place looked different at night. Bigger and somehow more silent. Too silent. I tripped on a root and Lindsey caught my arm.

Justin had to orient us. "There," he said, shining the light at the base of a tree. There were a few ribs and some leg bones. He swung the light around, talking more to Lindsey than any of us. "See," he said. "They're everywhere."

I didn't want him showing her, and I didn't like the way he was so casual about it.

"There are some in the perfect shape of a deer," I put in. I wanted to show those to Lindsey and asked Justin for the light.

He shined it into my face. "Don't get weird on us," he said, and then handed it to me.

I brought Lindsey over to where I remembered seeing an intact skeleton near a fallen tree, but when I shined the light on it, it was in pieces, the bones scattered. "But it was perfect," I said. "I saw it."

She said she believed me and then put her hand into mine. I looked around for Rachael and Justin and saw them standing under a tree, making out. I didn't like that. It seemed wrong to make out in a place like this. Lindsey moved closer and I felt her hair brush my face and I was going to tell her no, but there was the sound of a truck pulling to an idle on the road above. Headlights swept the trees around us.

I froze. We all froze. "Who's that?" Lindsey said.

I whispered for her to be quiet. Justin crept over to me and grabbed the flashlight, turned it off. We listened to the idling motor. I heard the voices of men but couldn't make out what they were saying.

"Devin," Justin said. "It's your cult. Your men in black robes."

I whispered for him to be quiet.

Then footsteps on gravel. Voices more distinct and I could tell there were two, drawing near.

"Shit," I whispered. "Shit, shit."

Rachael gave a startled look.

Lindsey said, "We should get out of here."

"We should hide," Justin said. We swept through the dark, until Justin's voice led us to a fallen tree. We crouched down in its shadow.

I felt the dirt beneath me and could hear Lindsey breathing. Our thighs touched. And then I saw two flashlights. At first it was hard to see. But then the two men became clear. They carried a tarp down into the woods where the other bones were. They wore orange sweatshirts and reflector vests.

"So we got in this huge fight because when I wake up, I piss with the door open." His voice was high and raspy, not like the voice I expected to hear in a place like this, in the woods, among the bones and the wind.

"And your wife's still in bed?"

"Yeah, she's still in bed, but she says she can hear the sound of the stream, you know. That it wakes her up. That it disgusts her. She doesn't want to hear it, she tells me."

I heard Justin stifle a laugh. The men moved in the night. We peered over the log like children and watched them dip the tarp they carried to one side, watched the deer slough off unceremoniously into the dirt, its shape already bloated and ugly, even in the darkness, and I heard the sound of their truck running, machine and steel mixing with the wind. I had a strange feeling then, not in my chest, but in my head, like reading a word that you don't know the meaning of but is still familiar.

The men stood there for a minute, looking at the deer. "It's just piss. It's not like you're taking a shit with the door open."

"That's what I told her."

They were about to walk away, but then one of them stopped. "Keys," he said, feeling his pocket. "I think I dropped them when we were holding the tarp." He walked over to the deer. "Shit. They're under its fucking body."

"I'm not driving," the other man said. "I'm not touching those."

Reluctantly, he reached down and picked up the keys. "Fucking disgusting," he said.

"Road workers," Justin whispered. "It's road kill, man. Your cult is a bunch of State workers worried about their wives." Justin started to laugh and the men were walking away. Lindsey giggled then, not too loudly, but loud enough.

I put my hand over her mouth and felt the cool of her lips part. I felt her lip gloss against my skin. I felt her twisting slightly under my grip, her slight smile underneath my palm. She reached a hand down and touched my thigh, running her fingers along my jeans. I pressed down harder and her hand brushed my groin and then I put all my weight into my palm. Her smile tightened. I heard her head and hair pressing into the dirt. I heard the truck start on the road overheard. I heard the wind and I kept pushing down until she was biting my palm, until she was just a muffled cry beneath my weight and I felt I could press her into the earth until she was gone.

But then there was Justin pulling me off her, prying my hand from her face. He held me while I kicked and grunted. Lindsey pushed herself to her feet. She wiped the dirt from her clothes and spit the blood from my palm on the ground. I know that she was staring at me, but I don't remember seeing her face. And I know that she said something, but I don't remember that either.

What I remember is the shape of that dead deer, bloated and mired in filth. I remember the men's voices and the feeling that they didn't belong there. And I remember feeling like I had been living in two worlds and that I needed to bring them together, somehow, that I couldn't continue on the way that I was. And I remember wanting to stay right there with that deer and the night and the quiet.

Brett Finlayson

Salt

For three days the radio had warned of an ice storm—the likes of Felix, they said, back in '73—set to hit the Eastern Seaboard on Sunday. The public had been advised to stay indoors except in cases of emergency. They'd been advised to fill their bathtubs, to stock up on batteries and stay tuned. Sick of warnings, Murph switched off the Casio boom box he kept on the radiator by the window for better reception. He'd finished the last of the brandy an hour ago, had already turned over the apartment three times and now he sat at the kitchen table in silence.

For a long time he'd told himself Ruth just needed time. That she'd get over it. Then one day he came home from the steel shop to find a note scratched on the back of an envelope:

Don't come looking for me because I'm already gone. You remember Mia, my girlfriend from work? She was the white girl. Well I don't think I need to write it down for you. Sometimes love just works like that. I'm not sure if I've always been this way. I don't think I always was, but if I always was then I'm sorry for putting you through this. And if I wasn't, well, then I guess we both know who to blame.

–Ruth

After reading that note Murph had fallen into a two-week bender that saw him total his truck and get fired from Eastman Steel. It was the lowest moment of his life. He might've gone on drinking himself straight into his coffin if the guys from work hadn't come by to check on him. They put on a pot of coffee and helped Murph into a tub. A few days later someone made some calls and Murph had a new job at SoCo Steel, a lot less money than at Eastman but close enough to walk to. That was two years ago. Murph hadn't seen Ruth since. No divorce, no separation. Just gone.

Then, earlier this morning, there'd been a knock at the door, and a thin voice muffled by the wood. "Are you in there? It's Mia."

Murph rose from the kitchen table. He stood at the door a long time staring at the shadows of Mia's feet disrupting the flow of light from the hallway. "What you want?"

"Jesus. You gonna open up?"

It took him almost 10 seconds to match the pale face in front of him with the memory he had of Ruth's lover. She looked horrible, like she'd aged 10 years in the last two.

"I tried to call. I couldn't get through," she said.

"They turned it off." He looked out into the hall. "You alone?"

Mia nodded. "Listen. Can I come in?" she said, rubbing her arms. "It's already coming down out there."

"I can hear you fine where you are."

She stopped rubbing her arms then. "It's Ruth. She needs to see you," she said. He went to close the door, but Mia stuck her foot out. The action seemed to surprise them both. "You need to hear me out," she said.

"If it concerns her, I don't need to do nothing."

With that, he forced the door past her leg and headed into the kitchen for the bottle. He uncapped the top and took a big sip of brandy. The purple syrup was a welcomed sweetness on his tongue. He picked up a cigarette and was about to light it when the door swung open again and Mia stared at him across the room. "She's sick." The news caught him off guard and he didn't know how to respond. "Do you understand what I'm saying?"

"Why're you doing this to me?" he whispered, wiping a wrist across his lips.

"Nobody's doing nothing to you, Murph." She leaned against the door, staying that way for a long time before she righted herself and got control again. "She's at my house. Thirty-three Laurel Street," she said, "in Trumbull," which was the next town over. "If you want to say goodbye." Then she'd walked out, leaving the address behind her while Murph sat there listening to sleet blow against his windows.

Murph thought about the night not long after he and Ruth had gotten married, when he was sitting with her father in Break Even's and the old man had touched his stomach. "My doctor, he says I got it here," he'd told Murph, shaking his head. "But I don't feel like I got it. I don't feel good. I ain't never felt good, you know. But I don't feel so bad either."

"Well maybe you ain't got it," Murph had offered.

"Yeah, maybe." Ruth's father was quiet as he thumbed the wet label on his beer bottle. Then he started to laugh. "Least it ain't my colon. I hear that's a pain in the ass."

Murph laughed at the joke as he waved over the bartender. Way he figured it, the least he could do was buy the man a drink. But the worst he could do was buy *only* him a drink. That would sound too much like sayonara. So Murph reached into his pocket, dumped all the cash he had left onto the bar. Then So-So Joe had moved down the bar flipping shot glasses in front of everybody: "On Murph. Murph's call. Murph. On Murph. Murph's orders." And one by one they nodded to him or held up a hand or said his name to the television. And Ruth's father got his drink, and pretty soon his picture on the wall, and the rest of them got an annual benefit picnic to go to.

Now, sitting at his kitchen table, Murph felt the shakes coming on, first in his hands, then up through his arms. Then into his core until he was rattling around the chair like a plate compactor. He paced the apartment, rechecking cabinets and drawers. He even checked the oven—a long shot, but a long shot that had come through once before. The best he could figure it, he'd mistaken the oven for the fridge one night, and since he didn't cook, the bottle had just sat there waiting for him to need it that bad.

When he couldn't take it anymore he put on his Starter jacket and a woolie, and left the apartment. Downstairs, he unbolted the front door, careful not to snag the weather stripping on the nylon runs in the carpet. Right away his neighbor's tabby darted out from behind the garbage stacked along the curb. The cat was crying. It scrubbed against Murph's calf, and he scooped it up and shouldered the door closed behind them.

He knocked a long time on Art's door. Art finally opened up, still cinching his belt. "What you need?" he asked Murph.

"Don't need a thing," said Murph, holding up the cat. "Less you got a drink." Art snatched the cat away from him and tucked it into his hip. The cat whined, writhing against his side. "I don't think he likes that," said Murph.

"It's she. Why you got her, man?"

"Damn thing got outside again. Found her in the garbage."

Art held up the cat, pressing his nose into its stomach. "She gets lost," he said. "A pain in my ass." He tossed the cat down the hallway into his apartment. It caught its balance and sprinted into the kitchen. Without saying anything else, Art closed the door.

Murph stood there for a long time. He knocked again and heard Art's faint reply somewhere in back, maybe the bathroom: "Why you houndin me, man!"

"You're welcome," said Murph, and he left.

He turned up East Main St. in the blank cold, past closed convenience stores and ethnic takeout joints, names like San Juan's and El Saha etched into the lightless billboards awning the sidewalk. Ice covered everything. It lay thick as resin on the power lines and tree branches, on the signs, streetlights, and roads. He stopped at Absolute Liquors, then Martin's News, but both package stores were closed, their overhead doors padlocked over the windows. On the corner, he knocked at the Oriental Spa where he occasionally paid girls to fill his nights with their small bodies and languages he didn't have to know, but though he heard voices inside nobody came to the door.

He kept to East Main St. 'til he passed Cooper's Garage, then cut through the Dairy Queen over to the Terrace. He stopped at the spot where Fat Daddy got shot down last year by some connect from the city. It took Daddy two days to die, but he never even gave the cops a name. Someone had hung an old wreath on the gate where it happened, but the wreath was crooked and Murph straightened it up. Normally there were people out here in the street, even in winter, sipping on something and passing the time. But tonight the Terrace was empty. He watched the sleet pass silently in front of the yellow squares of light that filled the projects windows, and then he headed south towards Break Even's.

With the ice, he could hardly see 20 feet ahead. He walked with his face tucked into the collar of his coat, wrists twisted in his pockets. Relying on deliberate, flat-footed steps, there was no avoiding the occasional wipeout, and each fall left his elbows and forearms bruised. Every time his mind wandered back to Mia's visit, to Ruth, he got angry, telling himself neither of them had any right, but always the anger was quickly subverted by a chill running up his spine, or the sting of sleet on his skin, and he would go back to worrying about what he was going to do if Break Even's wasn't open.

It wasn't until he was almost on top of it that Murph saw the accident. He'd come around a corner and walked right into a red Hyundai bent into its own windshield, most of the glass gone, the spider-webbed remains clinging white to the crooked frame. The whole front of the car was pinned beneath the chassis of an Expedition, the SUV hardly looking like it had been in a collision. Murph peered into the car. There wasn't anybody inside. Nobody in the SUV, either. He brushed off his pants and looked around. The ice fell on the metal with an almost peaceful hush. He thought about staying there, in case the drivers returned, but he didn't know what he'd do if they did, and with the shakes coming on stronger, and the storm getting worse, he eventually left the accident behind and focused on his own problems.

At Break Even's, all the lights were off except the blue, Bud Light neon throbbing in the window. The parking lot was empty, a square lake of glass that reflected the orange streetlights. Murph walked around the building and tried to jimmy the back door, but it wouldn't budge, and he slumped against the metal wall, pulling his legs under the short overhang of the gutter.

Across the street, a television glowed in the window of a dark apartment. A meteorologist stood black-suited, her lips silently addressing the camera while America glowed behind her, dissected by temperature. Without thinking, Murph found himself standing up and crossing the street to stand outside that window. Then there were boys, black boys dressed in desert fatigues, aiming rifles down dirt streets and fires molesting the sky. Black and Spanish boys, big white boys bleeding in dirt streets. Mouths open. Murph didn't want to be out in this storm all night. Men had gotten themselves killed for less. Already, he was probably close to frostbite. But there was one more place he could try. Jamal's Market was in the opposite direction and he'd have to backtrack, but the owner lived upstairs so there was a chance it might be open. It was a chance he would take.

Standing up, he jammed his hands into his pockets and headed back the way he'd come. He walked faster now, his anxiety growing with the ever-increasing probability he wasn't going to find a drink. Almost at the accident, he heard a loud noise ahead. The gray air turned a spectacle of red and blue lights and at first he thought they were towing the vehicles, but it was more than that. The machinery of emergency was at full throttle, gears turning over, pistons hissing in their steel casing, the whine of metal and popping glass.

The big SUV was rolled over onto its side now, and six or seven firemen surrounded the small red Hyundai. They'd already cut through the passenger door and had the jaws clamped between the dash and floor. Two paramedics stood behind them, their blue bags on the gurney, the ambulances idling white diesel smoke. Murph walked through the small crowd of cops talking to one another and to the few neighbors who'd left their homes in sweatpants and down coats. A young officer, Portuguese-looking, stood alone in back.

"Why they got them jaws out?" Murph asked the cop.

He shook his head. "She said she wanted ice cream sandwiches. Believe that?"

"Who?"

The cop pointed at one of the ambulances. A Spanish girl sat on the edge wrapped in a wool blanket. She didn't look good, but he could tell under different circumstances she'd be pretty. A paramedic was trying to talk to her, but she wouldn't lift her head up to look at him.

"There ain't nothing in there for them jaws. I seen for myself," said Murph.

"Who the fuck eats ice cream this time of year?" asked the cop.

The men at the car began shouting. There was a commotion of body parts, and one of the firemen pulled a boy out of the wreckage. Murph couldn't believe it. The fireman held him up for someone to take him, but nobody did, and he just floated there for everyone to see, his small shoes pointing at the ground. Finally, someone grabbed the boy and laid him on a gurney, but there was no point in doing anything else. He was already gone.

The Spanish girl shrugged off the wool blanket and tried to run to the boy, but the paramedic held her. She wasn't dressed for the weather, wearing only a light spring jacket and a pair of spandex cut at the calf. Then she began to scream. The sound was the worst thing Murph had ever heard, and it sent a shudder through his whole body. He turned and pushed his way through the crowd, which had more than doubled in size. Fighting for the edge, he bumped into an older woman, nearly knocking her over, but he didn't stop. He was almost free when a hand grabbed him by the arm and spun him around. He was face to face with the young officer.

The officer stared at him for a long time. Then he said, "Salt."

The word, so unexpected, seemed foreign at first, and Murph could only stare back at him, horrified.

"Drive three-and-a-half miles that way," said the cop, pointing west, "and there ain't no accidents. You know why?"

"What?"

"Because it's Trumbull. And they got a tax base."

"I didn't do nothing wrong," said Murph, ripping his arm free.

The cop looked at him like he was seeing him for the first time. He grabbed Murph by the coat, and it was all Murph could do to keep his balance under the young man's strength with the ice underneath them. Then the officer let go, and Murph stepped back. For a second he thought the cop would follow, but he stayed put, and Murph turned and ran. His foot slipped on the ice and something snapped in his knee, but he managed to stay up. Off into the storm he scrambled with the crowd watching in silence, except for the mother, who he could hear for a long time.

The plow driver could just as easily run him over as spot him hobbling down that dark and violent street. No doubt the driver was focused on the power lines collapsed into a lane of hemlocks along the side of the road. But Murph refused to move out of the way. His knee throbbed, and sweat poured down his face and neck. His head was on fire. He planted himself in the center of the street, in the huge lights of the plow bearing down, and waved his arms till the brakes squealed and the tire chains grinded to a halt.

The driver rolled down the window. He had a huge Italian face and the thickest, blackest hair, the blackest moustache. "You got to smile more in the dark. Damn near ran you over." He looked up and down the street. "Car broke down?"

"Ain't got no car," said Murph.

"You from Bridgeport?"

"My whole life."

The driver nodded like he knew it. "This is a long ways from there."

"Only on a night like tonight," said Murph.

The driver looked around, as if he were unsure. "Well, get in before you freeze to death."

Murph shook his head. "Hurt my leg."

The driver nodded, thinking for a second. Then he climbed down from the truck and walked around the plow and he was monstrous. He grabbed Murph and Murph was completely helpless in the giant man's arms. In one motion the plow driver opened the door and hoisted Murph into the passenger seat. Then he walked back around and climbed in himself.

"Look at you," he said, shaking his head. He leaned over, grabbed a fifth of vodka from the glove box. He gave it to Murph and Murph drank half of it, offering it back. "Finish it," the driver said, waving it off as he unhooked the radio from the visor.

Murph tilted the bottle and finished the rest of the liquor in one gulp. Already he felt the warmness spreading through his body. He was as strong as he'd ever been. The driver was calling in the downed power lines, asking after an ambulance, and Murph switched off the radio.

"The fuck you think you're doing?" said the driver.

Murph kept his hand over the receiver. "I got someplace I need to go."

"I don't want no part of any drugs. You can get right back out and freeze."

"It's my wife. She's checking out," said Murph.

"Join the club," said the driver, flipping down his visor to show Murph an old Polaroid taped against it of a woman smiling by a campfire. "Mine lives in Tempe, Arizona now."

Murph looked out the window. The ice fell on them. It fell around them, relentless and beautiful. "Then you know how much we miss 'em," he said.

A minute later the two were driving in the opposite direction, deeper into Trumbull. The radio was still off, and an ambulance bled into the night behind them. The ice exploded in their headlights. They had the plow raised up for speed.

Contributors

Jacob M. Appel's most recent publications include a short story collection, *Einstein's Beach House*, and a novel, *The Biology of Luck*. He is on the psychiatry faculty of the Mount Sinai Medical School in New York City and teaches fiction at the Gotham Writers' Workshop. His story, "Enoch Arden's One Night Stands," appeared in Volume 18 of *Beloit Fiction Journal*.

Michelle Donahue is a current MFA candidate in Creative Writing & Environment at Iowa State University. Her fiction has appeared or is forthcoming in *Cutbank, Baltimore Review, Whiskey Island, Paper Darts* and others. She was the managing editor for *Flyway: Journal of Writing & Environment* and is a reader for *The Adroit Journal* and *Revolution House*.

Brett Finlayson has an MFA from Syracuse University, and is presently a Black Mountain Institute PhD Fellow in Fiction at the University of Nevada, Las Vegas, where he is fiction editor of *Witness*. His stories have appeared in *KNOCK, New Delta Review, Stone Canoe* and *Third Coast*, amongst other publications.

Adrià Fruitós was born in Barcelona on 1984. He studied at *La Massana* art school in Barcelona and then traveled to France and Belgium to pursue other artistic horizons. He began his professional career in Barcelona on 2007, illustrating children's books. Today, based in Strasbourg, France, he works for many fields of illustration but especially for magazines and international newspapers. Additionally, his work has appeared in many group exhibitions in Spain, Italy, Japan, Iran, USA, France, England, Slovakia, Ukraine, Slovenia, Colombia and Portugal.

Steven Kurutz was born in rural Pennsylvania. He graduated from Penn State in 1998, and soon after moved to New York City. His journalism has appeared in such publications as the *New Yorker, GQ, Los Angeles* and elsewhere. Since 2011, he has been a staff features reporter for the *New York Times*. He is the author of the non-fiction book *Like a Rolling Stone: the Strange Life of a Tribute Band* (Broadway, 2008). "Party George" is his first published fiction.

Nicholas Maistros holds an MFA in fiction from Colorado State University. His work has appeared or is forthcoming in *Bellingham Review, Nimrod, The Literary Review, Colorado Review, Sequestrum, Sycamore Review, Washington Square* and *Witness*. He is currently finishing his first novel, *These Imaginary Acts*, and lives with his partner in Brooklyn, New York.

John Mandelberg works in retail and lives in Los Angeles. His stories have appeared most recently in *Southwest Review, Fiction* and *Northwest Review* and online in *Pif* and *Prick of the Spindle.*

John McNally's most recent books include his novel *After the Workshop*, his story collection *Ghosts of Chicago* and his craft book *Vivid and Continuous: Essays and Exercises for Writing Fiction. Lord of the Ralphs*, his first YA novel, will be published in September. He is Professor and Writer-in-Residence at the University of Louisiana at Lafayette.

Alain Douglas Park lives in Chicago, on the city's northwest side with his wife and two daughters. His fiction has appeared in the journals *Fugue, Folio* and *Zone 3,* and he's currently finishing a book, an episodic novel called *This is the Moment No One Remembers,* of which "Dig Deep Magnolia" is a part.

Eliana Ramage studied English literature and creative writing at Dartmouth College before beginning an MA in creative writing at Bar-Ilan University. She was awarded a Scholastic Art and Writing Awards silver medal in 2009, and later signed on as a fiction co-editor for *Compose Journal.* A Cherokee Nation citizen, she is at work on a collection of linked stories concerning indigenous girls and women. Her work has appeared in *Compose: A Journal of Simply Good Writing*, and is forthcoming in *Four Chambers.* This is her first published story.

Elliot Sanders lives in Syracuse, New York. His fiction is published or forthcoming with *Carolina Quarterly, Shenandoah, Sonora Review, Briar Cliff Review* and elsewhere in print and on the web.

Eric Severn is from Arcata, California, and currently lives in Moscow, Idaho. He has an MFA from The University of Idaho and has worked as the fiction editor of *Fugue.* His fiction is forthcoming in *Lake Effect* and *Moss.*

Anthony Spaeth's novella, *In the Reign of...*, will be published by *Iridum Sound* later this year. Other stories have recently appeared in *The Best of 10,000 Tons of Black Ink* (Vol. II), *Jelly Bucket, Red Fez, Spork Press, The View From Here* and *The Yellow Medicine Review.*

Laura Steadham Smith's work has appeared or is forthcoming in the *Gettysburg Review, Arkansas Review, Quarterly West* and other magazines. She was awarded an AWP Intro Journals Prize in 2014 and has been recognized as a notable emerging writer by *Glimmer Train* and the Southern Writers Symposium. She is originally from southern Alabama, and she currently lives and writes in Baton Rouge, Louisiana.

Michael Stigman grew up in Minnesota, has lived in both Virginia and Kansas, and now calls Missouri home, where he enjoys life with his wife and children. He teaches creative writing and literature across the river in Kansas. He has published stories in *Sycamore Review, South Dakota Review, and Suicidally Beautiful: A Collection of Sports Stories* (Main Street Rag Press), among others.